MURDER

IN$URED

A NOVEL

BY

J. STEPHEN REID

MAXAMY BOOKS
Seattle, Washington

Murder Insured
By J. Stephen Reid

Published by:
Maxamy Books
2566 12th Avenue West
Seattle, WA 98119 (U.S.A.)

ISBN Number: 0-9717691-0-9

Library of Congress Cataloging-in-Publication Data
Reid, J. Stephen
Murder Insured
ISBN: 0-9717691-0-9
Registration Number TXu 1-008-515
July 9, 2001

Printed by: One2One Direct

Cover design by Rocio M. Briceno

Printed in the U. S. A. 2002

Acknowledgements

First, I would like to acknowledge the life insurance business which has given me a fascinating career for nearly 38 years. Because most people have a fear of death, they don't like to think about this subject, and they certainly don't dwell on it. Over time, a certain mystique has developed, based on a lack of understanding. I have found that the average person will accept the status-quo, rather than question certain illogical or even ghoulish aspects of the business. So, while this is not rocket science, the reluctance to delve into the details of life insurance by the general public makes it possible for insiders to create some amazing schemes. My business provides so much rich material that it was hard to decide where to start. I hope you agree that I came up with a rather nefarious plot.

I want to thank several people who helped me during this novel's nearly two year journey to completion. Early on, Kathy Thompson, Albert Ravenholt and Dawson Taylor, Sr. led me to significant refinements. I must especially thank Natalie Lemberg Rothenberg who, as my primary editor, helped reshape the storyline and strengthen the characters. Natalie was a constant source of encouragement, while at the same time my biggest critic. I want to acknowledge Lynne Markova, computer whiz supreme, who helped me reformat the book, and Rocio Briceno of One2One Direct for helping me with the final printing and by designing the book cover. Finally, this project would have ended many times were it not for the constant encouragement of my wonderful wife, Alice. I have come to realize that while

4

writing a novel is a rather solitary endeavor, getting it published takes a larger collaborative effort from many people, some of whom I will never meet. I want to thank everyone who had a hand in the creation of this book.

PROLOGUE

November 1993

The view from Conrad Jenkins's northwest corner office on the fortieth floor of the Transamerica Building swept from the Golden Gate Bridge in the west, up north past Sausalito and Tiburon, then across the deep horizon to the Richmond-San Rafael Bridge. On those infrequent occasions when he stayed late, Jenkins had marveled at the variety of lights in the towns along the Marin coastline, and at the faint string of yellowish lights that marked the span across to the headland of Richmond.

Jenkins never tired of that panorama. He calculated that his office was the same height above sea level as his home in the hills above the town of Sausalito. He had mounted a telescope in each location aimed at its counterpart, and found that they were, in fact, exactly the same height. He had made careful measurements using a wrist altimeter bought for that sole purpose.

Jenkins was the managing director of Irving Bank and Trust, in charge of its private banking and financial services operations in the Bay Area. He reveled in this plush job with its title of Executive Vice President. Conrad had made the move from New York City three years earlier, in time to get in on the huge appreciation in real estate values on the Marin peninsula. As Jenkins looked around his office, he smiled at the thought of his good fortune. Jenkins knew that his old cronies at First Gotham Bank were envious of him; several of them had told him so after he had left New York.

Jenkins walked over to the window and looked down toward the North Beach neighborhood. Alcatraz Island was a pale smudge, nearly obscured by a paler veil of fog rolling in from the bay. Now that the clocks had been set back an hour, the sun was already dropping behind the western hills. The bank executive glanced at his watch--4:45 p.m. He had to wrap things up for the day and get down to the wharf to catch the 5:30 ferry which would get him to Sausalito by 6 p.m. Jenkins put on his suit-coat which he had carefully placed behind his office door the morning. He shrugged his bulky shoulders into his coat so that it hung just so, then smoothed out the expensive worsted material.

At 6' 2", 240 pounds, Jenkins was pudgy big. Even though he had his suits personally tailored, the man preferred to work in his shirt-sleeves. His massive arms and upper chest felt constrained in all that material. Jenkins grabbed his attaché case and umbrella and was off.

"Good night, Rose. See you in the morning," he smiled at his secretary.

He knew that Rose would stay until 5:30, then catch the bus to Oakland. Each of them followed a set routine. Jenkins had become a man of regular habits ever since he had suffered the onset of adult diabetes six years earlier. At the time, he had missed three weeks of work at First Gotham. That was in the late summer of 1987. It had taken that long a time for the doctors to stabilize his blood sugar level. It hadn't helped that Jenkins had weighed nearly 300 pounds. His regular and disciplined routine, along with an insulin shot each morning, had helped him reduce his weight by 60 pounds. Jenkins had managed to keep his weight down for over five years.

His wife Beverly was understanding and now prepared healthy meals every evening between 6:30 and 7. She would meet him at the dock in Sausalito in just over an hour, as she did each weekday.

Two weeks prior to that particular Wednesday evening, a slim Asian man with a scar over his left eyebrow had received a package from New York City. It contained a dossier on a Mr. Conrad L. Jenkins, Executive Vice President of Irving Bank and Trust of California. In it was a complete personal history Conrad Jenkins, down to his preference in music and even the breed of the family dog--a corgi.

For several days now, Duk Lon Ki had been observing Conrad Jenkins. A man of such regular habits was at once both an easy and difficult mark. His wife and secretary would always know where he was and would also become alarmed at the slightest divergence from schedule Jenkins had no bad habits which could lead to opportunity. It seemed he was never alone in an unobserved place. Duk had been instructed to make Jenkins's death seem as if from natural causes. The fact that his proposed victim was a diabetic created an opportunity. Dr. Ben Tom had told him that an overdose of insulin would cause a reaction similar to a drunken stupor which would be followed within minutes by cardiac arrest and death. Duk would have to find a way to inject his target without being detected.

A lifetime of training had prepared him for the task. His manual dexterity was superior; his devotion to repetitive practice second to none. He practiced the thrust and squeeze motion using a hypodermic needle until he could do it from virtually any angle, even with his eyes closed. After five days of concentrated practice he was fully prepared. Duk had decided on the time and place. He had visualized the complete scenario. Duk Lon Ki was confident and ready.

The passenger loading dock for the ferries to Sausalito and Larkspur Landing was always crowded in the late afternoon. Conrad Jenkins had mastered the routine, allowing just enough time to be sure to make the 5:30 crossing. That fog-shrouded early November evening, he was about five minutes behind his normal schedule, and had half-walked, half-jogged from his office to Pier 2. He was somewhat winded and sweaty as he joined the milling throng. Jenkins made his way through the crowd, turning his body sideways to work his way around the groups of friends who congregated there. When he had gotten up near the metal ramps, he slowed to a shuffle and relaxed, confident that he was going to make it. Jenkins was shoulder to shoulder with others now; they were all squeezed together in the final moments before the ramps were lowered to the ferry itself.

Jenkins felt a tug on the briefcase which he carried in his right hand. He turned in that direction, and yanked forward on the grip. In the same instant the smaller man behind him swung his left arm down toward Jenkins' buttocks in a well-practiced motion. The needle pierced his trousers and penetrated to the hilt. The plunger was squeezed tight and the needle withdrawn, all within two seconds. Jenkins never felt the deadly injection. He was distracted by being pushed forward with the surging crowd. He tramped across the ramp with the others, relieved that his briefcase had not been snatched. The swarthy Asian faded back through the oncoming crowd, unnoticed.

Duk did not get on the ferry. As it pulled away from the dock, he pushed open the door of a trash can and dropped into it the syringe that he had cupped in his left hand. Duk strode through the diffused light of the neon Sinbad's sign and across the Enbarcadero; his assignment completed.

Within ten minutes Jenkins began to feel disoriented and nauseated. He lurched out of his seat in the direction of the men's toilet. He staggered into the aisle, then fell in a heap. The crowd around him gasped. A young doctor came forward and turned him over on his back. Jenkins was frothing at the mouth, and his eyes were glassy. He was in severe insulin shock. A member of the crew brought a blanket. The crowd was now in stunned silence. Many of them recognized the large man from numerous crossings together.

His breathing became labored, then it stopped altogether. Jenkins had gone into cardiac arrest. A member of the crew began CPR immediately, and it was not the first time he had been called upon to perform that duty. The captain of the ferry called ahead and increased the speed of the craft to its maximum velocity. High above the Sausalito ferry dock, Beverly Jenkins heard the staccato blasts of the ambulance siren as she drove down the winding road to the town below on her nightly round-trip to pick up her husband. Their dog Daisy was startled by the noise and ran into the living room, bumping the tripod that held the telescope. The delicate instrument fell to the hardwood floor, shattering the glass lens. As things turned out, it would never be replaced.

The ambulance was waiting at the dock in Sausalito. After working on Jenkins at the scene, the paramedics drove him to the hospital. They had a very visible police escort. Beverly saw and heard the commotion, but it wasn't until the passengers were allowed to leave the ferry that she realized that Conrad was not among them. Only then did she begin to suspect that it was her husband who had been carried away in the ambulance. She ran to her Mercedes and headed for the hospital. By the time she arrived, he had been pronounced dead. There was nothing that she or anyone else could do to bring Conrad Jenkins back to life.

San Francisco Examiner: November 13, 1993

Conrad L. Jenkins, age 54. Born in Decatur, Illinois. Mr. Jenkins was an Executive Vice President of Irving Bank and Trust. He had formerly been a Senior Vice President of the First Gotham Bank in New York City from 1978-1990. Mr. Jenkins is survived by his wife Beverly, a daughter, Carolyn, and his parents, Mr. and Mrs. Horace Jenkins of Sun City Center, Florida. Services will be on Thursday, November 16 at Grace Cathedral. In lieu of flowers, please make donations to the National Diabetes Foundation.

On the day of the obituary, notice of Jenkins' death showed up on screen "D" in the offices of an actuarial firm in Chicago. The death was noted, and notification was sent to the two banks- First Gotham in New York City, and Irving Bank and Trust in San Francisco. Ms. Amy Maxey received the notice for Irving Bank and Trust, and Mr. Richard Trace for First Gotham. Ms. Maxey was distraught over the notice. On the other hand, Mr. Trace seemed gratified by the news. Of course, it was nothing personal. He didn't even know Conrad Jenkins

Duk Lon Ki sent a copy of the obituary, along with his bill for expenses, to a Mr. Pestrano in New York City in care of Johnny's Ristorante.

Chapter 1

September 1998

It had been one of those perfect Indian summer days in New York City, crisp and cool in the shade, bright and warm in the sunlight. On such days Richard Trace would often skip lunch and walk up to Central Park, covering a 4.5 mile route in less than an hour. For most people it would have been a forced march, but at a height of 6' 4 1/2" he had a long stride that made it a comfortable pace. He was pleased that at the age of 54 he could maintain such a pace in his business suit without raising a sweat.

On that particular late September day, however, Trace had stayed at his desk during the noon hour, poring over statistical reports. He didn't like the trend he had seen. Five year Treasury yields had dropped below 5 percent and were sinking daily. That day they hit 4.62 percent, which hadn't happened since 1993. He felt a trickle of perspiration slide down his armpit as he read those reports. Clearly, he would have to take action again. His annual bonus was dependent on achieving the targeted gain on those special funds entrusted to his department, the funds they called BOLI, Bank Owned Life Insurance. *Achieve the 6.5 percent and a $500,000 bonus would be his in January; fail, and he got zilch.* Failure was not an option.

Richard Trace realized after nine years experience working with this program that there would need to be an annualized 5.5 net return on the treasuries, plus another 1 percent from death claims, so the total would equal or exceed 6.5 percent. This meant that on the $500 million fund the death claim count would need to be around $5 million. Because of the size of the covered group, he could count on at least ten death claims. Actuarially, it was a virtual lock. The results of the previous nine years had given him faith in their predictive accuracy. So, while he could count on $5 million of death claims from natural causes, with treasuries off by at least 60 basis points, there would need to be closer to $8 million in death claims. If the results were as forecast by the math wizards, it would be necessary to have five additional deaths. It was crystal clear that he needed to do his research and take action.

At 5:30 Trace left his office and headed straight for the Maxim Bar in the lobby of the Mayfair Hotel, just two blocks away. The tall man did not pause to enjoy the afterglow of the beautiful autumn day; he was on a mission. Trace seldom went to bars. In his opinion they were for the weak, but on this day he needed to anesthetize himself against the task that circumstances had forced upon him. He stood at the polished bar and drained two Glenlivets. Neat. At 6:35 he returned to the First Gotham Bank building. His footsteps on the marble floor echoed in his head. Without the usual swarm of humanity to soften the noise, they sounded like hammer blows. Trace slid his access card into the elevator slot and punched floor 34, home of First Gotham Bank Insurance Agency, Inc., the bank subsidiary of which he was president. There was grim work ahead for him.

Before taking his seat, Trace removed his suit coat and hung it carefully on the coat hanger behind his office door. He stretched his long arms behind his back and grasped his hands together, rotated his shoulders, first forward, then backward, and held each position for several seconds. Then he rotated his neck several times in each direction. No one heard the popping sounds as his vertebrae were repositioned. These brief stretches had always relaxed him. The stressed-out man ran his large hands over his balding head, the pushed his powerful fingers into his temples seeking to press away the tightness, this time without success.

Trace realized that unless the death claim reports showed more than the usual results so far this year, he would have to arrange for at least four, possibly five additional claims. He crossed the office to the wall of locked mahogany, four-drawer file cabinets and opened the top left-hand drawer. He pulled out the folder for Death Claims-1998 (Year to Date), and leafed through the monthly summaries, January through August. The total number of claims was 11, for a total of $4,140,000. The number of lives was more than projected, but the average claim was somewhat lower, which meant that most were claims on older, lower-ranking men. Richard Trace knew that younger, more highly placed women would have larger average amounts of coverage because they represented a lower risk to the insurance companies.

Trace calculated that he would need an additional $4 million in claims to offset the treasury rate decline. Trace returned the file to its alphabetical place and retreated to his desk. He could count on two or three additional deaths from natural causes over the last quarter of the year, which would take care of $1 to 1.5 million. That meant that he would have to cover, at a minimum, about $ 3 Million. If he could find some high earners, at least one or two female, he reasoned that he could do it with four claims, which would average $750,000 each. He decided to aim for four initially, and increase the order if he came up short. The dark-complected man was now calculating death with detached, chilling efficiency. It was a rough business, but he reminded himself that it was strictly business.

Trace licked his lips, felt moisture on his tongue, and swallowed. His Adam's apple bobbed up and down. The brushed brass desk lamp cast an amber glow on Trace and softened the deep circles under his eyes and highlighted his prominent brow and oft-broken nose. Richard Trace knew that his height and powerful visage were often intimidating to other people. His appearance had served him well as a corporate executive, but it was his amorality that had led to his greatest success.

Over 5,000 First Gotham executives were insured under the program and were listed in Trace's desktop computer. He moved the cursor to a screen that showed there were 3,126 active employees, 1,403 who had left the bank for greener pastures, and 654 who had retired. *Geographical, sex, age and position diversity*, he thought.

Trace shifted forward in his chair. He glanced at the clock on his desk and saw that it read 6:54 p.m. He began to scan the list on his computer, methodically looking for amounts above $700,000 and for their status with First Gotham. By 7:45 he had winnowed the list down to fourteen. Without hesitation he chose three of these; they were slam dunks. He smiled at this observation. His nickname since high school had been "Slam Dunk." After a few minutes he selected a fourth name. It made him shudder inside. Trace had known this woman when she had been with the bank, but that had been many years earlier. As a young female executive the payoff on her death would be especially profitable, and besides, it would cut down the competition out west, an additional bonus. *Don't get all squishy and sentimental, Rich*, he thought, squaring his broad shoulders.

Trace picked up the phone and began to dial, then stopped himself. He cradled the phone, shut down the computer and turned off his desk lamp. For several moments the executive sat in the darkened office and stared out the window at Madison Avenue. Bright white-yellow headlights came toward him on the left; red tail-lights trailed away on the right. The thin slice of sky in the distance was a deep mauve on the horizon blending to dark purple above, but he was oblivious to the beauty of the colors outside. The clock now read 8:17. He remembered that his friend would be at his restaurant until well after midnight. Owners were predictable that way.

Trace collected his notes and slid them into his leather briefcase. He rose and strode out of the office. There was a phone booth in the lobby that he had used before for private calls. Trace closed the doors and sat on the bench for several minutes, collecting himself. Using his MCI calling card, the swarthy, sweating man dialed a Manhattan phone number.

On the second ring a deep European voice answered, "Johnny's Ristorante, may I help you?"

"May I speak to Mr. Pestrano?"

The wheels were about to be set in motion, again.

Chapter 2

Early summer, June, was the best time in the Kharchin territories of Mongolia. The wildflowers covered the grasslands to the east of Dalanjargalon, which was Duk Lon Ki's stop on the Trans-Mongolian Railroad. Each summer from the age of nine until he left Shanghai at age 14, Duk had made the journey by train through the teeming cities of the coast, through Peking, and then into the steppes on the route to Ulaan Bataar, the capital of Mongolia, to be with his mother's older brothers for the three months of the summer. They always met him at the train station in the tiny town of Dalanjargalon, their main city, 200 barren kilometers to the west of the wild, grassy homelands that they roamed.

The Mondars were a dirty, ragged band of three men, two women and their four children, traveling in a wagon that served as both home and transportation, the Winnebago of Mongolia. Traveling with this nomadic band were several sheep and goats, some cattle and, of course, the small horses that are so well known of that part the world. The Mondars had five. Duk had adopted Ning-Ning, the smallest of the ponies. She would still have her winter coat for the first few weeks of each visit. Duk was especially taken with her dark expressive eyes, the dark lashes set off against her dusky light brown coat. He could never get enough of the rides that were a part of every day life in the eastern grasslands. After the third summer, when he was twelve, he could have chosen one of the larger ponies, but by then he and Ning-Ning were like one, their muscles working together in unison on the long daily rides.

At night, his uncles would sit by the fire and tell the ancient stories of their people, eyes and teeth flashing with the wonder and merriment of it all. Duk recalled talk of mysterious adventures that seemed to have double meanings, and which always seemed to amuse his uncles the most.

"Someday you will pass through the Jade Gate," said Sandu, the oldest, to great laughter from his younger brothers. Duk's mother, Ming, had made sure that he spent this time with her family. "Never forget your Mongol heritage," she reminded him.

In Shanghai, during the other nine months of the year, life was very different. At the insistence of his father, Duk was in constant training to master several martial arts. They had become the very core of his life. After he had escaped to Hong Kong, he had come to appreciate his training, for it had saved his life in the back alleys and it had also led him to many opportunities with the white devils that couldn't seem to get enough of the thrill of violence that he was able to provide them through his instructions and demonstrations. In the late 1980's, while still in his thirties, he became the personal trainer of a wealthy Chinese business couple who introduced him into a world of travel and luxury that he had never imagined. Charlie and Candace Choi were generous in sharing him with their friends, and he soon had dozens of clients throughout the Pacific Rim. Duk came to know his way around in Hong Kong, Taipei, Tokyo, Honolulu, Vancouver, and finally, San Francisco, which to him was the epitome of the "Golden Mountain" that he had dreamed of as a youth in Shanghai. It was everything that his Mongolian uncles had fantasized about in their stories.

In time, Duk settled in the City by the Bay and his fortunes grew. He took advantage of his contacts and skills to open several martial arts studios. He was able to import talent from Hong Kong, and many of his instructors were from mainland China. While English was spoken to the clients, his staff meetings were conducted in Mandarin, and Duk was the undisputed boss.

His fortunes multiplied as he became a trusted confidant to many wealthy patrons. They admired his formidable skills, which had been developed to a masterful level through a virtual lifetime of concentrated training. His skills also attracted the attention of a nether world of sinister men who offered him substantial monetary rewards for accommodating their unique business needs. He soon discovered that one assignment a month allowed him to carry on his accustomed lifestyle without the necessity of putting up with what had become a tiresome routine, the drudgery of watching a middle aged executive pump iron or waddle through a miserable routine.

In 1993 Duk Lon Ki had done a job for the Pestrano family of New York City. The assignment had been a national bank executive. He had thought at the time that the banker must have turned down a loan request from the big boss or was threatening to reveal the family affairs to the authorities. Duk had successfully carried out that assignment and had favorably impressed Johnny Pestrano. That had been the beginning of a very lucrative business arrangement which eventually developed into a transcontinental partnership. From time to time Johnny had needed help on the West Coast, and rather than deal with a stranger, he had come to rely on

Duk. Once, in 1995, Johnny had met with Duk in San Francisco. They had enjoyed cocktails at his spectacular hilltop condo, then dinner in a private room at The Empress, Duk's favorite restaurant in Chinatown.

Johnny admired Duk's taste in clothes, automobiles (they had ridden in his Corniche that evening), and especially his taste in women. His companion, Ruby Ah Chee, was a genuine stunner, and she had a raucous sense of humor that Pestrano found exhilarating. He especially remembered her trilling laugh, which seemed to emerge from deep in her chest.

Duk had great respect for Johnny's straight forward business manner. There was no mistaking his power. The two men had remained fit and lean well into middle age; Duk understood and admired the effort that was required. He envied Johnny's sense of family and tradition. Having left his family behind, being part of the Pestrano organization was almost like being adopted by an American family.

So, in 1998, when Pestrano called him with a new assignment involving another bank executive, he was not surprised. But this time it was a female, and that did surprise him. She was president of the Central States Bank for the State of Washington, and, to his chagrin, she was a Chinese-American. He had been instructed to create a scenario in which the victim would appear to die of an ailment that she may have contracted on a recent sales swing through Singapore, Kuala Lumpur and Vietnam. Duk had been told that the lady would be attending a reception in San Francisco for the Chinese Chamber of Commerce before returning to her home in Seattle.

He would have to plan and execute his performance within a 24-hour period, although the death need not occur for several days.

"Johnny, I understand the assignment and I have just the solution," said Duk, "but may I ask why such a person has been targeted? Has she done something to offend your family?"

"Duk, this is strictly a financial arrangement. I don't even know this woman. Some guy I used to work with years ago has gotten himself into a position where it is to his advantage to have these bank officers eliminated. His bank has insurance on them, and his bonus is dependent on the return on their insurance investment, which includes claims."

"It seems strange to do this to an innocent woman. Most of our marks deserve their fate."

"It is bizarre, I'll admit. But this guy Trace pays top dollar; that is, I charge him top dollar."

"Sounds like a greedy creep to me," said Duk, with feeling.

"Yeah, greed does strange things to people, makes them lose all sense of perspective," Johnny observed seriously. "It even affects you and me on occasion, you must admit."

"Well, I'll do this because it is your request, and for us it is strictly business, but I've got to tell you that killing a hard working, innocent **Chinese** lady is not my idea of a good time."

"I know, Duk. I understand the conflict it causes you, and if you prefer, I'll go to another source."

"No, no, Johnny, I respect your position, and I am grateful for our arrangement. I just wanted you to know how I feel about this creep, what's his name? Trace, isn't it?"

"So noted, Duk, so noted." said Pestrano. He acknowledged Duk's distorted sense of honor.

When Duk migrated from Shanghai he brought several vials of germ culture which his uncles had obtained from the time they had been conscripted at Ro Block of Unit 731 in Manchuria, where the Japanese Army had experimented with prisoners, who they called "Maruta", during the Second World War. He had come to the United States armed not only with skills, but also with these unique weapons. His Mongolian uncles had presented him with these gifts as a means of protection against the round-eyes they thought might hinder his progress. He had used them before to advance his agenda, but never on an assignment.

Lily Yang Peterson was a slim, attractive and poised forty-four year old Chinese-American, born in Seattle to second generation immigrants. As she grew up she was only vaguely aware that she was different from the other kids as she was very popular in school and excelled both in the classroom and socially. She had a notably successful college experience at Cornell University and had gone to work for First Gotham Bank of New York right after graduation. Lily had risen through the ranks at First Gotham with ease, riding somewhat on the coattails of Sam Barry, who himself rose from vice president of business banking to executive vice president in charge of all retail operations in just five years. Lily had been his executive assistant in the business banking section, and then, as Sam realized her talents for organization and hard work, he promoted her so that by 1990 she was a senior vice president in his department.

The usual rumors of a romance between them, from Sam's perspective, were sadly untrue. He was very fond of her, and he also admired her talented and successful attorney husband. The Petersons had even named Sam the godfather of their son Rodney. No, there had been no romance.

In 1990 Central States Bank had approached Sam Barry with an offer to become Chief Executive Officer and within a year, chairman. Along with the titles came more stock incentives than he would ever have been able to get at First Gotham. So, after 23 years at the venerable old bank he decided to make the change, but not before convincing Lily to go with him. The move had worked out well for both of them, and when Sam retired in 1997, Lily and Rob Peterson had been among his cheering colleagues at the head table.

As one of his last official duties, Sam had negotiated a move to Seattle for Lily, as president of the retail operation in Washington. Rob was able to convince his Chicago partners to open an office in Seattle with him as managing partner. They had returned home to the Puget Sound area where they had indulged their passion for boating in a big way. Rob and Lily had share leased a 60 foot Windstar with their friends Ed and Shirley Leigh. The two families had begun to explore the waters around the San Juan Islands with great enthusiasm.

The dinner for the Chinese Chamber of Commerce was held in the ballroom of the Mark Hopkins Hotel and had been billed, ironically, as a "Night in Shanghai." The guest list included 1,500 of the movers and shakers of San Francisco with an emphasis on the

Chinese community. Lily Yang-Peterson had been invited by her old friend and competitor Robert Han, the U. S. Manager of the People's Bank of Hong Kong. He had known that she would be in town and had tipped off the organizers. While Lily would not be an honored guest and sit at the head table, having Lily attend was a real coup as she was regarded as one of the prime success stories for the Chinese business community on the West Coast, and, for that matter, in the whole country. She was one of only seventeen Asian bank presidents in the United States, and one of only three Asian women.

Robert Han knew he would gain significant face by squiring Lily around the ballroom and introducing her to his business associates. It didn't hurt that she was very attractive, and her off-the-shoulder gown of yellow silk, recently purchased in Kowloon, made her a magnetic attraction even in this room full of beautiful people.

Duk Lon Ki had surveyed the teeming crowd before him and calculated that it was just a matter of time before Lily would make herself accessible. He had secured a seating chart in the event planning office and had noted that Robert Han was hosting a table of eight near the front left-hand side of the room, near the head table, but far enough back so that he and his guests would have a good line of sight to the speaker's podium.

The ballroom had access to hallways that led to the service areas and halfway down these halls were the men's and ladies' restrooms. These hallways were crowded with guests and waiters at all times as the room was filled to capacity. The guests were gorging on food and drink and would soon be in need of relief. This would be the perfect place to bump into her, seemingly by accident. She would never know that the brief and, for all appearances, inconsequential encounter with one of the waiters would cause her death within five days.

Lily had just finished talking with Mayor Willie Brown and had asked Robert where to find the women's room. He had guided her across the room and pointed to the crowded hallway.

Lily released his arm and told him that she would only be a few minutes. "Please hurry back, Lily, my friends will be bored just talking to me," he whispered, laughing.

Robert raised his hand in recognition of another guest and was off on another mission. Lily was somewhat relieved to have some time alone away from him and his mad social whirl. She turned and began to find her way through the throng and down the hallway. She saw the illuminated sign for the *Ladies* up ahead and stepped around a couple who were standing still in the middle of the passage. As she stepped around them, the laughter of the girl caught her attention, and she looked backward toward her.

At that moment, Duk, dressed as a waiter, sprang forward in a flash and bumped her just hard enough so that she lost her balance and began to pitch forward to her left. He made a lightning quick thrust and scissors-like move with his hands that pinched the skin of her bare shoulder. In the same instant, he pushed the special injector tool, specially designed to fit over his index finger, into her shoulder, pushing just hard enough for the deadly Manchurian germ cultures to penetrate the skin. The unexpected bump, and Duk's frantic grabbing to hold her upright, made it impossible for Lily to feel the fatal insertion. When she felt herself falling forward, Lily bent at the waist. At the same time she felt the rough grasp of a waiter grabbing at her bare shoulder and waist. She was pulled upright by his strong arm, reaching across her hips.

It's a good thing that I'm so slim, she thought, marveling at the strength of this man's hand and wrist as he gently, but firmly, pulled her to an upright position.

"Duibuqi! So sorrie, Missa!"

She looked down at the top of the waiter's head as he bowed in supplication.

"That's all right, thank you. I should have looked where I was going," she stammered.

Duk held his head down and backed away, appearing humbled and embarrassed.

"It's OK. Meishir," she said.

Duk had glanced up at her when she addressed him in Chinese. She noticed the dark scar over his left eyebrow, but never saw his face, only his forehead and the scar. He had quickly turned and walked away. Lily Yang-Peterson was once again jostled by the crowd and continued on to the restroom. Once inside she straightened her gown and checked her makeup. Everything seemed to be in order. Her shoulder was irritated from the encounter with the waiter, she speculated because of being grabbed there to prevent a fall. She ran her fingers back and forth over her bare shoulder and it felt rough, so she had licked her fingers and smoothed out the skin. This seemed to soothe the dull ache and as it subsided she turned slightly and looked in the mirror at her back to see if there was any kind of cut or abrasion. She was relieved that there appeared to be only a reddening of the area around her shoulder blade, nothing to be concerned about. Lily lifted her fingers to her lips and flicked at the edges of her open mouth.

Deadly spores of the century-old germs were released directly into the open pores of her tongue and palate. They would now attack two areas of her body, and the normal six day cycle would be reduced to five, possibly four days. The beautiful banker applied more lip gloss and returned to the ballroom to find Robert Han.

Duk had backed into the service area and walked straight through the crowded room to the far end where a hall turned back to the freezer units; then to the delivery alley behind the hotel. He shed the waiter's uniform which he had worn over his dark trousers and turtleneck and stepped into the empty alley. He lit a cigarette and calmly made his way down the dark passage to California Street. He turned down the hill, taking deep drags on his cigarette; from all appearances he was just a slender Chinese man out for an evening stroll. A few minutes later, after several turns, he arrived at his car, which he had parked on a side street. Once in the plush seat of his Jensen Interceptor, he put on the leather jacket he had left in the front seat, and emitted a deep sigh.

Such a pretty woman, he thought. *I wonder why Trace chose **her** for this fate?*

He turned the key and guided the powerful car onto the quiet side street. The City was just turning from dark pink to lavender; it was 7:35 p.m.

Duk turned onto Chestnut Street and headed for his apartment on Telegraph Hill. He licked his thin lips, touching the bottom hairs of his dark mustache, then licking up the sides of his Mandarin cut beard. The feeling was sensual and stimulating. As he drove up the winding hill, he put the events of the evening behind him and thought of Ruby Ah Chee waiting in the apartment not five minutes away. He had called her before the assignment and knew that she was preparing her playthings, and the warm oils with which she plied her craft. Of all his imports from Shanghai, Ruby was his prize. She was his woman, by ownership and control, not by any conventional means. Duk wheeled the powerful car through the final turns with only two fingers on the wheel. The classic car glided effortlessly along the cobbled street and approached the bronzed gate at the entrance of his condominium complex. He punched the electronic opener and sped forward through the portals, turning sharply left as the wheels of the Jensen squealed. The automatic garage door was just then reaching the fully open position. The electrician had timed the interval between the gate and the garage just right.

On his left in the four-place garage was the Rolls Corniche that he rarely used, and on the right the Jaguar that he had given to Ruby for her shopping expeditions, an electric-blue coupe that turned heads even on the streets of San Francisco. Ruby and the Jag were both exquisite. Duk pulled the heavy sedan into its customary middle space and pushed the clicker that closed both the garage door and the private gate, and at the same time opened the elevator at the far corner of the garage where there was one empty parking space.

He contemplated the idea of adding a Navigator to his stable of cars, and labeling it his "Urban Assault Vehicle." Again he laughed quietly to himself.

Duk Lon Ki got out of his car, hitched up his Armani slacks, adjusted his belt, hunched and squared his shoulders and smoothed down his wispy mustache and beard. Then he ran his fingers through his salt-and-pepper close-cropped hair and finished by sweeping the back of his left little finger along the dark scar over his left brow.

The private elevator hummed into action and transported him the forty feet up to his penthouse. The doors slid open to reveal a marble and glass entry area leading into a raised living room and the lights of the city beyond and below.

Ruby Ah Chee emerged from around the corner of the living room and folded into his arms.

"Ah, Duk," she purred.

He placed a hand at her waist and tilted her up. She moved her hips into his and lifted herself to receive his eager lips. He nuzzled the hollow of her shoulder, then raised his head and looked in her eyes.

"Ruby, I..."

She placed a finger over his mouth. "Say nothing, just come with me."

As she turned she loosened the silver rope belt around the waist of her silk nightgown and with a shrug of her shoulders it fell to the marble floor. Duk suppressed a smile of satisfaction as he followed the beautiful naked woman—his woman—through the carpeted living room. Ruby turned toward him, looking back over her shoulder. He could see the taunt nipple of her right breast. He marveled at the firmness of her muscular body.

Ruby was pulling him along now, gliding quickly toward the bedroom in her silk slippers. Duk removed his leather jacket and threw it on the divan as they went through the large living room. They entered the bedroom, and Duk saw that Ruby had made her preparations. Four small candles gave the white and mauve furnishings a golden glow. There were vials of oil on the side tables that curved out from the elaborate half-moon shaped rosewood headboard. He peeled his black sweater over his head and let it fall to the floor. Ruby turned to him and they embraced.

She unhooked his belt and tugged at his dark gabardine trousers. Duk pushed them down and stepped out of the legs. Ruby led him to the waiting bathroom. He could see the steam rising from the Japanese furo that he had imported and installed in the apartment. The bathroom was dark except for the candles whose flames were reflected over and over in the mirrors. His lover scrubbed his back and neck in the shower stall, then sprayed him clean with a thin flex-metal hose.

Only then did Duk lower himself into the deep furo. The intense heat had the effect of making his body feel as though it had melted away. Ruby Ah Chee massaged his neck and the back of his head. Duk reached for her and she slipped down into the scalding water beside him. The furo was only large enough for both of them because of their slim physiques. Some of the water spilled out over the edge onto the stone floor. They were locked in an embrace that neither could fully discern due to the enervating effect of the heated pool, but one that was all the more spiritually intense for that very reason. Duk could feel the tension of the night melt away. He kissed her eyes, her cheek, the lobe of her ear. They remained melded for a long time, their bodies soaking in the soothing waters which Ruby had perfumed. An intoxicating aroma rose with the steam from the bath and permeated the room.

After what seemed an eternity, Ruby rose past Duk and sat at the edge of the tub. She held out her hand and he followed, allowing himself to be pulled from the still steaming waters. They patted each other dry with huge white bath towels. He knew that the bath was only a prelude of things to come. She walked to the bed, pulled back the cover and languorously stretched out on the sheets. Her thick blue-black hair spread out like a fan on her pillow. Duk followed and lay down beside her, hands behind his back. On the ceiling above he watched the shadows play a game of hide-and-seek caused by the interaction of the candle flames all around them. In a few minutes their bodies again had feeling. They began to touch each other, lightly at first, then with more intensity. Their recently languid bodies became turgid and almost painfully sensitized. Duk rose up on his knees.

"The oil, Ruby….now!" he gasped.

His lover rose to a kneeling position beside him and reached over his body to a side table, inserting two fingers in the warm oil. She inserted her index finger into him and began to move it up and down, slowly and carefully at first, then deeper and faster.

Duk grunted, "Yes, yes!"

Ruby knew what most pleased her man. Her ministrations were exotically sensual. He relaxed into the rhythm of it and floated off into another world of pleasure.

"The beads, Ruby," he groaned.

She reached across the bed with her left hand and felt for the string of onyx beads, and, catching the end of the string, reached back and dipped the foot long strand with its six marble-sized black beads into the hottest oil. She made sure each of them was thoroughly doused in the oil and then returned her hand to Duk, first inserting her index finger, then her middle finger. She could feel that he was now moist and ready.

"Yes, now Ruby, do it!" he commanded.

She inserted the first bead with care, then pushed in the other five. She resumed her rhythmic oral stimulation. He moaned aloud.

"Now, Ruby!"

His legs began to jerk in cadence with her rhythm. The shadows overhead appeared to dance across the ceiling. Duk thrashed wildly on the bed.

"Please, Ruby....now!"

At his command, she tugged at the string of beads.

"Oh, yes," cried Duk.

His legs lashed out and hit the side table a glancing blow. A candle shook in its holder and white, molten wax spilled out onto the table. As it hardened, more splattered on top and then still more, as his legs trembled again and again. Duk closed his eyes and let out a deep sigh.

"Ah, Ruby, that was so good," he whispered.

Ruby Ah Chee smiled and handed Duk a second set of beads, smaller than the onyx ones, about the size of cultured pearls. He dipped these shiny white beads in the hot oil and inserted them into her.

"Now, Duk," she sighed.

He tugged on the string and soon the first bead began to emerge.

About halfway she cried "Oh Duk. Oh, my God."

He pulled harder and the rest came out in a rush.

"Oh, it hurts! Oh, my God!"

He used his warm, oily fingers to soothe her ache, then to stimulate her again. She responded by rolling on top of him. Once again the shadows danced in a rhythm that had been projected on the ceiling of their bedroom many times. At first they were slowly riding up and down, in time they extended from corner to corner as Duk thrust hard and deep, reaching the limit of her tiny body. The candles quivered and once again splattered milky wax on the end tables. Ruby collapsed herself over Duk and humped wildly until he receded.

Duk rolled her over and sat on the edge of their bed. He rose and went into the bathroom and blew out the flickering candles there and shut the door. When he returned to the bed, Ruby was already asleep. He pinched out the candles on the night stands, then pulled the covers over her and walked into the living room, leaving the bedroom door ajar behind him. He sat on the sofa and looked out at the city. He thought of his assignment earlier that evening, and it sent a shiver through his still naked body. Duk instinctively found the cigar humidor and extracted an El Conquistador #2. He snipped off the end and lit the aromatic tobacco, allowing the smoke to fill his mouth, but suppressing his throat so that it could not reach his lungs. The taste mingled with the perfumed steam and Ruby's oils.

In his sensitized state the effect was mesmerizing. Duk concentrated on the lights of Coit Tower, trying to erase the image of that woman in the yellow silk dress. He knew that she was still alive and not yet aware of the deadly germs that would ravish her body in a few short hours. Duk blew a smoke ring toward the ceiling. It was just barely visible in the reflected light from the city lights outside his apartment. He heard Ruby murmuring from the bedroom. It was ever so quiet here; the only sounds were the muted muttering of car horns on the Embarcadero nearly a mile down the hill from where he sat, not too far from where he had needled that fat banker five years earlier. Why couldn't all of his assignments be that satisfying? That mark had been a pompous capitalist. He was the very kind of American who always tried to keep Asians in their place, that lower state of joss which the white men perceived to be our fate. Maybe someday he would get a chance to ply his skills on that man who ordered the hit on this Chinese lady. What was his name? Duk struggled to recall what Johnny had told him about the banker who he had known in a previous life when suddenly it came to him.

Oh yes, Trace, that was it. He smiled at the remembrance.

He saw Lily's yellow dress; he heard her soft voice speaking Chinese to him, ye Gods! *Yes, if I am given the chance, Mr. Trace, you will pay big for this.* He stood up and took a long pull on the cigar, exhaled, and strode to the window. An intermittent red-orange glow illuminated his hard, naked body as he stood transfixed in a murderous trance, oblivious of his surroundings. He was trying to suppress the thought of killing a model Chinese woman, but try as he might he couldn't get her out of his mind.

Seattle Post Intelligence: Saturday, November 7, 1998

Lily Yang Peterson, President of Central States Bank for Washington, passed away on Wednesday, November 4, 1998 at age 44. Mrs. Yang-Peterson grew up and attended secondary schools in the Seattle area. She then went on to Cornell University in Ithaca, New York, where she graduated with honors in 1976. She began her career in banking with the First Gotham Bank in New York City, rising to the position of Senior Vice President. In 1990 she joined Central States Bank in Chicago,

Illinois, and since August 1997 had served as its President in the State of Washington. Mrs. Yang Peterson was active in civic organizations in the Puget Sound region, serving as District Director of the American Red Cross— King/Pierce County, Secretary of the Business Leaders Round Table, and Deputy Director of the United Way of Seattle.

She is survived by her husband, Robert R. Peterson, son Rodney P., and her mother Sui-Lin Pang of Everett. In lieu of flowers, the family requests that donations be made in her name to the American Red Cross."

The following Monday morning when Shelly Martin saw that her cursor was blinking on Program "D", she knew that could only mean there was a new death claim. Shelly was used to having important messages waiting for her on Monday morning; it came with the territory, but she could never suppress the feeling of apprehension when this particular program signaled activation. Program "D" was designed to find a match, by social security number, whenever any of the insured employees of their client banks was reported as deceased. She opened the program and clicked twice to engage the window that would give her the vital information. She called it "the window of death."

She saw the first entry on the screen: 576-55-2385. It was a West Coast social security number. The name was Lily Yang-Peterson, age 44, female, Chinese-American, married, current position President, Central States Bank for the State of Washington.

"Wow!" Shelly whistled.

Place of death: Seattle, WA. Cause of death: Unknown disease (most likely contracted on a recent trip to Asia). Date of Death: Wednesday, November 4, 1998, 10:05 a.m.

The cursor indicated that there was a second page. When she saw that the same information was on the other page, Shelly uttered, "Oh boy, she's a double dipper, also covered by First Gotham of New York." *I'd better check on the coverage so I can bring Mr. Harkness up to date when he gets in*, she thought. Shelly was able to access the coverage files for First Gotham as they had already converted them from the file folders over the summer. She scrolled down the list of covered employees page by page as a Lily Yang-Peterson would be near the end of the coverage pages.

Ah, there she is. Check social, 576-55-2385. Yep, it's the same gal. OK, premium at inception, age 33, $ 54,900.00,, death benefit, $825,000. It seems high. Oh yeah, Mr. Harkness had explained that, at inception, the young females would have the highest coverage and the older males would have the least coverage. She must have been way up in the hierarchy of the bank even at age 33. This would be a bonanza for First Gotham, she reasoned.

Shelly got up and went over to the file cabinet marked Central States Bank and unlocked the safety lock. She went to the third drawer down and pulled out the Y file. There she found the file for Lily Yang-Peterson, same social security 576-55-2385. *OK, premium $50,500.00, age 37, death benefit, $700,000*, she confirmed to herself.

Shelly couldn't remember such a young woman dying, and the coverage was nearly the largest she had seen. Shelly had just settled back into her chair when

Harry Harkness walked by on his way to his office at the end of the hall.

"Mr. Harkness, we had a message from Program "D" this morning, a young woman executive at Central States. Oh, and she is also covered by First Gotham."

"Yes, I saw the obit in the New York Times this morning, Lily Yang-something"

"Lily Yang-Peterson. And she was the President of Central States for Washington State!"

"Okay, Shell. What are we talking about on this one?"

"$700,000 at Central States and $825,000 at First Gotham."

"My God, she must have been a pretty high exec. How old was she?"

"She was 44, and the Gotham coverage was done in 1988. She went to Central in 1990, and her coverage there was done in 1992."

"What was the cause of death, did it say?"

"Let's see, yeah, unknown disease, possibly contracted in the Orient."

"What a way to start a Monday morning," he muttered.

"How do you think her family feels?" replied Shelly.

"Yeah, well. OK, Shelly, notify the companies about this. I'm sure they know, but we need to contact them about making a claim. That would be George Turner at Central States. Send him a nice letter, condolences, and so forth. And Richard Trace at First Gotham, just send him an e-mail. He's been at this a long time and their program is large enough that he sees plenty of death claims. Besides, Trace is a rather unsentimental type."

Chapter 3

By the time the e-mail from Shelly Martin of Smith, Hay and Ward appeared on his computer screen that Monday morning, the death of Lily Yang-Peterson was old news to Richard Trace. He had gotten a call the previous Wednesday evening from Sam Feldman, a former First Gotham Vice President who was then with Central States. Sam had remained on friendly terms with "Slam" after leaving First Gotham three years earlier. He had been someone with whom Trace saw eye-to-eye, and not just because they were both ex-basketball jocks and were about the same height. Trace saw no irony that, in his mind, Feldman was a "good guy" while all other Jews were "heebs."

"Yeah, died this morning. They think it was some oriental virus. She had just been on tour in Southeast Asia," Feldman had reported.

"Wow, she was so young and dynamic." Trace feigned shock.

"Right. A big loss for this bank, but probably a big gain for you though," Sam replied.

"What do you mean?" Trace responded cautiously.

"The insurance. The BOLI."

"I don't really know about that. It's a big program," he lied, knowing full well that Lily represented an $825,000 bonanza for First Gotham.

During the days and weeks that followed, Trace had a hard time pushing the image of Lily Yang-Peterson out of his thoughts. When he got the e-mail from Smith, Hay and Ward it had brought it home to him again with a finality that was jolting. The enormity of his crime staggered him. It **was** a criminal act that he had arranged. He shook his head in wonder that such crimes had been committed by him nine times now, five in 1993 and four more in 1998. Somehow, this one had more impact. He had known Lily personally. They had worked together on several committees. She had always been supportive of his work with the bank, even when many other old-time bankers were skeptical of the "insurance guy." She had gone out of her way to introduce him to other executives at company functions. Now, she was only a death claim, $825,000 for First Gotham Bank! *I should have chosen someone else,* he shuddered.

Trace had tried to carry on with his normal business, without success. He decided to take his walk early and left the office at 10:45. The traffic patterns, both pedestrian and vehicular, were quite different compared to the noon hour, not so crowded and much less frenetic. Within minutes he found himself walking alone in Central Park South. He strayed from his usual route and wandered down a path through a grove of maple and oak trees. His shoes scuffed at fallen leaves with every step. The sidewalk had been permanently stained by the wet leaves which were now being blown away, the heavier gusts of wind tearing at the parchment thin remains. Lily remained in his thoughts like the ever present heaviness he felt in his left shoulder where he had once had arthroscopic surgery. While the pain had been eliminated, he still remained cautious about ever extending it. He had felt the same kind of caution when he got the call from Sam Feldman. Trace was a man with something to hide, and it had begun to cause him to withdraw within himself. *I've got to get over this. It had to be done,* he rationalized.

A sudden blast of wind blew a large wet maple leaf into his face. Trace raised his hand to fend it off and lost his balance. The large man stumbled forward, but regained his footing almost immediately. Looking over at the trees blowing in the wind, he saw yellow and red leaves flying off the branches and swirling down toward the pond on his right, landing and floating away like a colorful armada. Trace came to a small bridge and leaned on the concrete siding, watching the leaves float over to the bridge, and then down below into the darkness underneath his vantage

point. His thoughts turned back to another autumn more than thirty years earlier across the Hudson in New Jersey where he had recruited and trained Johnny Pestrano.

—

That November had been the precursor of what turned out to be the almost Nordic winter of 1969. He recalled a particular morning outside the East Coast Life office when the last of the leaves had been blasted off the maples and elms along Ridgewood Avenue by a fierce northwest wind. The trees in that usually leafy suburb had become stark naked that day. The locals shuffled about outside like so many aged snowmen, their necks buried in their dark overcoats, their hats pulled down hard over their heads. Even the young men looked like old gray men. This kind of weather was a great equalizer when it came to appearance. It would have been bitter cold, even without the wind. Richard Trace and John Pestrano had hurried toward the inviting warmth of the Ridgemont Coffee Shop just a few paces ahead.

"Whew, it is really cold, Mr. Trace!"

"Just starting, kid, just starting. We've got four or five more months of this, to say nothing of the ice and snow that we can expect. You may even long for 'Nam before this winter is over."

Johnny gave him a look that said "off limits." It made Trace realize that he would have to be more careful about that subject since Johnny seemed so sensitive about it.

"Let's grab a booth, Johnny."

They hung their dark coats, cloth for Trace, mohair for Pestrano, on the hooks on the aisle end of the booth backs. Their coats served almost like a curtain, giving them a sense of privacy in the crowded restaurant. Rich and Johnny slid in on opposite sides of the anchored table and faced each other.

The older young man noticed that Johnny seemed distracted and was avoiding eye contact. This gave him a chance to study the features of his newest recruit more closely. The bridge of his nose was too wide for him to be considered handsome in the classic sense, but it did give him a strong look that would likely become a powerful visage as he got older. His skin had a golden hue that Trace at first had thought was a tan from the sun of Vietnam, but it didn't seem to be fading and he had been back in the States for over two months. At first Trace thought that his recruit might be using a sunlamp, but on further reflection realized that he was no pretty boy. He surmised that Johnny was what he had heard described as a "golden guinea."

Trace admired his slim physique. Every part of Pestrano's body looked taut and fit, ready to spring--like a sleek leopard. It was unnerving, even though Trace was a much larger man.

Just then Johnny's eyes came up and met his manager's gaze. He smiled and his boss relaxed, unclenching his tight fists. His height usually intimidated new recruits, but John V. Pestrano didn't seem intimidated by anyone or anything. Maybe it was Vietnam, or maybe it was the streets and alleys of Lodi, New Jersey, or possibly something deeper, something to do with his family. Someday he would find a way to get Johnny to open up on that subject and satisfy his curiosity. Before Trace could pry, Johnny opened the conversation with a question.

"How did you get the nickname "Slam Dunk?""

"Oh, that, well that goes back to high school. My junior year I was already 6' 4" and very skinny. I had a lot of enthusiasm, but not much talent at that time. Our team was a good one and we made it to the Nassau County championship that year. 1960 it was.

I was the number ten man on the squad, out of ten. We had nice purple uniforms and warm-ups, and I loved the pre-game drills when we were all dressed up, but I hated taking off the warm-ups because the uniforms showed how skinny I was. They weren't the baggy things the kids wear these days.

"Things have sure changed for you," observed Pestrano.

"Well, yes. After the experience that I am about to tell you, I vowed never to be embarrassed in public again and hit the weights. I gained 40 pounds of muscle between my junior and senior years, made the All-Nassau County team my senior year and got a basketball scholarship to LIU," bragged Trace. Johnny nodded with respect.

"Anyway, let me finish the story of how I got the nickname. Well, I didn't really expect to play in the championship game and was content to ride the pine and look cool in my purple warm-ups. In the second quarter the coach yelled, *Trace, get that warm-up off.* It took what seemed like an hour for me to struggle out of the warm-ups and go into the game. When the buzzer rang I went in on defense, guarding a kid throwing in the ball from under the basket. I shifted left, then right, then left again just as he threw the ball in-bounds, and somehow I intercepted it. Everyone took off down the floor, but I whirled and shot for the basket, the wrong basket. Up it went, straight up, touching nothing, an air ball. By then everyone turned and were racing back to me. My teammates were yelling, *No Richie, No!* But I was so excited and determined. Up I went for the ball, and it came down in my hands, then up again."

At this point Trace was up off his seat and reaching up, up as if reliving the scene of eight years earlier.

"I strained with all my might and made my first slam dunk, my first ever, and it was in the wrong basket for the other team. In the confusion the whistle blew and the Coach came out to me, put his arm around me and said, *Son, you're a little too excited. Put on your warm up and sit down.* Trace laughed and shook his head as he recalled the scene.

"All the guys began to call me "Slam Dunk" and it stuck. My senior year, and especially in college, it took on a whole different meaning. I came to enjoy the power image it conveys."

Johnny looked across the table. "You know, I was never into team sports."

Richard "Slam Dunk" Trace stared at him without a word as he realized that Pestrano had not related to anything he had just said. He was both unnerved and peeved at his arrogance.

"Oh well. Listen, I want to run an idea by you that you may want to talk to your dad and uncle about. This is the latest insurance sales gimmick. Ray Engleman, East Coast Life's biggest producer, has made $ 1 million in production credits on this idea alone so far this year. Here's the deal: you buy a regular whole life contract and pre-pay, say, ten years of premium. This is for rich guys like your uncle. Well, the company puts the extra unused premium to work at 7% interest, and because it is with an insurance company, it grows tax free. This makes it a better investment than a CD or other fixed investment, after taxes. We should show this to your uncle Carlo."

"Well, I don't know. Uncle Carlo don't like to pay taxes."

"Hey, Johnny boy, that's what we're talking about here, a tax dodge!"

"Uncle Carlo just says, 'Johnny, I don't pay no taxes'."

"Well, think about it. It's a cool idea, and we can get nice premium growth with it. How about you're other prospects?"

"My father told me to call on Mr. and Mrs. Metstaff. He says they want to buy some coverage. We can see them tonight. Can you come with me?"

"Sure, Johnny, my pleasure!"

—

Richard Trace stretched his long legs, locked his fingers together, and rolled his wrists up and out, holding this position for a few seconds. This exercise always seemed to relax his upper torso and, somehow, cleared his mind. He was 6' 5" in shoes, his preferred measurement, and at age 54 still weighed within ten pounds of his college playing weight of 195 pounds. Trace remembered that at the time he was working with Johnny he was still able to hold his own against the younger guys at either end of the basketball court, but he didn't get up and down the floor nearly as fast. Yes, it had proved true that you lose a step each year.

He ran his long fingers through his dark, tightly curled, short-cropped hair. He recalled that even in his mid-twenties, a bald spot was beginning to show at the crown of his head, and his hairline was receding in front. The thought of shaving his head had occurred to him, but he was self-conscious about his ears. As a kid he had been teased about them. *Dumbo, Dumbo* they would yell. So he preferred to leave as much hair above and behind them as possible. His face was angular, with high cheekbones, a strong jaw-line, wide mouth and slanting forehead. This Vulcan like visage was perched on a long, powerful neck. His appearance was definitely that of an ex-basketball player.

Along the way, largely because of his participation in team sports, he had picked up several nicknames. Rich (never Rick or Dick,) and Richie when he was younger. Then "Slam Dunk" and its shortened versions: Slam, Slammer, Slam-man, Dunk, and Dunk-man. Most often he was called Rich or Slam. Over the years he had grown comfortable with these nicknames. He came to enjoy telling the story of how he got the

"Slam Dunk" handle. It gave him an excellent opportunity to appear at least somewhat humble about his basketball prowess. It also revealed his need for acceptance, and his motivation to impress and succeed. For Richard Trace, dissatisfaction was a far greater motivator than satisfaction; he could never be satisfied about anything in his life. He was a classic type A personality, a driven man. His height and intense bearing impressed superiors and subordinates alike. But, thinking back on these early days with Johnny Pestrano, he realized that it was **he** who had been intimidated, even though Johnny had been four years younger and five inches shorter. He had never before seen such coolness and calm assurance. He now knew that it was both Vietnam and, more fundamentally, the knowledge that he was destined for a succession to a family tradition, a tradition of power that in Vietnam had been reinforced as within his capacity.

Johnny Pestrano knew, even at age 21, that he would be a successful Don some day. He had been a very successful soldier, loyal to his country and to his unit. When the time came to perform his duty as a trained killer, he did so with efficiency and without emotion, just as his father Harry and Uncle Carlo had instructed. He had returned to Lodi as a young war hero, the perfect image for their extended family. They had arranged for him to secure a sales position in the upper class neighborhood of Ridgewood, knowing that they could supply him with leads that would give him a good income for those first two or three years back home. The family business could be put on hold for a while.

At the time, Trace had marveled at how all of Johnny's prospects were so eager to buy. They would often insist on buying even more than he recommended. He had eventually come to understand what had been happening, and why these customers had been so motivated. Those had been some of the most satisfying months of his sales career as a trainer, success on virtually every appointment. He had enjoyed those months in spite of what had been the worst winter weather before or since.

In August, after a first half in which Johnny had led the territory among the newer agents, Harry and Maria Pestrano had invited the Ridgewood office to their house for a celebratory dinner. It promised to be a very festive evening. Richard and Diana Trace were excited and curious about attending a party in Lodi at the home of what they had come to believe was a Mafia family. Diana had become somewhat anxious as the day approached.

—

Richard Trace leaned back and pressed his fingers into the back of his neck. The muted sunlight reflected off the multihued leaves in the pond, turning them silver and gray. They floated beneath the stone bridge as he stood there in a trance. Trace again closed his eyes and recalled that night in Lodi.

—

"Where the hell is 619? We should be there by now, Diana. 619 Parkland Avenue. I'm sure this must be it. Did you see the street sign back at the last corner?"

"Oh, Rich, I don't like this part of town," she whined.

"Never mind! This ought to be some show, these Pestrano folks throwing a party for their kid hero and his district office. It should be a blast!"

"It looks like a seedy neighborhood to me."

"Anything looks seedy to someone from Scarsdale, dear."

Diana Trace was tall and well put together; she had a long lean face and an athletic look that gave her an earthy sexiness. Her voice had a twang, part Scarsdale, part bone structure. She shifted uneasily in the Mustang. It bothered her that Rich insisted on such a small car. Power and style be damned, she would rather have had a four-door Lincoln, like her father.

"Here it is, and it looks like others are already here. Wow, this is the biggest and best house on the street, by far! On with the show, dear girl. Let's be on our best behavior. His family is loaded."

"I'm not impressed, Rich. My father could buy this whole neighborhood."

"Well, you had better learn to start depending on Richard Trace rather than Walter Underhill. Let's go impress these paisanos."

Trace spotted Johnny greeting Larry Matriano, a young agent who had started just the week before Johnny, and his wife Mary. Larry was one of the "pulse count" agents, hired because a so-called "debit" collection area needed filling, and since he had a pulse count, he got the job. He had surprised everyone by lasting this long through hard work and perseverance. Larry worshiped Johnny for his ability as a salesman. They had formed a big brother-little brother relationship even though Larry was six years older.

"Mary, it is so great to meet you. Larry talks about you all the time, and now I know why."

Mary blushed, "You are so nice to invite us to your party, Johnny."

"No problem, Mary. Hey, I want you to meet my mother. Ma! Come meet Mary and Larry."

Maria Pestrano came from inside the house and shook hands with Larry, then held out her hand to Mary and pulled her into the entry, placing a protective arm around the young woman as they went into the house. Her husband watched her go with a look that bordered on panic.

"Mary is in good hands, Larry. Mom is the greatest."

Rich and Diana Trace approached Johnny, and Rich greeted him. "Johnny, my boy, meet the love of my life. Diana, this is Johnny Pestrano, my best agent!"

Johnny gazed into her blue eyes and she felt a power that she had seldom encountered. "It's great to finally meet you, Diana," he said *sotto voce*, taking her hand.

She felt a cold shiver run down her back even though it was a very warm August night. "And you too, Johnny," she whispered, as his stare spoke volumes in return.

The setting sun shone directly on his face and illuminated his golden skin. Was it a tan after a summer in New Jersey? She made a small bow and passed by into the entry. Trace patted Johnny on the arm and said, "See you later after you finish your official duties."

Once inside, Trace saw the district manager, Manning Klein, talking to an older version of Johnny Pestrano: the same taunt body, slightly bent forward, the same wide nose and coal black hair, and the same golden skin. He was moving his hands in a circular motion as if to depict some sort of race. As he walked toward them, he realized that it was Harry Pestrano. He was regaling Mann Klein and his wife with a story about how he had chased young Johnny around when he was just a little boy. It was obvious that the father had great love and admiration for his son.

Trace just barely tolerated his manager. Klein had been promoted out of his original territory as a way of getting rid of him. He had inherited the Ridgewood District of East Coast Life virtually by forfeit. The man was wet wood, a real zip! When Trace had tried to explain the interest rate play to him he just sat there with a fish-eyed stare. *Some people just don't get it,* he thought.

Harry stepped forward to greet him, "You must be Richard Trace."

"How did you know?"

"Well, no other basketball players in the room. You got to be him," barked Harry. He took Trace's hand in his strong grip. Harry "Slats" Pestrano was indeed much like his son, golden brown and slim, with an easy confidence about his presence.

"I like what you're doin' for my son. He's a good boy, war hero, you know? Apple of his mother's eye."

"Hey, Maria! Come meet Mr. Trace." Harry yelled over the din in the living room. Maria came over to him, Mary Matriano in tow.

"Mary is going to help me with the set-ups, Harry."

"Oh, OK Maria. Say, I want you to meet Rich Trace, Johnny's boss."

"I thought that Mr. Klein was the boss."

"Nah, he's the big boss. Trace, here, he's the one that's trained Johnny and goes on all the sales calls with him."

"Nice to meet you, Mr.Trace. You take good care of my boy! He's a war hero, you know!" She nodded proudly. "A real hero in Vietnam, Mary."

"Yes, Larry has told me," She nodded, as if in awe.

"Oh, I'm just so happy to have him back. Was your Larry in Vietnam, Mary?"

"No, Mrs. Pestrano, he has a bad back and couldn't go," said Mary, almost apologetically.

"Well, don't you worry about that, young lady. He's a fine young man."

Maria looked at the tall blond next to Trace, "You must be Diana."

"Yes, Diana Trace."

"Well, why don't you join Mary and me in our kitchen. I want to show you girls what we are preparing for dinner."

Diana's departure allowed Rich to circulate among his friends. Spotting his buddy Joe Dolan across the room, he yelled. "Hey, Joe D!"

"Slammer! How're they hangin?"

"Not bad. Say, you know that interest rate play that we talked about some time ago?"

"Yeah, I have already pitched it several times; could be a winner."

"Well, I tried to explain it to the boss, and well, it was, you know, a small step for man, but a giant leap for Mann Klein."

"A giant leap for Mann Klein. Clever, clever Slammer! Great line. You've got that turkey pegged. Yeah, that interest rate idea is the kind of thinking we need in our district office. The trick is to figure the angles, Dunk-man, figure the angles. That's how Engleman and his heeb buddies lead the company every year. They work the angles."

"Dolan, have you been down to the rec-room? I guess that is where the feast is to take place."

"Let's go, Mr. Dunk; I'm ready to eat a horse."

Joe Dolan and Richard Trace went down into the fully finished basement that covered almost the entire footprint of the spacious Pestrano home, nearly 3,500 square feet. They were amazed at all the marble; it was like walking into a Roman bath house. In each corner of the room there was a column of pure white Carrara marble. The floor was some sort of multi-colored inlaid granite and in the middle was a section of cherry wood, set up like a dance floor. There were four long tables set for ten each, two on either side of the center section. At the far end of the room was an enormous fireplace that covered about a third of the wall. Trace could see that there was a room beyond the fireplace, as it was an open hearth affair with an opening on each side. Serving ladies in white uniforms were busy preparing the meals in the far room, and on a grill in the opening, huge steaks were being grilled. The room was now nearly filled with guests. Some had already taken seats and were busy with their salads. He saw that Diana and Mary were seated with Maria, across from Mann Klein and his wife Millie. Harry was at the fireplace with Johnny and Larry.

Slam and Joe went over to the fireplace to admire the steaks, urged forward by their sizzling aroma.

"Good God, look at those honeys!" observed Dolan.

"Only the best for my Johnny," answered Harry Pestrano.

Dolan gave Johnny a punch on the arm. "How're they hangin, Pesto?"

Johnny grinned widely. "Mighty low," he whispered in a deep basso.

"You must be gettin' some then," said Joe D.

Johnny laughed loudly. He loved the earthy, good natured humor of "Irish", old Roger Lindahl's nickname for Dolan.

"Looks like your dad has made quite a haul here."

Johnny gave him a glance that said *out of bounds*.

Harry heard Dolan, and said with a good-natured laugh, "We hijacked 'um!"

"I don't understand, Mr. Pestrano," said Diana, who had come to join her husband and the others at the fireplace. Trace tried to signal his wife to back off, but to no avail. "But Mr. Pestrano, those steaks...."

"Let's just say that you really don't want to know, young lady, and leave it at that," smiled Harry.

Maria came up to the group. "Come, come my dear, let's let the men talk man-talk," as she led Diana back to the table. Diana looked back at the men and saw that Johnny was again staring intently at her. She returned his gaze for a moment, and quickly turned away. Her heart pounded in her chest. She knew what that look meant and it excited her.

Slats watched the women go, then turned to Trace and Dolan and said, "Boys, I'm in the interstate trucking business. I call it the fuckin-truckin' business, and from time to time little gifts just seem to drop in my lap. Verstace?"

The insurance men nodded, their heads bobbing up and down in unison, eyes wide.

"Yes sir, we get it," said Trace. "And we appreciate your doing this for us and for Johnny. We really appreciate having him with us."

"You're a big basketball star, huh Trace?"

"Well, I played some ball at LIU a few years ago."

"Yeah, well I follow the Knicks. Can make a few bucks on the spread wit 'em, get my drift?"

"Yes sir, we do!" said Trace and Joe in unison.

"Well, boys, time to get the meat on the table and have a feast. Nice talkin' with you. Keep your powder dry and you, Trace, take care of my boy. Capise?"

Richard Trace nodded, perhaps the most sober acknowledgment of his young life.

Harry Pestrano waved to two large young men who were standing near the entrance to the kitchen area. They were not part of the district office group, but seemed to be very comfortable in the Pestrano home. They made no attempt to talk with any of the invited guests. They merely watched. Trace noticed that they seemed to keep Harry, Maria and Johnny in their sight at all times. The smaller blond man also had an eye for a beautiful younger woman who had joined them with her infant son. Trace guessed that he was likely to be her husband.

"Did you 'get his drift'?" asked Dolan.

"Yes, Joe we are in the presence of the family, if you get **my** drift."

"Slammer, I would make sure that Johnny continues to be a big success, even if you have to write the business yourself and hand it to him on a silver platter. Slats is frightening."

"Dolan--I'm lucky. Whenever I go on a call with Johnny, the prospects seem to talk us into even more coverage than we recommend. It's as if they are ready, even anxious, to buy, and now I know why. Whew! This is too much pal, too much. See you later."

Trace sat down at the table with Diana and Maria. They were joined by Maria's daughter Sophia and her son Alfredo. The ladies in starched white uniforms brought the steaks to the table. In a few minutes Harry joined the party, seated at the head of the table with Johnny on his right, then Millie and Mann Klein and Maria, holding her grandson and finally the voluptuous Sophia. Little Alfredo kept pulling at her blouse.

Trace was having a hard time keeping his eyes off the buxom young woman.

Maria squeezed the infant Fredo. "Isn't he the most adorable baby? Look at these blond curls, and the eyelashes, Mah-rone! Will this kid be a heartbreaker, or what?"

Sophia blushed, "Now, Mom, stop, you're embarrassing me."

They all nodded in agreement; he was indeed adorable. As far as Trace was concerned it was Sophia who was adorable. This cute little kid would probably grow up to be a killer some day.

What a year, thought Trace. *An American walks on the moon, and now I have the Mafia in my life. I only hope Diana doesn't go asking Slats any more questions about his 'business.'* To his relief, the conversation seemed to center on Johnny as Mann and Millie had a presentation arranged, along with a congratulatory cake. The focus of attention was on the man of the hour, Johnny Pestrano, as it should have been. Richard Trace was grateful for this organized structure since it kept Diana from dominating the conversation as she was so prone to do, especially among strangers.

On the drive home, Trace berated her for asking Harry Pestrano about the source of the steaks.

He growled at her. "Don't you realize who they are, Diana? You just don't ask those kinds of questions."

"I'm sorry, Rich. Maria seemed so nice."

"She is nice, Diana. All the Mafia wives are nice. It's Harry I'm talking about."

"Well, he seemed nice, too!"

"Forget it, Di. It's not important."

"You always talk down to me like that, Rich. It's not fair!" she cried.

"Diana, drop the 'oh poor me.' Now!" He raised his hand and gave her a backhand smack across her cheek. She momentarily saw stars, the side of her face erupted in stinging pain.

Diana gasped; she began to sob.

Trace stared straight ahead, thinking that if she wasn't going to inherit a fortune someday he would dump her in a heartbeat. Diana had clamped her arms across her chest and turned away from Richard. He vividly recalled the silence of that ride home, a precursor of thousands of such rides to come.

—

Richard Trace had been at the bridge for nearly thirty minutes. The laughter of a young couple, oblivious to anyone nearby, brought him back to the present. He turned and retraced his steps, taking the shortest route back to his office. It was nearly 12:30 and he would get back at 1:00. He realized that there was no real reason to rush, his work for the year had been completed. Pestrano's network of professionals had completed their work in just over one month.

Lily had been the last of the four assignments. In addition to her, Bill Nellison had suffered a fatal car crash in Orlando, Florida ($725,000); Shelly Turland, EVP, had committed suicide over the death of her husband, William, in Irvine, California ($800,000); and Samuel Spencer, retired, had been shot in a failed bank holdup attempt in Detroit, Michigan ($700,000). The total had been just over $3 million. Natural, "unassisted" deaths had totaled $1.3 million, for a grand total of $4,350,000. Yields on treasuries had turned up at year end and the First Gotham Insurance Agency, Inc. had achieved a 6.6 percent return on the BOLI account for 1998. Richard Trace would be paid his bonus of $525,000 in January, 1999, in accordance with his contract.

The call he had made to Johnny Pestrano in late September had been an expensive one. In the five year interim between 1993 and 1998, the price for each "hit" had increased from $25,000 to$60,000. Trace had seen his bonus shrink by $240,000. Still, $285,000 was far better than zero **and** the possible loss of his gravy train. He had reasoned that two years out of nine was not too bad. But he had definitely decided that if had to do it again in the future, all assignments would be on strangers.

—

Johnny Pestrano's career with East Coast Life had lasted only 18 months before he was called back into the family business. During his only full year with the company he was the new agent of the year for the Mid-Atlantic Region, which covered a five state territory. Johnny had left for a family emergency in the Midwest the following April. While he had received considerable recognition in the company bulletins, he was unable to attend the convention in Atlantic City where his accomplishments were publicly recognized in front of his peers.

While Richard Trace had accepted his recognition plaque with glowing praises for him, Johnny learned that he had also taken the opportunity to tell several of the agents that it had really been he, Richard Trace, who had made all of those sales. Johnny also had heard that Trace had told his fellow managers that, *you just couldn't count on new people being grateful for the help of their managers*. All of this had been reported to Pestrano by his sources in the company.

Trace had, of course, mailed the plaque, with its large silver 'number one', to him with an ingratiating note. His manager's insincerity had angered Johnny, but since he was completely absorbed in critical business, he didn't have time to dwell on the slight. Johnny Pestrano knew that he could deal with Richard Trace in the appropriate manner should the occasion arise in the future. Then, of course, there was another reason for his antipathy; Diana Trace had told him all about her husband's abusive tendencies. She still had a purplish bruise under her left eye that first time they had been together, and a few weeks later she had showed him bruises on her upper arm. Johnny had responded with appropriately gentle lovemaking that would leave her weeping with passion

Chapter 4

The murky underworld of business practiced by Richard "Slam Dunk" Trace during the mid-nineties was entirely unknown to Chris Masters. In 1993, he was not yet in high school. By 1998, he had just entered his second year of college. The closest he had come to the business world was mowing lawns in the summer for $3.00 an hour. Sports and study were his two primary concerns.

Chris had always been fascinated by numbers. As a child he had learned to count to 100 long before being able to recite his ABC's. He felt a certain comfort in the certainty and logic of mathematics. Addition, subtraction, multiplication and division came easily to him, and he found that he could mentally calculate rather complex combinations of numbers at a very young age. Statistics, algebra, and calculus added further refinement and new challenges and rewards. Geometry, trigonometry, spatial math and then physics enhanced his respect for and love of numbers and their relationship to one another.

When Chris went from place to place, he would silently count the number of paces, the number of stair steps, the number of repetitions in gym class. He would shoot baskets and keep a running tally of his percentage made. He discovered baseball with all of its fascinating statistics, and scoring a game became a summer ritual. He loved to fill in the little diamonds, which, when marked on all four sides, represented a run. Math was certainty, completion, coming full circle. It was always true, logical, predictable, reliable; all the values which he related to and admired. He had known by age 12 that he wanted to make math a lifetime pursuit. In high school, he took every advanced math and science course available and was usually the top student in his class. On his first try at the SAT's, he scored 780 in math and 560 in English. When he took the second round of tests in his senior year, he scored a perfect 800 in math and 540 in English.

His academic strength was obvious to all. He won the Harold Stern Math Prize his senior year as the outstanding math student in a class of 450. He also won an academic scholarship to Dartmouth College, and when he entered as a freshman, it was with advanced placement in mathematics and physics. Upon graduation four years later, Chris calculated that the scholarship had paid 68.73% of his expenses. True to form, he had figured it to the last percentage point.

While at Dartmouth, Chris had met Sarah Hardy. They were sophomores at the time, and now, several years later, they were still together. Sarah's academic strengths complemented his own, and while she was not a math whiz, she understood some of his world and provided a good balance with her interest in the arts and literature. After undergraduate studies they decided to live together while attending graduate school at McGill University in Montreal. Sarah got her MBA while Chris pursued his master's degree in advanced mathematics. Chris had expected to go on for his Ph.D. in preparation for a position in academia.

As luck would have it, the last summer before graduation he had been an intern at Smith, Hay & Ward, an insurance consulting firm based in Chicago. They had given Chris responsible duties in their actuarial department where he had impressed them by excelling in the precise actuarial work. This experience helped Chris to make the decision that a career in business was preferable to a career in academia, particularly since he would have to spend an additional five years getting his Ph.D. Sarah was also ready to escape the academic grind.

During the early winter of his last year at McGill, his supervisor for the previous summer, Benjamin Schoen, had called with an invitation to come to Chicago to discuss a permanent position as an associate actuary with Smith, Hay & Ward. After living on a student budget for two years together, Sarah and Chris were ready to get off a campus and join the army of working couples. They began to speculate what life would be like in Chicago. Sarah re-focused her job hunting efforts toward firms with offices in the Windy City. She found that all the major consulting firms had significant operations headquartered there. Their optimism about employment prospects made even the darkest winter days bearable.

Chris and Sarah had flown to Chicago in early February on what seemed to them to be a brand new Air France jet. Chicago was cold and very blustery, but at 20 degrees seemed almost tropical after ten straight days of below zero temperature in Montreal. Chris had his interview set for 9:00 A.M. at the Michigan Avenue offices of Smith, Hay & Ward. He got up early and went through his exercise routine, counting off 20 repetitions of each procedure and holding each of the stretches for thirty seconds. He was careful to do exactly 28 push-ups, having calculated that even if he missed seven days a year, he would do 10,000 each year. After carefully shaving his heavy beard, he showered and put on a starched white shirt, rep tie and dark blue double-breasted suit. He checked the mirror for razor nicks and was relieved that there was only a small scrape below the jaw line which didn't show. He brushed his hair straight back. With his clear brown eyes, dark brows and square jaw, he looked strong and healthy, not like the nerds that usually haunted math classes.

"How do I look, honey?"

Sarah rubbed her eyes with the back of her wrist yawning deeply, "You are my cuddle bear!"

"Sarah, the interview, how do I...."

"You'll knock them dead, handsome. Come kiss my cheek and go impress!"

Thirty minutes later Chris was greeted by Ben Schoen.

"Morning Chris, Coffee?"

"Yes, thanks, black with sugar."

"We are going to talk with Harry Harkness first. You probably remember him from last summer. He is head of our BOLI/COLI division, that is, Bank and Corporate Owned Life Insurance. Then we will have a few minutes with "Red" Smith, our founder. Did you get to meet him?"

"Well no, not really. I did see him two or three times at company meetings, but never actually met him one on one."

"Red is not only our founder, he's still involved, hands-on, with each facet of a complex business, and he puts it all together. Rather well, I might add. We have come far considering our first sale was in 1984, and that one took Red three years to close. Are you ready to go see Harry?"

"Sure, let's go."

Harry Harkness stood as they entered his office and came out from behind his desk to greet Ben and

Chris. He was slightly hunched and rail thin. Chris guessed that he would be six feet if he stood up straight. He had a way of looking up from his brow that gave his gaze an intense hawkish quality, a bird-man in modish clothes. The effect was quite disarming.

"Hi, Ben. Good morning, Chris. Nice to see you again. How was the trip down?"

"Good morning, Mr. Harkness. It was great. Our first flight on Air France...."

"I'm glad. They are also a favorite of mine. Why don't we all sit down over here and get more comfortable?" Harry craned his neck toward the couch and chair in the corner of his office.

After they were settled, he continued, "Chris, Ben and I are aware that you will be getting your M.S. in June and that you may be considering the Ph.D. program there at McGill. We were hoping you might be persuaded to abandon that plan and come to work for us sooner, on a permanent basis, of course."

"Well, Mr. Harkness, I ...."

"Harry, please. My father is **Mr**. Harkness." They all shared a chuckle and the tension level eased. However, this attempt at informality was belied by his pedantic demeanor.

"Actually, um, Harry, my fiancée, Sarah, and I, have had several talks about whether or not to continue in school for another 5 years. We have been students for 18 years, and it does get a little tiring after awhile," Chris managed. It would be the last time he would call him Harry.

"Yes, go on, Chris."

"Well, we talked last night about what I should do if you wanted me to join Smith, Hay and Ward, and we are both open to a new adventure."

"Chris, Ben has told me how impressed he was with your work last summer. Frankly, some of our interns in the actuarial area have been real geeks. Isn't that what they are called?"

Chris showed amusement, "Well, yes, I know what you mean. Sometimes it seems to be an occupational hazard. I have always loved math, and even in my sports the numbers have always been important to me. One of my most satisfying memories involved a close basketball game where we had a three point lead with ten seconds to go. When the other team threw the ball in-bounds, I waited for a few ticks of the clock then fouled my man. He got two shots, but I had figured that even if he made both, we would get the ball back with only two or three seconds left in the game. That way there was no possibility that they could have hit a three point basket to tie the game. When I had made the foul my coach had been furious, but after we won the game and I explained the logic of my foul, he just stared at me for a few seconds, then got a big smile and yelled, *you're a genius! Way to go, Masters. Way to go!"*

Harry and Ben nodded in unison.

"We like the fact that you are a regular guy, that you were a jock and frat man. You will get along well with our sales group. In the past we have had some conflicts because our sales guys have tried to bully some of our numbers guys, the geeks," said Ben.

"Last summer I got to know Charlie Anton and Bill Robertson in sales. They are great guys!" Chris noted.

"Ben and I have discussed our proposed offer and we have agreed that we should start you at $75,000."

Chris tried to hold back a grin, not very successfully.

"That would include full benefits, medical, life insurance, disability insurance, pension and401(k) along with time off with pay in June for your actuarial studies. We assume that you will be going for your FSA."

"Oh, yes. I planned to take two parts this coming summer, as Professor Stanton at McGill had suggested, then probably one part each year because of the three-year experience requirement. At the end of the three years I would be eligible to become a member of the society, a fellow, as they are called."

"That is a good plan and what I would have expected of you," said Ben, as he tapped his head with two fingers, looking over at Harry.

"Oh, and Chris, there is one other item. We know that you and Sarah will need some help to get moved here and settled, so we will throw in a $15,000 signing bonus. That would add up to $90,000 the first year, and with raises you should be pushing $100,000 in two years. What do you say?"

"Wow, Mr. Harkness, I, I, yes— yes. Of course I will want to talk to Sarah, but I'm sure that she will also say yes."

Harry Harkness adjusted his steel-rimmed glasses, ran his fingers through his long silvery hair and leaned forward. "Chris, my primary requirement is that you pay attention to detail and report anything that doesn't make sense from an actuarial point of view. Even a few basis points can adversely affect our bottom line, and Red

Smith doesn't have much of a sense of humor about failure."

Harkness was staring intently at Chris during this admonition, as if in a predacious trance.

Wow, he is really intense on this point, thought Chris.

Ben Schoen shifted his considerable bulk to the front of his chair and also leaned forward toward Chris.

Chris sat up straight and said, "Mr. Harkness, Ben emphasized to me last summer the critical importance of the role of an actuary not only in predicting the future, but especially in the monitoring of actual results. To me, math is a pure science, and when things get mucked up it shows up like a blazing red alarm." Chris stared back at Harry and Ben.

They nodded with satisfaction. "Ben, I think we have found our man. Let's go see the boss."

—

Russell R. "Red" Smith was a powerfully built man of medium height. At 5' 11', 180 pounds, Chris was taller by two inches, but was at least 25-30 pounds lighter. He felt like a midget next to the chairman of the board of Smith, Hay & Ward.

"Good morning, young man. I understand you are a Canadian!" Smith roared.

"Well, no, Mr. Smith, he is an American, just attending grad school in Montreal," corrected Harkness.

"Oh! Well, yes. Where did you grow up, boy?"

"I'm from Pittsburgh, sir."

"Great town! You a Steeler fan?"

"Well, yes. They had really great teams while I was growing up, four Super Bowls. Bradshaw, Swann and Stallworth and the "steel curtain" defense, and..."

"And Franco Harris?" asked Red.

"Yes, 'the immaculate reception,'" added Chris.

"Good town, Pittsburgh. We have some real good cases there. Were you a football player, Chris?"

"I played football in junior high school, but switched to cross-country in the fall of my sophomore year. Then basketball in the winter and baseball in the spring."

"I played linebacker at Wisconsin, second team All-American in 1958. You must be a Pirates fan if you played baseball."

"Yes sir. They're my team! Things haven't been the same since Stargell retired and Bonds was traded. Then Jim Leyland left, and, well, baseball is getting to be a big-market dominated sport, and Pittsburgh is being left behind."

"You think you've got troubles. I have been a Cubs fan for years. Once, in '69, probably before you were born, they had a huge lead at the end of August and then..."

"The Miracle Mets?" asked Chris.

"How did you know that, kid?"

"Well, it was the biggest come from behind pennant win in history," Chris observed.

"Yes, well now they are paying the homerun king, the Dominican Babe Ruth, I call him, Sosa, $40 million or some amazing amount, but I guess he's worth it. At least he seems to be a fairly good citizen both here and back home. Well, you do look like an athlete," he observed, pausing, "You sure don't look like an actuary. They are usually little pimply guys with thick glasses."

Chris chuckled. "An occupational hazard. I just grew up liking math."

"It's nice to meet a potential actuary who looks as if he could stand upright in a windstorm. Have these gentlemen made you an offer you can't refuse?"

"Well, yes, I guess they have, although I need to be sure it will be OK with my, uh— fiancée."

"OK, young man, that is the politically correct response, but I think I have heard a definite yes."

"You probably have, sir. I'm sure you have!" Chris enthused.

—

"Honey, ninety grand, can you believe it?"

"Oh, Chris, we can have a life. I'm tired of classes. Let's do it! I'll start looking for a job in Chicago right away. I'm sure all the big accounting firms have large offices here, and my finance and accounting professors have all said that they would give me a top recommendation. I love you!"

They walked hand-in-hand into the bedroom of the Embassy Suites Hotel. Their dinner with Schoen and Harkness would have to wait.

—

Back in Montreal Chris and Sarah settled into the final weeks of the school year. Secure in the knowledge that Chris had a great job nailed down, they enjoyed the coming of spring during May and into early June.

Sarah had offers from three of the top five accounting firms and chose Andersen Consulting, which had an office in the Loop only five blocks from Chris' office on Michigan Avenue. The late spring brought forth all the flowering trees and bushes. Outdoor study became a joy, and their long twilight walks were like strategic planning sessions: housing, transportation, investments, even marriage and family. They talked of things they had not dared talk about before when they seemed so remote with the specter or five more years of school. Yes, they were about to have a life.

McGill University had a noted pre-actuarial program which Chris had pursued. He would be able to take two of the five actuarial exams soon after graduation and S-H+W, Inc. had agreed to pay him for the month of preparation time prior to the exams in late June. The Montreal spring Chris and Sarah had enjoyed so much during the last few weeks grew into a glorious early summer, but Chris had little time to enjoy it as he was buried in statistics and formulas. His professors at McGill had inspired the graduate math students with the story of Garland LeRoy, a legendary actuarial student who had sat for and passed all five exams in 1978, the only person to ever pass all five in one session. It was well known that now, at age 41, he was the chairman of the board of Atlas Life in New York City. The professors were understandably proud of Mr. LeRoy's accomplishments and used his story to inspire young students toward careers in business. Chris needed no such encouragement. The job waiting for him at Smith, Hay & Ward was all the motivation that he needed.

He had enjoyed preparing for these first two exams, in part because he knew he would be using this knowledge at his job in a few short weeks. The exams were held in the last week of June, and while he would not get the results until late August, he was sure he had aced them both, such was the nature of the subject and his confidence about mathematics and statistics.

He and Sarah were to start their new jobs in the middle of July. They had enjoyed a relaxed drive to Chicago by way of Niagara Falls, a sort of pre-honeymoon. Within two days after their arrival in Chicago, they had found a nice apartment on Erie Street in the western close-in suburb of Oak Park. Their apartment was only three blocks from the nearest Metra station.

By early August they had fallen into a routine. Up at 6:30, Chris did his stretching and push-ups for twenty minutes while Sarah showered. Then she applied her makeup while he shaved and showered. By 7:45 they were at the "L" station for the 7:51 train into the Loop. The eight-mile trip took sixteen minutes, straight east to the Eisenhower Freeway overpass, then south to the Northwest Station. The train was always crowded as Oak Park was the last stop into town from the western suburbs. The multilayered station was on the west side of the Chicago River. Chris and Sarah would walk quickly from the train platform through the building with its many shops and kiosks and, after a kiss good-bye, Sarah would head off to Washington Street to cross the bridge over the river into the Loop. Chris would head straight across the concrete balcony to the *Wendella Boats*, then down the stairs to the river taxi that would take him around to the Miracle Mile. Chris counted each morning,

35 steps down to the river, and 37 steps back up to Michigan Avenue at the other end. The launch usually stirred up some breeze on the short eight minute trip, making this part of his commute almost comfortable, but it was a typical muggy Chicago summer, hot and humid even at this early hour. Once he hit the street, his office building was exactly 241 paces, just over one block, at 450 Michigan Avenue. The national headquarters for Smith, Hay & Ward was on the 28th floor, and he was their newest Associate Actuary, as it read on his brand new business cards.

At exactly 8:26, Chris was greeted by Sally Bell, the receptionist who had started just two weeks earlier.

"Hello, Christopher, have a great day!" chirped Sally. Chris was used to having girls raise their voices on the last word of a sentence. It was a signal. A signal he had worked at ignoring ever since he had been with Sarah.

He arrived at his cubicle and turned on his computer. He hit on an icon and up flashed his e-mail. Six messages. All but one were administrative detail. That one was from Harry Harkness about a new account. Chris now reported to Harkness, manager of the BOLI business for all of the banks in the Northeast and Central Regions. Harry had been with S-H-W, Inc. for 18 years and was one of the top officers, a senior vice president. Only three executive vice presidents, the president, Joe Weinstein, and Mr. Smith, the chairman, were above him on the organizational chart of the company.

Harkness had explained the basis of BOLI, Bank Owned Life Insurance, the first day that Chris had reported to the office.. Their job was to project values and monitor results. While it was exacting work, Chris enjoyed the precision and purity of the way the various elements came together. Bank Owned Life Insurance had become popular during the 1980's as the banks had been educated by men like Red Smith about the advantages of using life insurance as an asset to offset certain emerging liabilities on their balance sheets, such as the future cost of health care and retirement benefits to retirees.

Harkness had explained that while the primary stated reason for banks to purchase life insurance on the lives of their employees was to offset these emerging future costs, the real reason was that they could shelter earnings on invested assets from tax by putting them inside an insurance "wrapper." With a corporate tax rate of 35%, this represented a whopping tax saving! In addition, banks could insure their employees for life, even if they left and went to work for a rival bank. Unlike Key Man insurance, this coverage could be maintained. Furthermore, since large groups of employees were insured at the same time, the usual medical exam associated with large amounts of individual coverage was waived. Thousands could be insured by the simple submission of a list of employees to be covered. The amounts would be determined by age, sex and the amount of premium. When Chris had heard this the first time his instinctive reaction was that it couldn't be true, but Harkness had confirmed that it was, in fact, true, and a key impetus for the BOLI program, which he described as a boon to American business.

"It seems ghoulish to me," said Chris. Harkness pursed his lips and shrugged his shoulders.

"Well, yes, some people make that point, but trying to track terminations and cash-in policies would be an accounting nightmare. Then there is the tax problem because these policies are MEC's."

"MEC's?" asked Chris.

"Oh, I'm sorry. Modified Endowment Contracts. Because these are single premium policies they would receive less favorable tax treatment if they are surrendered than regular annual premium policies. It is a moot point because they are never surrendered, except at death. Here we are getting at the heart of why life insurance is attractive to the banks.... They can defer taxes virtually forever because they don't withdraw any funds, and at the time of death, the proceeds are tax-free. With a group of 10,000 employees, for example, they can reasonably expect 10-12 deaths on a brand new policy, and many more as the years go by. That is why BOLI is such a hot item. We are talking billions of premium annually, my boy, billions!"

"How much is each employee insured for?" asked Chris, incredulous at the amounts..

"That will vary from policy to policy and within each case by age and sex. But, let's say, $100,000 to $1,000,000 per person. It's somewhat unusual for someone to be covered for over $500,000, but a younger, say under 40, female executive could push $1,000,000. Her cost per thousand would be quite low— lower risk, lower cost."

"How much of a factor would death claims amount to in a typical case?"

"That would vary depending on the aging factor, and how long the policy had been in force. New policies will have lower death claim rates because the group starts out younger and healthier, but from the tenth year on, the death rate accelerates. Remember, we continue to maintain coverage even on the retired employees, and in ten years some of them are well into their 70's. So, to answer your question, new groups should have death claims around half of one percent, at ten years maybe one to one and one half percent and then on up from there. The death claims can become really lucrative after a while."

"And the other factor is the tax-deferred return on invested assets within the plan?" asked Chris attentively.

"Yes, most are invested conservatively in the low interest arena, and it is hard to get a very high return using treasury bills or government notes. Many banks are reluctant to take any risk in these volatile market conditions, so we have some plans that are just not making it to the satisfaction of their management."

"For example?" asked Chris.

Harry Harkness sighed. "If the five year treasury rate is 5 percent, then the value of tax-deferral, in the 35 percent tax bracket is 175 basis points. You do know what I mean by basis points, don't you?"

"Sure, it's one hundredth of one percent," replied Chris brightly.

"Right, so if the cost of administration, taxes and other fees is 145 basis points, the net gain is only 30 basis points. Since the banks can borrow money from the Federal Reserve in a ratio of 6.5 percent equity to 93.5 percent debt, their return-on-capital (ROC) would only be 4.6 percent, not very exciting. Now, if they were able to get 8 percent on T-bills, the tax saving would be 280 basis points, which against a cost of 145 would yield 135 and, voila, the ROC would be 20.8 percent with no additional investment risk. When they can achieve that rate they often will increase their commitment to BOLI."

"I thought that the reason for BOLI was to offset the emerging liability for employee benefits, plus..." said Chris.

"Don't believe it! This is a pure tax dodge as far as the bank treasury departments are concerned. Their interest is the bottom line, and return on capital is their watchword."

"So, how does the death benefit factor in? Oh, yes, new cases have 50 basis points, older cases 100-150 basis points, which is certainly significant," said Chris.

"How about an existing case that started in the late 80's when T-bill rates were over 8 percent, and they are now down around 6 percent. The ROC was expected to be over 20 percent without death claims, and now it is down to around 10 percent. If this case were ten years old and yielded an additional 100 basis points from death claims, the ROC would be right back up over 20 percent. As long as T-bills yield over 5.5 percent, our more mature cases should perform OK, although some of the newer ones may have losses even at 6 or 6.5 percent. I sure hope these treasury rates don't go much lower. They should be near the bottom. However, in 1993, and again in 1998, they got down to almost 5 percent for a while and it was very tough to get a decent net performance on these plans. Those were the only times in the last thirty years that the T-bill rates dipped below 6 percent. The current rate of 5.65 percent is about as low as we have seen except for 1993 and 1998, and the rate in the late 80's was as high as 8.5 percent," Harkness continued, "Chris, this BOLI deal used to be even sweeter. The banks used to be able to deduct the interest on borrowed money they used to fund the premium. So, for example, if they had borrowed $100 million at 4 percent from the

Fed, their 35% tax deduction would have been worth $1.4 million, and their net cost of the borrowed funds would have been 2.6 percent."

"$2.6 million on $100 million of borrowed money, almost like a Yen loan today," contributed Chris.

"Those plans started before June 19, 1986, were grandfathered and still got the deduction until recently. We only have two plans written prior to that time. As you can see there are lots of moving parts. Most of our bank clients are well into their plans and can offset those low returns. We have many clients who have been with us for over ten years."

The older man adjusted his jacket lapels with a short tug of his thumb and forefinger. "Chris, I will give you some material to read that will explain the more esoteric aspects of the legal background of these plans. That should give you all the background that you need to understand how the concept emerged as a viable insurance strategy." He hesitated for a moment, then said, "I want you to work on five banks: National Heritage of Denver, Heartland Bank of Kansas City, First Gotham Bank of New York City, and two banks here in Chicago, Central States and Midwest Freedom. Over the next several months I'll make sure that you meet the key people at each of them. We can start next week with Central States and Midwest Freedom. They're the closest and easiest. Many of the insurance execs have become good friends over the years."

"What do you want me to do for starters?" asked Chris.

"It would be very helpful if you could compile the death claims over the life of each plan as to how their return-on-capital (ROC) has worked out after all costs.

You would have to take into account their investment performance, their cost of money, including tax savings, the cost of all fees and taxes including the various state taxes, and, of course, the death claims to come up with a net-net return. It is exacting work and will take some investigative digging on your part, but the result will be that you will really learn about BOLI and will be the expert on these five banks.

"How long do you expect me to take on this project?" asked Chris.

"This may be an ongoing process, as things will evolve as you go, part current, part historical. I have often wanted to do it and, well, other priorities have always come up and, you know, it just slipped away. I think if we isolate these five and develop a model for gathering this information, we may be able to do all of the other banks more easily in the future." Chris's boss spread his bony hands in a gesture of hope.

"I will try to handle the day-to-day details and you will have mostly clear sailing. This seems the best way I can think of to help you really understand the entire workings of not only each of these banks plans, but also the overall scope of our operation. While BOLI plans have some unique features, they are similar to our COLI, that's Corporate Owned Life Insurance, that you will be able to understand and even assist Bill Cody and his group, if necessary. We often help each other when it comes to crunch time," Harkness smiled and continued.

"I'm sure that you will have lots of questions as we go along, and I'm right across the hall. My secretary, Shelly, has been with me for over five years and knows the ropes pretty well. She's not your average nine-to-fiver. If you need help with a letter, I have told her to expect you to ask from time to time, and she said she would be glad to help. Shell's a gem, more like an associate than a secretary. We are all so wired into the computer today that formal letters are rare, usually just a cover letter when we send our reports."

"Are there files on the five banks that I will be working on?" inquired Chris.

"Chris, right behind you are five steel four-drawer files, one for each bank with mostly old reports. The last year is loaded into your computer. I'm afraid you are going to have to go through those files and transpose the information into your computer in order to develop an accurate history."

"Do you have a model developed for recording this information?" asked Chris cautiously.

"I was hoping that you would develop it for us; then we could have all our bank cases standardized. After these five, there are 47 others, $30 billion or so of cash value in our section alone, and probably about $150 billion of potential death benefit."

Chris whistled, "Whew!"

"We expect you to earn that $90,000, son!"

—

Chris could hardly wait to get back to the apartment to tell Sarah about the events of the day. His head was swimming, such incredible numbers. Billions of dollars of insurance and millions of bits of information to assemble, organize and analyze. This was a dream job!

"Honey, this is wild. I have these five banks to work on and, and I am going to develop a model for us to use to analyze over fifty cases, and each bank has a four-drawer file cabinet full of past historical information and...."

"Whoa, boy, slow down! Start from the beginning."

"OK. First, Harry told me about the history of BOLI; that's Bank Owned Life Insurance. It may seem a little ghoulish to you, but banks and other large corporations, those are called COLI, Corporate Owned Life Insurance...." he gulped.

"Slow down." she purred.

"They can own life insurance on their employees and they do, by the billions."

"Yes, we studied that at McGill, Key Person Life Insurance. I seem to remember that the main aspect of it was something called "insurable interest." It was a test question on my business-law final this spring."

"Well, not quite, Sarah. This isn't Key Man, uh, Key Person Life. That is called class A. The bank regulations allow for Key Person coverage only on active executives and directors. This is class B, uh — no, test B, and it was test A, not class A," he stammered.

"Test B says that companies, or banks, can own life insurance on any employee to cover the cost of their future emerging liability for employee benefits like health plans and retirement. Not only that, but they can select only certain employees under a group concept to develop the required benefit, and, here's the ghoulish part, they don't ever have to drop the coverage, even if the employee quits or retires, even if they go to a rival bank."

Sarah seemed puzzled and observed, "I thought that insurable interest has to exist in order for there to be coverage."

"It only has to exist at inception, not when the claim is paid. Harry explained that it would be too hard to track changes in the insured group and that cash surrenders would be especially difficult because of tax considerations. It gets a little complicated. Besides, most states now have statutes upholding this definition of insurable interest."

"Do you mean to tell me that there are people walking around insured by their former companies?"

"Well, yes. And come to think of it, as mobile as the banking industry is, there are probably plenty, maybe thousands, who are working for rival banks. There are probably even some who are insured by two banks, maybe even more. Can you believe it?"

"Wow, this sounds like something out of Kafka, at least potentially," Sarah whispered.

"Honey, we are talking about professionals."

"Yeah, sure. Professionals who would just as soon cut your throat as look at you."

"Oh, I don't think...."

"Well, I don't like the idea!"

"Anyway, my job is to set up a model so that we can get the history of each bank. There are fifty-two of them on our computers. There is certainly nothing sinister about that. Now is there?"

"I certainly hope not!"

"Let me hear about your day, Sarah."

"The people at Andersen are fabulous. What a nice crew.... My boss, Kelli Burns, is a doll. She is just three years out of law school and totally relates to me and Beth, the other girl who is starting with me. We are going to have three weeks of training and then we'll be assigned to a consulting team working for a large client of the firm. Kelli has stressed professionalism. That's what the clients hire us for, and that's what we must be, both in terms of knowledge and also in appearance. They always have an experienced team leader and at least one other senior analyst for every two analysts. Here's my new business card. It's even embossed! Way cool, babe!"

Chapter 5

Chicago in the summertime, with its oppressive heat and frequent afternoon thunderstorms, tried the patience of most of its residents. But, for Chris Masters, the weather patterns were no more than a minor annoyance. He had a dream job for a mathematician and he had the happy choice of two major league baseball teams. Not only that, each had a genuine superstar at the apex of his career, Sammy Sosa for the Cubs and Frank Thomas for the White Sox. Sammy was having another monstrous year with over 50 homers by mid-August, and the "Big Hurt" was having his best overall season, with an outstanding .650 on-base percentage. Each would threaten the big league record in those categories. Chris followed as much of the game action as Sarah would tolerate, and each evening he would check the baseball statistics for both hitting and pitching on the Web. Even so, he would re-read these same statistics in the morning paper on his commute into downtown Chicago.

The conversion of the BOLI records from paper to computer on the five assigned banks was tedious work that required much cross-checking. Chris had spent his first month at Smith, Hay & Ward devising a program that would organize all of the pertinent data in such a way that each of the banks could be tracked using the same set of input criteria. After two weeks of input, he had to fine-tune the program to accommodate certain unforeseen fact patterns. It became obvious that there was considerable executive migration between banks, and there were far more double and even triple-dippers in the BOLI ranks than he had anticipated. Since the coverage was for life,

he had to account for these potential multiple claims.
There were even a fairly significant number of executives
who had left one bank for another, only to return to the
original bank.

Sometimes this would result in an employee being
covered a second time by their original employer.

Chris had been initiated into the claim procedure
by Shelly on his second Monday morning at Smith, Hay
& Ward. She had called him over to her work-station at
8:10 to view screen "D", which, she explained to Chris,
was known as the "death screen." The deceased had been
a retired executive, age 74, male. He had been a vice
president in the corporate loan department of Midwest
Freedom Bank in Chicago. The cause was liver cancer.
His coverage was $345,000, written in 1989 with a single
premium of $105,000. Chris had marveled at the large
amounts.

"This is actually a rather small policy," said
Shelly. "The older men are, in most cases, the smallest
amounts."

"How about the largest claim?" asked Chris.

"Well, the largest I have seen was a 45 year-old
executive vice-president," she replied.

"Man or woman?"

"It was a Mr. Elroy; the amount was $912,000. He
was a big exec. It made all the Chicago business pages
with his picture, I think because of his being so young
and still very active."

"What was the cause of death?"

"Here, I can pull it up on my monitor. Let's see: it
was Poland National Bank, 1999. February, I think. No,
March, here it is. Merle M. Elroy, age 45, Executive Vice
President, Poland National Bank, coverage $912,000,

year of issue 1997, single premium $180,000, cause of death, cerebral hemorrhage."

"Wow, they took out the coverage less than two years earlier!"

"Yes, and that made the claim contestable."

"Why would that be?" Chris asked.

"If the insured dies within the first two years of the policy, the issuing insurance company has the right to contest the claim. Basically, it means they investigate to be sure he didn't have a pre-existing condition that was not revealed on the application."

"How did it come out?"

"I have no idea, but we did get a claim check for Poland National so I guess they found nothing wrong," she replied.

As the summer played out, Chris came to expect the frequent brief obituaries that appeared on screen "D". With over 50 banks, there would be several hundred claims annually. The actuarial forecast for the five banks he was specifically assigned to had predicted 76 death claims that year. Some weeks there were three or four, some weeks none. He got used to the Monday morning claims.

Somehow, more claims came in on Monday than any other day of the week. If someone were to be overly sensitive about the subject of these news items, it could get to be a very depressing business. Chris, Shelly and all of the others in their section had no actual contact with any of the deceased parties and concentrated solely on the process. The company execs in charge of the particular BOLI program had to be notified, claims procedures initiated with the various insurance carriers, investigations conducted when necessary, follow-up procedures carried out and claim checks delivered. It was very well-organized and detail-oriented. It was also a statistical paradise for Chris Masters.

While it had taken him several weeks to set up his initial program, and then an additional three weeks to adjust to unforeseen fact patterns, by the end of August he had a program in his computer that could organize virtually any input for each of the five banks. With the help of Shelly and an ultra efficient "temp," Sammy Sorrell, the process of entering past data was going well.

Sammy was a tall, skinny art student with a fantastic facility on any computer and a need for a "day job." At nineteen, his ambition was to become the black LeRoy Neiman, although his skin tone was closer to Creole orange. With dreadlocks and wispy facial hair, and his rangy physique, he resembled a large hairy spider. Sammy and Chris had discovered a common interest in sports, and when Chris took him to Comisky Park to a White Sox-vs-Texas Rangers game, his reward several days later was a large, brilliantly illustrated acrylic painting of Alex Rodriguez diving for a hot grounder in the hole. The technique was like viewing the real play through a multihued prism, with splashes of light emanating from the surface of the canvas. Chris was awed by Sammy's talent, and grateful for his efficiency on the computer. He vowed to get him to a Cubs game at Wrigley Field, as the other Sammy, Sosa, who was Sammy's hero, was having a fantastic season. Of course, that made a Cubs game the hardest ticket in town. He decided to prevail upon Mr. Harkness at the first opportune moment.

His new program could accommodate each bank equally well, and since historical data was filed by year, he and Sammy had decided to work backward from the present by date, completing all five banks for each successive year before moving on to the next year. Records went back to 1984, but not for all five banks as some had started their BOLI programs more recently. By the end of August they had inputted back through 1997, and the volume of input was reduced with each succeeding year. Chris calculated that they should be able to work back to 1992 by the end of September, and then finish the job by the middle of October. He reported this news to Harry Harkness, who was both pleased and amazed.

"You are doing a great job, Chris. How is that tall youngster, Sorrell, working out?"

"He is just perfect. He's got a great attitude and he's incredibly fast and accurate. Oh, Mr. Harkness, speaking of Sammy, he is a big Sammy Sosa fan. It could be because they have the same first name. Anyway, is there any chance that you might be able to help us get some tickets to a Cubs game? For him, that is?"

"Chris, it just happens that the firm has two season passes, and I'm sure we can arrange it. Why don't you go with him?"

Chris could not hold back a grin that lit up the room. Five minutes later he reported the good news to Sammy, and they bounced up and down together like kids on a playground. Harkness had followed Chris at a distance, and when he saw this scene fifty feet down the hall, he altered his course and turned into a side hall. Harkness was pleased at the enthusiasm of his young charges, but didn't want them to see the smile that showed how happy he was with these young men. He was from the old school that believed one should keep one's employees at arm's length. It was a rule of conduct which had stood him in good stead for many years. Maturity had its advantages which one should not squander by familiarity. Harry's rules! They defined his personality. He would always strive to keep his customers and his bosses happy. Employees, even talented ones, were expendable and replaceable. Another rule!

Chapter 6

By the end of September, Richard Trace knew that he was facing another crisis year. Yields on treasuries were down significantly, and sinking. Death claims had been modest. He had developed the habit of checking each week, ever since 1998. He thought back to that November day when he had gotten the confirmation of the death of Lily Yang-Peterson. An involuntary shudder ran through him.

"Never again with someone I know," he vowed aloud, his voice low and trembling.

Trace had accumulated a net worth of over $5 million and now lived in the toney suburb of Alpine, New Jersey, just minutes from the George Washington Bridge. The annual bonus for a successful year in the BOLI plan was now just a shade under $1 million and was the key element of his compensation package. All that he had was made possible by this bonus, which he had never failed to achieve, albeit with a big price-tag in 1993 and again in 1998. He was sure that the fee for the service charged by Johnny Pestrano would be well up from the $60,000 he had charged in 1998. He decided to visit Johnny in person, hoping that he could appeal to his sense of loyalty. After all, he had been a loyal client to Pestrano, never seeking these services from anyone else, and never questioning the price. Trace actually convinced himself that logically he deserved a break on the fee due to volume. After all, the insurance companies often did so, and he had given Johnny a lot of business.

It never occurred to Trace that Johnny would take this appeal as a sign that he was beginning to lose it and worse, that his recidivism had become a potentially dangerous liability. This reaction was further exacerbated by the personal visit. Trace's arrogance made him oblivious to Johnny's disdain.

"Did you say Richard Trace is in the waiting area?" asked Johnny Pestrano incredulously.

"Here is his card. President of First Gotham Insurance Agency, Inc." answered Salvatore Graffini, who was Johnny's attendant and bodyguard.

"OK, have him wait downstairs. I'll tell you when to bring the dumb fucker up here," he said.

———

Johnny Pestrano wove his fingers together and placed them behind his head, and leaned back in his chair. He closed his eyes and thought about the last time he had seen Trace. He had brought Diana here to the restaurant, in 1996. They were celebrating Diana's fiftieth birthday. At that time it had been nearly 27 years since he had last seen her.

———

The day after that long ago district office party at his parent's home in Lodi, Diane Trace had called him at the office. They had met at that Chinese restaurant in Fort Lee--the one in the shopping mall just north of the freeway. He couldn't remember the name. She had worn sun glasses even in the darkened room, more to cover the bruise under her left eye than to hide her identity. He remembered that the booth they had sat in had red velvet upholstery. Johnny smiled and shook his head slowly.

She had wanted to talk. He listened. *Rich* was a brute, a bully and not a good provider. She was from a prominent family in Scarsdale and was embarrassed at his crudeness. She told him that he seemed to be more refined than her husband. Diana had removed her sun glasses, revealing the dark shiner. Johnny continued to gaze directly at her, never turning away. She looked older than her years back then. She was a big-featured girl, tall and athletic, and well-tanned even in the late autumn, but she was not what one would describe as beautiful. He had heard such women described as striking or handsome. To Johnny, her relative maturity was enticing. He instinctively reached over and felt her cheek.

"I'm sorry," he had said.

She covered his hand with her own and replied "Thank you, Johnny, that's sweet of you."

They had ordered family style and he had insisted on chop sticks as he was an expert in their use. He soon had Diana laughing at her ineptitude with the sharp-pointed ebony utensils featured at Jade East--that was the name of the place--Jade East. Johnny had taken her hand and demonstrated the proper way to squeeze the two sticks together, but she couldn't seem to hold the slippery morsels. He began to pick up the succulent food and place it onto her tongue. She allowed herself to be fed this way. He would alternate feeding her and himself, often from the same loading. He demonstrated how to load the grains of rice by saturating them in gravy, holding the two sticks very lightly and slightly apart to form a trough. The chunks of chicken or pork needed to be squeezed, but not too tight. He was particularly adept at the slippery mushrooms, and she delighted in having him pop them into her waiting mouth.

Some oily sauce from the rich sweet and sour pork had run down her chin. He scraped it up toward her lower lip with the edge of one of the chop sticks. She grabbed the end of the stick and sucked at the sticky orange liquid with puckered lips. Their eyes never left each other. He poured hot tea, first for her, then for himself, and showed her how to interlock their arms and serve each other. When they had finished the hot dishes the waiter brought fortune cookies.

Hers read:

"The longest journey always begins with a single step."

-Confucius

She showed it to Johnny.

"Where are we going with this?" he asked.

Diana had reached under the table and up between his legs. She knew right away that she was not the only one who had been aroused by the sensuous meal.

"Let's go find out," she whispered huskily.

They had shared many afternoons over the next several months, usually in the city where everywhere was *"the cheating side of town."* Diana had taken him to museums and concerts, exposing him to a world of art and music that he had previously not known. When they took a hotel room, Johnny would stay overnight. Diana would be with him in the afternoon, return home to New Jersey for the night, and then come back to him in the morning to resume their lovemaking. He did not have much recollection of their trysts except that she had pear-shaped, very heavy breasts and insisted that he actually chew on her nipples. Johnny smiled at this eccentric remembrance.

The following spring he had met Anna Soriano at a family gathering. At eighteen she had an exotic beauty, with lashes and brows so dark that they needed no artificial enhancement. The first time he had seen her, she was in a polka dot sundress. As she turned toward him with a shy smile, it literally took his breath away, as if he had been hit in the solar-plexus by a fist. He knew in an instant that this was the girl for all time, and the luminous look in her eyes told him that she felt the same way.

He later found out that their mothers had conspired to get them together. He was, by that time, ready to pursue a serious relationship. His affair with Diana had been exciting and erotic, but it was beginning to become a burden. She had become possessive and demanding. He had grown tired of her constant berating of her husband. It was a strain to have to work with him under the circumstances. He had lost any respect he ever had for the man, knowing how he had abused his wife, but he was beginning to understand how it might happen, given her selfish nature.

Johnny had taken Diana to dinner in Manhattan and had told her that the family had introduced him to the young woman who was to be his wife, and that they would have to stop seeing each other. She tried to argue that they could continue the affair and he could cheat on his bride-to-be just as she was cheating on Richard, reasoning that it would *balance* their relationship. Johnny explained to her that, in his family, the marriage vow was sacred and they could have no more contact.

He had said, "Diana, you have helped me become a man, and I appreciate all that we have had together, but it is time for me to move on. I hope you will understand. There is nothing either of us can do to change it. I must do this for my family."

Diana had nodded numbly and turned away, shoulders slumping. When she turned back to look at Johnny, she saw, even through her blurred vision, that he had an unmistakable spring in his step as he walked away.

"You bastard, you don't have to be happy about it," she muttered under her breath.

—

Anna had given Johnny two lovely daughters. Over the years her slim figure had thickened, and she was now rather matronly. To Johnny she was still the most beautiful woman he had ever known, and she only got more beautiful as time went by. He had been completely faithful to her from the beginning, in spite of many temptations. Anna was the heart and soul of both their immediate and their extended family. They had all come to depend on her for all matters within the family, just as they had come to depend on Johnny for all matters of business outside the family.

—

When Richard and Diana Trace had come to his restaurant, he had been amazed at how little Diana had changed in appearance. At twenty-five she had looked ten years older than her years, and at fifty she had looked at least ten years younger. Her blond hair had been frosted and cut short, but her jaw line was still firm under her large, wide mouth. She still had a very athletic appearance even though he was nearly certain that she got little exercise. *Her legs still went all the way to the floor*, as the men in their insurance office used to say.

Diana had stared at Johnny boldly during their visit, and as they left his private quarters she had palmed a note to him when he shook her hand goodbye. The note said simply, "Gramercy Park Hotel, Wednesday--2:00". It had been one of their rendezvous sites. He understood the implications. Johnny had not gone to meet her. The phone call came at 3:10 that day, as he knew it would.

He had said, "Diana, I told Richard not to come here again, and I'm telling you the same thing. Be warned, both of you are out of your depth."

She heard a coldness and menace in his voice that didn't make sense. What had her husband done to offend Johnny?

Pestrano knew at the time that she would probably not fully understand this stern admonition, but he also knew that it would frighten her enough so that he would not likely hear from her again. He opened his eyes and loosened his fingers. Trace had been given the same warning, an unequivocal warning, but here he was again. Pestrano summoned Graffini to his office.

—

Richard Trace sat in the ornate Italian armchair in the inner lobby at the back of the restaurant, out of sight from the dinner patrons, hidden by gold velvet curtains. He perched forward, a fierce grip on his wide-brimmed old fashioned felt fedora. He had begun to wear a hat ever since John Baker at the bank had teased him about how red his ears were when he returned from a vacation in St. Maartens. He had forgotten to apply sun block along the top edge of his ears even though he had habitually covered his baldness with 15 power sun block every day.

Trace recalled the last time he had seen Pestrano. It had been several years ago. He remembered that he had brought his wife to Johnny's Ristorante as a special treat to celebrate her 50th birthday, so the year would have been 1996, about halfway between the crisis years. Johnny had been charming to Diana and very gracious. He had come down-- *That's right*, he recalled, *he has a private elevator just down the hall*, and had greeted them at their table. After dinner he had asked them to come back to his private dining room for an after-dinner drink. Trace looked to his right and saw the shiny ebony door with the small, circular window that led to that special room. He remembered that the room was furnished entirely in leather, including the walls and even the ceiling. They had reminisced about their days together with East Coast Life, and that had been 25 years in the past. Johnny reminded Trace about their visit to the boardroom when they had led the North Jersey Region in sales in the early 70's. "It also had a leather ceiling," said Johnny with pride.

When Diana excused herself to go to the ladies room, Pestrano had told him *sotto-voce* that he should avoid coming to the restaurant because of their previous business arrangements. He had asked, with resolute firmness, that they conduct all business by phone, and insisted that Trace always call from a pay phone so that calls could not be traced.

"I'm extra cautious about these things," said Johnny, a bright smile lighting his rugged, bronzed face.

Trace had returned the smile, but it had been a troubled smile because he realized that his calls had been made with his personal calling card number. He had tried to submerge that thought as being irrelevant. Who would ever suspect? The assignments had been carried out all over the country, at different times and the victims were not known to each other. He had chosen names for both randomness and profitability. Geographical separateness and tenure differences were also a factor. Most had left First Gotham years earlier. *No, there was nothing, nothing, he* repeated in his mind, *to worry about.* Johnny Pestrano could be as cautious as he wanted to be, so what!

"Mr. Trace, please follow me!" commanded Graffini.

They went down the hall to an elevator which, Rich noticed, went up three floors. He had asked about the second floor, "What's on two?"

Sal growled in a low voice, "You don't wanna know."

The elevator opened onto a marble entrance hall with a shiny ebony door at each end, and what appeared to be a polished metal door directly across from the elevator. Graffini knocked respectfully, three light taps. Trace heard a faint buzzing sound, and the metal door clicked ajar. Sal pushed it forward, and the insurance executive saw that it opened into a large, richly furnished living room. When he walked in he heard Johnny's voice on his right and turned to see him coming out from behind a huge marble desk. His mouth, he discovered, was so dry that he could hardly speak.

"Richard Trace, the old Slam Dunk," Johnny snarled, menace in his voice.

"Hi, Johnny boy, how you doin'?" he sputtered.

Johnny signaled Sal to leave them with a single, silent nod. The large man complied with a parting response: "I'll just be right outside."

Again, Johnny nodded.

He rubbed his chin, "What's the problem, Mr. Trace?" His voice rose as he spoke the name.

"Well, Johnny, I need your help again."

"I figured that, but I thought I told you never to come here in person." It was not a question.

"Yes, but...."

"Yes, but, my ass. I told you Slam, never come here in person. How do you know you weren't followed? Someone might start asking questions."

"Johnny, how could anyone know anything about..?"

"You learn to be cautious in this business. Even the least little slip-up can be fatal. *Capice?*"

Trace thought about the MCI calling card, and gave a muted nod.

"Do you have a list with background and particulars?"

"Yes, here it is. Five names this time, all spread out like before; no way to link them."

"Except that they all are insured by First Gotham. That's not a link?"

"Well, OK, but some are retired, and two have moved on to other banks."

"Still, it is a link, and some smart son-of-a-bitch may figure it out someday."

"Johnny, I don't think...."

"That's the problem, Slammer, sometimes you don't think. You're a 'ready, fire, aim' kind of guy and that makes me nervous. So, tell me, what's so special about these assignments that it requires a personal visit? You didn't come for the food or the scenery."

"Well, Johnny, I have a somewhat limited budget for these jobs, and...."

"Your limit, as you call it, better be $125,000 per. That's $625,000 total. The price is up for this kind of work, and since I use only the very best operators, they demand top dollar, and I get it for them."

"Johnny," huffed Trace, "that's really steep. It doesn't leave me any margin."

"Trace, you don't understand, this is not negotiable."

"But, Johnny, we go back over thirty years. I was hoping that because we have had a successful, uh--that's financially successful...uh, history, that you would cut me some slack."

"On what grounds?" Pestrano spat back.

"Sort of like a volume discount?" he queried with false bravado.

Johnny leaned back, his eyes rolled, and a deep laugh emitted from his solar plexus.

"Sal, get in here!" he shouted.

Graffini burst into the room, his hand inside his formal jacket.

"No, no, it's OK, but you've got to hear this. Mr. Trace says he deserves a discount for volume."

Sal looked puzzled for an instant, however with Johnny's urging, getting him to understand by raising his eyebrows, Sal also doubled over in laughter at Trace's impertinence.

"Trace, you are some poor dumb fucker. It doesn't work that way. If anything, the price goes up because the risk goes up...not down! Now, do we have an agreement for the $625,000...or not?"

Richard Trace nodded mechanically. His legs actually shook. It was an effort not to loosen his bowels on the deep mahogany carpet in Johnny's office. So much money!

"OK, hand me the list. It'll be taken care of by the end of November. Payment will be in the usual way, through a drop that will be sent to you in due time. Don't, I repeat, don't ever come here again, and don't contact me direct again. I will contact you through a Mr. Manfredi. That's spelled M-A-N-F-R-E-D-I. He will know your mother's full name, which is?"

"Uh, um, Viola Manson Trace."

"OK, got that Sal? Now, Sal will escort you downstairs and out through the garage. Don't come here again!"

Trace reached out his hand toward Johnny. Pestrano looked down at his poised open hand and shook his head. Turning away he muttered, "Poor, dumb fuck."

———

Richard Trace trudged down 44th Street, his hat pulled down heavily over his ears, which still burned with those words "Poor, dumb fuck." *I should have known he would be a prick!* he thought. *What a stupid idea!* He realized that his greed had overtaken his sensibility. As he walked back to his office, it also hit him that after paying Johnny, and then the taxes due on his bonus, his net take for the year would be practically zero. This was going to cost him his entire bonus. They would have to put off the purchase of the condo in St. Maartens for at least another year. But it had to be done, otherwise he might lose his job.

Thank goodness these weak investment returns only come along every five years or so, he thought. *Those damn condo prices are going up every year, through the roof! Maybe next year we will be able to swing it if I get to keep my bonus.* A cold west wind was pelting him with heavy raindrops. There was no hint of an Indian summer revival in the weather. September had fled, and October promised to be grim. Richard Trace pulled up his collar and cursed his bad luck. It had all the effect of a piss-hole in a snow-bank.

Chapter 7

John S. Barton was the picture of contentment as he took his early morning stroll down Palm Canyon Drive. The stillness in the air foretold a warm, breeze-free day on the Palm Springs Golf Club course. Maybe today he could nudge his score into the 80's for the first time in more than a decade. Retirement was beginning to grow on him. He had coffee and a Danish every weekday morning at Rosie's Diner and was often her first customer right at 8 a.m. He made a check of the local rag and then read the Wall Street Journal to see what was happening in the world of business. After all, it had been his world, night and day, for 43 years until Friday, last March 13th. He had retired as senior vice president in charge of trust administration for Midwest Freedom Bank on that glorious day. There was nothing unlucky about that particular Friday the 13th as far as Johnny Barton was concerned.

Barton recalled his last six years with a smile. He felt so lucky to have gotten such a great offer from Midwest Freedom at age 59, after all those years at First Gotham. There was no way that he would have received the same value of stock options at First Gotham. Then, when the California real estate market tanked in 1994, he and Helen had been able to pick up their little hacienda in Las Palmas for a song— well, a $350,000 song, with only $70,000 down.

The ex-banker looked up at Tahquitz Mountain as there was something moving against the mottled gray background of the rocky cliffs. He finally realized that it was a hot air balloon, probably at about 1,500 feet. Someone had told him that commercial balloon flights were only available in the early mornings or late afternoons because the midday heat often caused convection air currents that could take a balloon straight up to 10,000 feet without a hope of stopping. He mused about taking one of those flights with Helen, but it was just so hard to get her up early anymore.

He felt great contentment in their financial situation for the first time in their married lives. They had sold their Park Ridge, Illinois, home for $420,000 on the second open house, and with the new tax law they were able to payoff the mortgage on Casa Camino Sur, here in Old Palm Springs, and bank the difference of $140,000. Their stock options provided another $600,000; they had a nest egg of over $750,000. This cache provided an annual yield of over $45,000, and his pensions from the two banks plus social security brought their retirement to just under $100,000 a year with a paid-for house.

"Good morning, Rosie," he said, happy in his contentment.

"Will you have the usual, Mr. Barton?" she asked.

"No need to change anything now. The ol' engine seems to be running fine."

Rosie giggled as she poured his decaf from an orange rimmed pot. "Danish coming right up." John settled into the Palm Springs Herald, saving the Wall Street Journal for later.

Outside Rosie's another early riser watched John Barton's ritual with Rosie as he had for the last three mornings. Nothing changed. Barton would sit and read for 25 to 30 minutes, then, after three refills from the coffee pot, he would get up, make some little joke about the men's room keys and amble down the hall, usually for about five minutes. After another session with the Journal, his wife would come by around 9 a.m. in the Sedan De Ville, and off they would go. This was going to be almost too easy.

Charlie Smith had gotten the call from Mr. P's West Coast man, Duk Lon Ki, just last Thursday. The pre-payment of $20,000 had arrived. The four different money orders had already been converted at different locations. The balance of $25,000, plus expenses, would arrive within a week after the job was completed. With expenses the total would come to just under $50,000.

Charlie was a professional "arranger." He had been at this work for eighteen years, and now, at age 43, he kept busy enough to earn $350,000+ tax free each year. He was 5' 11", 180 pounds, with regular features and sandy blond hair. Sometimes he wore glasses; sometimes he had a beard and/or mustache. He could dress up or dress down. He was "everyman" from his common name to his bland appearance.

Duk had suggested Charlie "The Needle" to Johnny Pestrano for this assignment primarily because of his ordinariness. Duk knew he would stand out in the lily-white world of old Palm Springs. If he were Mexican or American Indian he would have done the job himself. As it was, Charlie Smith would be perfect, and he had full confidence in his ability. John S. Barton had a history of angina and high blood pressure. Barton was 5' 8", 220 pounds, an ideal candidate for a heart attack, which Charlie Smith would make sure would happen.

Over the last few days Charlie had devised his plan. He had patronized Rosie's on Monday morning well after Barton had left in the Cadillac. He had borrowed the key for the men's room. It was a standard

Schlage key attached to a plain wooden grip marked "Men's". Rosie was quite busy with customers by now and didn't even look up when he asked for the key. He knew that the door at the right rear of the restaurant led to a hall that connected Rosie's to other stores in the complex. The men's room was down the main hallway and then down a short back hall on the left, just before the elevators and around a corner to what would be the back of the elevator shaft.

As Charlie suspected, this was a one-man affair with an open toilet and wash basin. One customer at a time. The linoleum floor picked up the sound of most approaching footsteps, and light from the main hallway also cast a shadow that would indicate someone approaching the door. He could wait here for Barton concealed from sight until his victim made the last turn to the right. He saw that the main hall continued to the back of the building and double-glass doors led out to a covered cloister-like walkway on the outside of the building. This Spanish architecture had apparently been adapted by each of the subsequent developers, and the cloistered walkway ran along the back of several buildings on this block. His escape route was clear.

Other than Rosie's, which opened at 8 a.m., none of the shops off the main hallway opened for business until 10 o'clock. There was a dress shop, an antique store and a hair dresser off the inside hallway, and a jewelry store that opened to the back archway. Charlie hadn't seen any activity before 9:30 in any of them, and then just the proprietors arriving and bustling about in preparation for their business days.

On this third day Charlie Smith moved swiftly through the covered walkway and pushed open the glass door with his gloved hand. He proceeded to the short sub-hall on his right just past the elevators, then down into the small alcove leading to the men's room. No sound, no shadow, no one had seen his entry. It was now 8:20, and all he had to do was wait for his mark.

At 8:35 he heard a slight shuffle and saw a wide shadow, the sound and sight of a large bodied man approaching. John Barton coughed as he approached the last turn, and with this signal Charlie's right arm went around his shoulder and his left hand went to that spot on Barton's neck that he knew from years of experience would take him out. The ex-banker could only manage, "What the heck?..." before his throat was choked shut and he sagged against Smith.

Charlie reached across the slumping body for the key, felt the wooden grip, and wrenched it from Barton's hand. He twisted while trying to balance the heavy, limp body and managed to turn the key in the lock, squeezing open the door. He let his load fall the rest of the way to the floor of the bathroom.

Working with noiseless efficiency, he pulled his unconscious victim all the way into the small room and closed the door. Barton was heavier than Charlie had calculated, and he was sweating from the effort. He pulled the capped needle from his jacket pocket, removed the rubber tip, pulled back the plunger, and inserted the needle deep into Mr. Barton's left shoulder just beside his clavicle. With firm resolve he pushed the plunger all the way to the collar.

"That should do it," he muttered.

Charlie Smith then unbuckled the large man's belt and pulled down his slacks and underpants. Barton was now shaking, the potassium was taking effect. Charlie stooped and lifted the ex-banker onto the toilet. His bulk made it possible to balance him in a slumped sitting position, although he wanted him to fall off at some point. That would be a normal result of the heart attack he was having, and to anyone investigating this matter the fall would simply be a case of an overweight 65 year old retiree with a history of heart trouble coming to his expected demise.

Charlie looked around the neat restroom, saw nothing that concerned him, and placed the key grip on the wash basin. No fingerprints, no scuff marks, nothing fell out of any pockets. He looked in the mirror and brushed his hair back into place. He put on dark sunglasses and pressed opened the door.

There were no sounds in the small entry hall. Charlie took a long step and stretched forward to see around the corner. It was clear in the sub-hall. He let the restroom door click shut and walked calmly out to the main hallway, turned toward the back of the building and swung open the glass door leading to the covered walkway. His stride lengthened through this passageway to the adjoining parking lot. He got into his car at 8:42 a.m. No one had seen him.

Everything had gone as planned. John S. Barton, retiree, would be dead within 10 minutes, and likely would not be found until after 9 o'clock. Rosie would be too busy to leave the restaurant. She might send a customer to check on Mr. Barton fairly soon, then get alarmed and probably either call 911 or the police.

The hit man drove slowly down East Ramon Road to the freeway and turned west toward Los Angeles and home. It was 8:58 a.m. and the job had gone off without a hitch.

Rosie had gotten preoccupied with her latte machine. Sometime around nine a customer had asked for the men's room key, and she remembered that Mr. Barton had needed it around 8:30. "My God, he has been gone for nearly half-an-hour and his wife will be here any minute," she said, mostly to herself.

"I gave the key to another customer some time ago. Could you check the men's room? It's just down the hall."

"Yeah, sure. I'll go knock on the door. Is it OK if I get the key from him and bring it back later?"

"Sure, sure. No problem," replied Rosie.

The man hurried down the hall and found that in spite of repeated loud knocks on the door there was no response. He returned to the restaurant frustrated.

"Sorry, miss, no one there. I've got to go, sorry," he said, as he hurried off on a personal mission.

Rosie picked up the phone and called Bill Williams, the building manager. His voice-mail answered, "This is the Santa Custino Management Company, Bill here. Please leave a message after the beep."

Just then, Rosie remembered that she had a duplicate key made a few months ago.

Now where did I put it? she asked herself.

She looked through the drawers under the register, then remembered that it was in the bottom drawer in an envelop marked "men's." Sure enough, there it was, to her gratification.

Rosie spotted Joe Klein, another regular. "Hey Joe. Would you take this key and check the men's room?

One of my other regulars went down there over half-an-hour ago. I think something may be wrong with him."

"OK, Rosie. For you I'll do it."

Joe took the key from her and shuffled off down the hall. In less than a minute he was back.

"Rosie, Rosie, call the ambulance! There's a guy lying on the floor and he don't look so good."

She called immediately, but it would be some time before the medics arrived. Rosie noticed that the lady in the Cadillac had arrived, and seemed to be looking anxiously into the restaurant. Rosie ran out to her.

"Mrs. Barton? Something has happened to your husband. You'd better come," Rosie cried.

"Oh, no! Not my Johnny! Where is he, miss?"

"He is down in the men's room, but I'm not sure you should go there until the paramedics get here."

Just then the medics arrived at the back door and rushed into the building. Joe Klein and some of the other men waived them around the corner to the men's room. They checked Barton for vital signs and found nothing. They hit him with the defibrillator, nothing. This appeared to be a classic heart attack. From what they could determine death had been immediate, before he hit the floor.

"Anyone know this man?" asked the supervisor of the paramedics.

"He is John S. Barton, my husband," sobbed Helen.

"I'm afraid we got here too late, Mrs. Barton. We just got here too late."

Helen cried, "Not my Johnny. Oh dear, what will I do?"

———

Charlie Smith, cruising at 51 miles per hour, looked in his rear view mirror and saw the last of the windmills that welcome visitors to the desert communities disappearing from view. Three and a half days for $48,500. He would save Mr. P and Duk $1,500 with his efficiency. He breathed in and pushed out a sigh. He nodded, his lips pressed tightly together. It was another job well done, and it had been easy.

———

Chicago Tribune: Saturday, November 21.

John S. Barton, formerly of Park Ridge, Illinois, died Wednesday, November 11. The cause of death was a heart attack. Mr. Barton retired as Senior Vice President of Midwest Freedom Bank in Chicago earlier this year and was living in Palm Springs, California. He is survived by his wife Helen, sons Gregory and William, and three grandchildren. Private services were held last Sunday in Palm Desert.

———

On arrival Monday morning the Program "D" cursor was blinking on Shelly Martin's computer console. She dialed up the screen and opened the window of death. Since Chris was already in, she called him to her desk.

"Hey Chris, we have another Program "D"," she yelled.

"OK, what do we have?" he asked as he pulled up a chair and sat next to her.

"Social Security 235-46-0937; Name: John S. Barton; age 65; male; Caucasian; married; current position: retired; place of death: Palm Springs, CA; cause of death: heart attack; date of death: Wednesday, November 11, 8:50 a.m." she read methodically.

"Which bank?" asked Chris.

"Midwest Freedom," Shelly answered.

"Oops, wait a sec, let's see, yes, also First Gotham, another double dipper."

"How much this time?"

"Premium $ 65,000; death benefit $280,000 for Midwest. Premium $89,000; face amount $595,000 for First Gotham."

"OK, Shelly, notify, let's see, a Ms. Felicity Jordan at Midwest, the usual condolences, and of course, our dear friend Mr. Trace at First Gotham. You know the routine."

It sure seems like the deaths are coming fast and furious at First Gotham this fall, he thought.

Chapter 8

Chris Masters and Sammy Sorrell had completed entering all of the data for the five banks by the second week in October. The Cubs, led by Sosa and Wood, had made it to the World Series for the first time in 80 years, and while slugging Sammy had broken the record for homeruns in a six game series with 7 dingers, they had lost to the Seattle Mariners. The boys had secured tickets from Mr. Harkness for one of the National League Championship games against the Mets, and had seen Mike Piazza crush two homers and a double. Their summer had certainly ended with fireworks at the ballpark.

Chris had begun to analyze the data to determine actuarial trends. He was particularly curious about how close the death claims came to the actuarial tables, given that these bank groups numbered in the thousands of participants, while the tables were based on millions of lives. Given the homogeneity of the bank populations, well educated, ages 35 to 65, mostly white, relatively affluent, which assured the availability of good health care, good lifestyle habits with regular exercise and little tobacco use. He had expected better than normal results.

He found that while there was a slight improvement over actuarial expectancies, it was almost too small to be statistically significant, less than a 2.5 percent gain over the 20-plus year period under observation. As expected, in the early years there were very few death claims, but as the insured groups matured, the claims increased. While the overall claims rate for the five banks had been predicted with significant accuracy, there were certain anomalies that puzzled Chris.

First Gotham Bank, for example, had significantly higher death claim rates, both in number of claims and amounts in 1993 and again in 1998, and all other years were at or below normal rates. Central States had excess claims in one year and that was also in 1998. Chris checked the actual claims for that year and found that two of the deceased bankers had, ironically, worked for and had been covered under the BOLI plans of both banks. One of them, Lily Yang-Peterson, had been a young female executive with each, and the claim amounts had been among the highest he had seen. He reminded himself that young, highly ranked female executives would always generate the highest claims because the same premium would purchase larger amounts of coverage. As this was primarily a tax-equivalent yield play for the banks, the strategy was premium driven. Face amount, at least at inception, was virtually irrelevant to the banks. They counted on the tax-sheltered return to make the programs pay off, and this was especially true in the early years of the programs. Death claims were secondary and only became a statistically significant aspect of the program in the later years, or in years when the investment performance was weaker than expected.

Chris Masters had a logic-driven mind, and he had always been able to pull together what may seem unrelated data to come to the unexpected, but correct, conclusion. Therefore, when he observed that First Gotham had actuarially significant excess claims in 1993 and 1998, it triggered his memory of fluctuations in the yield on treasuries over the years, and that there had been two or three dips in the mid-nineties. He logged into Bloomberg on his computer, and within seconds, there it was; treasuries had indeed dipped in 1993 and 1998, and were above 6.5 percent in all other years. Only First Gotham had managed to offset those dips in both years. The only other bank to hit an excess claim year was Central States in 1998, and that was a double-dip that they shared with First Gotham on two of the larger claims. He scrolled down the column of numbers and soon realized that the yield on treasuries had been dropping weekly and was now at 5.63 percent, which was the lowest point since 1998, and only the third venture below 6 percent in the last twenty years. Could there be more that the random influence of nature at work? He called to his assistant, "Sammy, I want you to pull up the death claims for First Gotham this year," then added, "by month of occurrence."

Chris reasoned that if there was manipulation going on, it would occur late in the year, after the trend in interest rates would be known, and when combined results could be calculated. As he did so the face of Richard "Slam Dunk" Trace came to him. The man had given him the creeps. He had looked like a living version of Ichabod Crane, tall and gaunt; dark stubble of beard and wide mouth emphasizing his bony, raptor-like jaw line. They had only the one, rather short meeting in the First Gotham office in New York City. Harkness had asked Chris to describe the program that he was working on for First Gotham and the four other banks. The banker had questioned the need for such detail, dismissing it as "make-work," to the embarrassment of the young actuary. Unlike the other bankers he had met, Richard Trace seemed hostile to his work and anxious to change the subject when Chris brought up the preliminary actuarial results. It was as if he had something to hide.

Harkness had remained silent throughout the exchange. It was clear that he was not going to say anything that would upset such an important client. Later that night after they had returned to Chicago, Chris had told Sarah that if anyone would abuse the system it would be someone like Richard Trace of First Gotham Bank in New York.

He clicked to the window on his screen showing annual death claims for First Gotham in 1993. Of the 16 death claims, seven had occurred after September 1; 43.75 percent in the last quarter. He then checked 1998: 8 of 19, or 42+ percent in the last quarter.

"Sammy, what have you found for this year?"

"Let's see, the total is 14 so far. The latest was just last week, Mr. John Barton in Palm Springs."

"Any others this month?"

"Yes, one on the 3rd and another on the 9th."

"How many more since September 1st?" asked Chris.

"That would be one, two, three, four, plus the three in October so far--a total of seven."

"50 percent since the 1st of September, right?'

"Un-huh," Sammy nodded, scratching his rust colored dreadlocks. "What's this all about, Chris?" he asked.

"I don't know yet. I just don't know," he whistled half under his breath. "But when the numbers lose their randomness, something very strange is going on."

———

Chris put down the thick novel, "Sarah, do you want to play?" he asked thoughtfully.

"Sure, why not. I'll be back in a couple minutes."

When she returned, her blond hair hung straight down below her shoulders, and she was in her teddy nightgown. She turned off the bedside lamp and pushed back the covers.

Chris nuzzled her neck and began to kiss her cheek. She rolled toward him and their lips came together, her kiss was warm and wet. He felt himself start to stiffen. He maneuvered her onto her back, even though he knew that she preferred to be on top. What he had in mind required the traditional missionary position. He stroked her gently until she was silky smooth and wet. By now he had a full erection and glided into her. Slowly, he began the ancient ritual, long, slow strokes, lingering on each. She moaned in appreciation.

Chris counted in his head: 8....9....10....

Suddenly, he speeded up and rocked her with ten violent strokes, as fast as he could manage. She gulped in surprise, but before she could react, he was back to the long, slow strokes that she preferred.

Again he counted: 8....9....10....

Then, again he abruptly speeded his strokes for ten quick bursts.

For the third time he slowed down and again fell into the more pleasurable slow, lingering strokes. At the count of ten, he started to speed up again.

"Chris, what the hell are you doing?" she yelled.

"I, uh, what do you mean?" he stammered.

"What's with this fast-slow stuff?

He had lost his grip on her and had slipped out during this exchange.

"Well, I, um-- well..."

"Well, what, goddamnit?"

"It's in the book Sarah, here, in Shogun. The Toronaga character makes love that way. He counts the strokes, ten slow and then ten fast until he gets to 100, then he comes."

"You and your fucking numbers," she muttered. "You are such a gooner!"

He laughed at himself, "Yes, well, I guess I should have warned you or something."

"Why don't you just forget about the counting and do it the regular way."

Chris eagerly complied, and they ended up panting from the exertion.

"You are a great lover without the new techniques. Just keep doing what comes naturally."

—

The next morning on their way to the Oak Park El Station, Chris turned to Sarah and said, "Honey, remember that we talked about the BOLI program being ghoulish when I first joined Smith, Hay & Ward?"

"Oh, yes. I just don't like the idea of being insured by a big corporation, especially after leaving."

"Well, Sammy and I have loaded in all of the data now, and the numbers indicate that there is a possibility that one of the banks is maneuvering the death claims to make their results come in on target or higher."

"What do you mean by maneuvering?" she asked tentatively.

"I think they are having people murdered," he replied.

"Oh, come on, Chris, is that your imagination talking?"

"No, Sarah, it is my logical mathematical brain telling me that the randomness of nature would not give us the results we are seeing."

"You've got to be kidding me!"

"I wish I were, and I hope I'm wrong, but circumstances in existence right now may provide additional evidence between now and the end of this year."

"Are you going to tell Mr. Harkness?"

"Not yet, I want to see how things develop first, and besides, he is so protective of the clients. As far as he is concerned, they walk on water. He is totally driven by corporate profit."

"Would he have anything to do with these murders?" she asked nervously.

"No way! Harry Harkness is as straight-laced as any man I have ever met. It's just that he is such a straight arrow that he will not be able to bring himself to believe that anyone would take advantage of his precious BOLI program."

Chapter 9

The sun was just beginning to rise on the eastern horizon. Flickers of light flashed on the dashboard of the new Chevy S-10, each flash blinding Bunky Owens as he drove due north. *Thank God I'm not driving straight into it,* he thought. *It's too damn dark for my shades.* With three days until the winter solstice, it was still dark at 6 a.m. and would be dark again by 4:30 p.m. that afternoon. These ten-hour days were a challenge to be endured.

Bunky's truck floated along the two-lane rural road, its headlights revealing nothing but macadam and the dirty remains of a late November snowfall. It had a rhythm like a gentle mare, rolling over the rough spots with a smooth rocking motion rather than the jolting ride of his previous pickup. He held the steering knob with his right hand and ran his left hand through his sandy blond hair.

He would get to Midway by 6:30 at this rate. Bunky was accustomed to early mornings. He was a professional pilot hired by large corporations. Many companies had their own jets all to themselves, usually under a lease agreement, while others share-leased with other corporations. Having one's own pilot on retainer was a luxury most companies could not afford, especially after the downsizing of the 1990's. Some of Owen's friends were single-company Sky-Jocks, which had its advantages and disadvantages. While they were able to participate in company benefits, they became slaves to the needs of that particular corporation. There was no way to say no, even if it meant leaving one's family at the most inopportune times.

Being an independent meant that Bunky had to pay for his own health and retirement plans, but he had much more control over his schedule. Most of his trips were lined up well in advance. First Gotham Bank was a particularly good customer. He usually was called on to haul from four to six executives on trips to two or three cities in a day. Sometimes this meant an overnight stay in a hotel with a return flight the next day, but most of these flights were one day round trips. He surmised that the purpose of most of these junkets was to get the word out to the troops on a hands-on basis. Every once in a while there would be a looker aboard which made the venture at least somewhat rewarding, over and above the usual fee, of course.

Today's assignment was Chicago--Milwaukee--Minneapolis/St. Paul and back to Midway. Out at 8 a.m. and return home by 6 p.m. He would net $2,000. Not bad for a pleasant day of flying. Bunky looked at the dimly lit sky outside his driver's side window and noticed that the western horizon had that slate-gray heavy look associated with a storm front, perhaps fifty to seventy-five miles away. Up ahead at 11 o'clock he could see that the sky was even darker than normal at this hour, and that the massive nimbus clouds rose up to what he estimated to be at least 30,000 feet.

He had a feeling that it would be a little bumpy unless the weather cleared. He would know soon enough after getting a look at the weather maps on the computer in the shed. The shed was a brightly lit control room attached to the Munger Air terminal on the southwest corner of Midway Airport. Bunky parked his truck in a designated spot close to the entrance and jogged the twenty feet to the door. Once inside he blew on his hands, which had managed to get plenty cold just closing the door of his truck and opening the door of the control room. He glanced at the thermometer outside the side window which registered 3 degrees Fahrenheit, and that meant that it would be below 10 degrees when they took off.

Bunky Owens strode to the coffee machine and flicked on the switch. As usual, at 6:25, he was the first to arrive. He sat down at a computer terminal and punched in his code name and the color monitor lit up immediately. He called up the weather map for the area and saw that the storm front was indeed fifty miles west and extended for another fifty miles. It was thick and heavy and reached heights of over 30,000 feet as he had suspected.

The pilot knew that this pea soup weather would really test his bird. He looked through the inside picture window at the gleaming white Cessna Citation parked in the attached hanger. It was a beautifully balanced aircraft nearly 50 feet from stem to stern and from wingtip to wingtip, with two well-positioned Williams-Rolls engines on either side of the fuselage just behind the wings. It could accommodate six passengers, and while there was a seat for a co-pilot, Bunky almost invariably flew solo. The entire round trip was well within the range of this Citation CJ2, the second generation Citation Jet his consortium had leased brand new in the year 2000.

Bunky returned his attention to the computer screen and determined that the front had been mostly stationary throughout the night and was now moving eastward at about three miles per hour. He surmised that by 8:00 a. m. it would be between forty and forty-five miles to the west, and at that rate, they could fly north to

Milwaukee without any direct intersect with the storm. He would have the First Gotham execs to their first meeting site by 8:45 with little more than a few bumps along the way.

The schedule called for them to leave Milwaukee between 11:00 and 11:30. He checked to see how far north the front ran and found that it was nearly to the Canadian border. Without a doubt the Milwaukee-Minneapolis leg was going to be a challenge. *So much for a pleasant day of flying.* He would earn his stripes today!

He got up from the computer and poured himself the now heated coffee, then walked out into the hanger. While it wasn't freezing, the hanger was noticeably cooler than the shed. He always had his corporate customers get on board here in the hanger where they were sheltered from the elements. Bunky waved hello to Chester and Conroy. He called them the C boys. They were the mechanics who took care of both of the Citations in their fleet.

"How're you C boys this morning?"

"We're cold as mackerel this a.m.," replied Chester.

"I can accept that as long as you don't smell like mackerel. How's our bird?"

"Fit as a fiddle and ready to roll," said Chester.

"Looks like we may have some weather today; may need to climb her quite a bit."

"No problem. Checked out the engines yesterday, greased all the struts and landing gear, and tested the stabilizer. She's in fine shape."

Owens was now circling around and beneath the body and wings of the craft, conducting his visual exam.

He could see his own blurred reflection in the bright white skin of the fuselage.

"It's a shame we have to get her dirty in this weather," he said. "I really appreciate the way you guys care for her."

"It's simple, Bunky. We love her as much as you do." It was Conroy.

It was true. They did love her, as much as anyone could love a machine.

Of all the airplanes that he had flown in his career, the Citation CJ2 was his favorite, a true state-of-the-art gem. Things had changed quite a bit in the twenty-five years that he had been an aviator. He had hit the 25 year mark on May 15, and he smiled at the thought that next March 17 he would hit the big five-oh!

Bunky remembered that June 27 would be his 24th wedding anniversary. He tugged at the scarf that Evelyn had given him for an anniversary present after they had seen the movie *The Great Waldo Pepper*. Ever since, he had always worn the scarf under his starched white uniform shirt. They called the scarf "Waldo." He and Evelyn had no children which gave them the freedom to live a very peripatetic life. They did have a cat named Pepper. He pulled at his sandy mustache with the thumb and forefinger of his left hand, then ran them down over the collar of his shirt, feeling Waldo. He sighed and took a last sip of coffee.

At 7:45 the gang from First Gotham Bank arrived in two cars. There were six executives, five men and a woman. She was a handsome lady, but not the kind of looker that Owens had thought about earlier this morning. Senior Vice President Elmer Galloway was in charge. He was the head of Corporate Banking for Gotham here in

Chicago. Bunky Owens had piloted for Galloway on several occasions.

"Good morning, Captain Owens. It's certainly a brisk one," said Galloway.

"Yes indeed, sir. Would any of you like coffee before we get going?" Bunky asked.

While they took turns at the coffee machine, Galloway introduced them to Bunky. There were two group V.P.'s, Bill Johns and Carol Krebin, and the division marketing V. P., Andrew Haskell. Krebin and Haskell were taking their first trip on the corporate jet. Owens could have guessed without being told by the look of awe in their eyes as they looked out at the Citation waiting in the hanger. Besides these members of the Corporate Banking team in Chicago, Galloway also introduced Bill Barnes and Steven Schwartz, two company attorneys who were hitching a ride to Minneapolis. They, too, were also on their first flight in the company jet.

Galloway let it be known that the attorneys would be staying on in Minneapolis and not returning in the company plane. He also made it clear that they were not part of his coterie. Bunky was used to these split groups. Clearly there was competition for use of this perk, and the various executives did not relish sharing their good fortune with others in the corporation.

Bunky led them out into the hanger which was now noticeably colder as the C boys were in the process of opening the hanger doors electronically. They all scrambled up the stairs and into the waiting airplane. The wiry pilot closed the door behind him and made sure everyone was comfortable. Then he took a few moments to cover the safety features of the Citation, and show them some of the finer appointments of the interior, especially the well-stocked galley. Elmer Galloway, being the senior passenger both in terms of corporate rank and company jet experience, was asked to help Bunky with these explanations. He enjoyed showing his "expertise." When his passengers were settled, Bunky told them that the trip to Milwaukee would take less than 45 minutes, and that they could expect some bumps because of a weather front a few miles to the west. Then he entered the cockpit and went through his pre-flight routine, checking all of the avionics. In a few minutes the Cessna rolled smoothly out of the hanger and into the chilly morning air. It was an uneventful trip to Milwaukee with an easy landing at 8:41.

While the bankers went into the city to visit their troops, Bunky went to the computer to check out the weather between Milwaukee and Minneapolis. He could immediately see that the front had not moved more than ten miles since 6 a.m. and was now about 30 miles deep. It was as though all that heavy muck was piling up behind a stable front, so that what used to be fifty miles of bad weather was now consolidated into thirty miles. He would have forty miles to approach the storm front and then would need about five minutes to get through it. Since the Citation had a ceiling of 45,000 feet he filed a flight plan to start out flying east and circle up to 35,000 feet before heading west and climbing as high as needed to fly over the storm.

When the bankers returned at 11 o'clock, nothing had changed on the weather computer. This time he warned them that they would be going through and over some very turbulent storm clouds and that they should keep their seat belts fastened until he gave them the all clear signal. The plane roared down the runway and turned out over the lake as Bunky pulled his yoke back to the max to get the greatest possible rate of climb. The Citation responded as expected and within minutes he was at 32,000 feet and began a slow turn around to the north. When his bird had traveled a few miles along the shore of Lake Michigan and was at 35,000 feet, he turned west-northwest and headed toward the front, now 50 miles distant. He could see that the storm clouds were higher than his altitude and began to climb. In ten minutes he began to feel the first turbulence and continued his ascent. The Citation was now at 41,000 feet and the clouds were, incredibly, still higher. He eased the yoke back to get still more altitude, knowing that he was nearing the maximum ceiling for his craft.

As they entered the storm front, the windshield began getting blasted by sprays of ice, and he fought to keep control as they plunged into the clouds which he now estimated to be upwards of 50,000 feet. It was becoming clear that as the storm pushed against the stationary front with no forward progress to be made, the clouds rose upward to almost unheard of heights. Within less than a minute he was well into the storm clouds. The ice in these clouds ripped at the beautiful white skin of the Citation.

Suddenly, he felt a shudder and realized that his starboard engine had blown out. He quickly concluded that ice must have clogged the intake.

Bunky now had to compensate for the lack of power by trying to counterbalance his port-side wing. He calculated that he would need another four minutes to get through to the west side of the storm which would be difficult even with both engines fully operational, and worst of all, he was losing altitude at an alarming rate. Bunky realized that he was in a desperate situation. All of these thoughts were processed in a few seconds. He decided that he would negotiate a turn to starboard and swing down, around and out of the storm and return to Milwaukee. He punched the radio to the proper frequency and spoke calmly.

"Milwaukee, this is CY 394. We have blown our starboard engine. I am turning back and request emergency landing assistance, over."

"Roger, CY 394, we read you and have you on radar."

"Milwaukee, I'm very busy up here and need to focus on flying my way out of this mess."

"Roger, CY 394, we will stand by."

Bunky tried to raise the nose of the Citation by pulling back on the yoke as they made the turn out of the storm, but ice had accumulated on the wings and was weighing them down. The altimeter began to plummet.

In the cabin the bankers had, at first, grown very silent. The two attorneys were in the back bulkhead seats. They looked at each other with serious concern etched on their faces. The four corporate lending officers were in the central four seats that faced each other.

Andrew Haskell was the first to speak after the shuddering bump that accompanied the starboard engine blowout: "That can't be normal, and it can't be good."

"Does this seem normal, Elmer?" asked Carol.

"This is definitely not normal," he growled.

At that point the plane began to drop precipitously. Bill Barnes was the first to react. He retched before he could get the vomit bag up to his face, and the gravity of the downward fall pushed his discharge back into his face.

Carol, who was facing him, saw this and immediately followed suit, throwing up all over the table between the two pairs of seats. She loosed a gurgling scream that echoed through the cabin.

Bunky heard the commotion and yelled, "Try to keep calm. I'm going to get us out of here." The ice on the starboard wing caused it to cant over and the Citation went into a slow downward spin. The aft passengers, the two attorneys, Elmer Galloway and Bill Johns, were now hanging by their seat belts, hovering over Carol and Andrew. Johns moaned and covered his face. Haskell noticed, to his dismay, that Johns had soiled his pants and excrement was running down his pant leg and falling on him. The plane began to spin more rapidly. The clipboard that Bunky had laid on the co-pilot seat flew up at his face and he instinctively threw up his right arm to fend it off. The sharp metal clip bit into his wrist, opening a deep two inch gash. He tried to re-grip the steering yoke, which was shaking violently, but he had no strength in his hand.

Bunky became confused. Blood was all over him, and he didn't know whether it was coming from above or below. He realized that his wrist was probably broken and useless.

"I'm cut. I'm cut real bad," he yelled into the radio.

He let go of the yoke with his left hand and clawed at his collar. He would try to use his scarf as a tourniquet and stop the bleeding, but working with one hand it was nearly an impossible task. He yanked Waldo free and tried to bind up his wrist using his left hand and his teeth. The Cessna shook so hard his teeth banged together and he lost the scarf. It fell away, and he didn't know whether it fell up or down.

Again he yelled into the radio, "We're going down. I've lost control!"

Those were the last words heard by air traffic controllers in Milwaukee. For Bunky Owens, everything was turning bright white, then red, and finally, pitch black.

The Citation plunged straight down, taking only ninety seconds to fall the final 20,000 feet. It hit the ground at .95 mach. Most everything forward of the aft bulkhead was vaporized. Only the tail section was identifiable. The frenzied activity that had taken place inside the cabin would never be known. None of the victims was clearly identified. The investigators did find a Star of David medal forged into the steel frame of the back bulkhead on the starboard side, leading them to surmise that Steven Schwartz had probably been in the back left seat. They also speculated that the force of the impact had probably caused the gold chain on which it hung to cut through his neck like a garrote.

By the time Enoch Israelson, the farmer on whose forty-acre farm the plane fell, had made his way cautiously out to the crash site, the wreckage was a gray bubbling mass, getting more soupy by the minute as the icy rain pelted down upon it. Enoch sat in the seat of his John Deere tractor and held a small black umbrella over his head with one hand and a Chesterfield in the other. In about twenty minutes, the local sheriff and his deputy arrived in their squad car. They sat in the car with the windshield wipers at full speed and listened to country music. It wasn't until the county ambulance arrived in answer to their summons that anyone had the nerve to approach the wreckage, and that was an hour and fifteen minutes after the officially calculated time of the accident, 11:26 a.m. on December 20. The paramedics poked around the outskirts of the wreck for a few minutes and then retreated to their ambulance and left. Enoch had one last cigarette and then headed back to the barn. Sheriff James and his deputy stayed at the scene.

—

Chris and Sarah had been back to Pittsburgh for the Christmas holidays when the airplane crash deaths of six First Gotham executives was broadcast as the lead story on the evening news. Chris didn't need to hear the details from Shelly to add to his already heightened suspicions about the death claim rate at that particular bank. The totals through the end of November had already confirmed his initial calculations. The totals were burned in his brain: 9 deaths since September 1 for a total of $4.65 million, and only 7 deaths for $3.13 million for the first eight months of the year. This same pattern had been recorded in 1993 and 1998, the only other years when the claims seemed to be enhanced by other than natural randomness. Now, with 6 more deaths, the total would be 16 since September 1, for how much more?

The next Monday morning at 8 o'clock Chicago time Chris made a call to the office. His fingers trembled as he punched out the number for Shelly Martin's extension.

"Hi Shel, I'm sure you've read about the crash in Wisconsin."

"Yes, Chris, it was awful."

"Have any reports come in over the weekend?" he asked anxiously.

"Chris, I just got in. Let me check screen D. OK, let's see here….Oh, yes, there are reports on five of the seven victims."

"No, Shelly, it's only six. The pilot was not an employee and wouldn't have been covered, and, of course, we don't know for sure that all six employees were covered. I don't need detail until I get back to the office on Wednesday, but could you give me the claim totals on each of them?"

"OK, ready?"

"Yeah, go ahead."

"Barnes--$450,000; Galloway--$650,000; Krebin--$700,000; Haskell--$600.000; and Johns—$420,000. Total--$2,820,000," she read.

Chris calculated in his head: $2.82 million, added to the $4.65 million he already knew about, meant that the claims since September 1 now totaled $7.47 million, a real bonanza for First Gotham Bank.

"Any double-dippers, Shel?"

"Let me check. No, all are fairly long-term employees of First Gotham."

"The newspaper report also mentioned a Steven Schwartz. Could you check to see if he is on the BOLI program?"

She switched to another window in the program and scrolled down the coverage list, which, fortunately, was in alphabetical order.

"No, Chris, he isn't listed."

"That means he is either new or didn't agree to be covered," Chris surmised.

On the most recent round of additional BOLI coverage conducted in 1999 at First Gotham, the employees had been offered a $5,000 personal paid-up policy as an incentive reward for allowing the bank to add them to the BOLI program. Somehow, Schwartz must have declined to be covered. *It didn't do him any good, though*, thought Chris.

"Everything else OK there, Shel?"

"Well, Sammy is off this week, so other than this stuff, it is pretty quiet. Processing these claims will keep me busy."

"All right, Shelly, I'll see you on Wednesday."

Chris cradled the phone and whistled softly.

"Sarah, the murders at First Gotham are getting out of hand!"

"Chris, you're calling them murders again," she half-shouted.

"It's hard not to with the statistical evidence," Chris replied.

"What statistical evidence?" asked Sarah.

"The number of death claims at First Gotham was far beyond our actuarial expectation even before this accident, and now it is completely off the chart. The thing that bothers me is that most of these excess death claims have come in years when the investment return is down due to lower interest rates on treasuries. It's as if the claims always make up for an investment shortfall at First Gotham."

"Do you suspect that creepy Mr. Trace, honey?"

"I don't know who else it could be," replied Chris Masters.

"Well, you have told me that Harry Harkness doesn't like any questioning of his program, so I would be very careful if I were you." she warned.

"You're right, Sarah. He always seems to defend his clients, particularly Trace. They have known each other for eons."

"I'll find the right time and circumstances to talk to him."

"I'm sorry you are in such a mess, honey. I really am."

"I'll figure a way to get this done, Sarah, but it is a tough situation, I must admit."

Chapter 10

When the Cessna went down, Ralph Murphy was on the road to St. Louis. He had left Chicago early that morning for an accident site just south of the Hillsboro Municipal airport. He had arrived at the scene just before noon to meet with the local officials and planned to be at the crash site for the rest of the afternoon.

This promised to be a routine investigation of a single engine Piper Cub that had hit some power lines and flipped on its back. The pilot, a 22 year-old novice, had a broken arm and smashed wrist, but otherwise was fine. She had escaped the cockpit by dropping about eight feet from the upside-down door. This had been her fifth solo flight. She had never ventured more than ten miles from the airfield on any of the flights, and as far as Ralph could see, other than the 30-foot tower and a few rather tall trees, these power lines were about the only aboveground obstacles for miles.

His plan was to take measurements at the scene, check out the aircraft, and have it removed so the telephone repair crew could do their work. After that he would interview the pilot, one Annie Mae Howe. She had been taken to the Jefferson County Hospital to have the arm set and the wrist operated on by a local orthopedic surgeon. Ralph had been told that she could be seen by late afternoon. He figured that the interview would take less than an hour and that he could be back on the road by 6 p. m. and home in his apartment in Des Plaines by 9, totally routine. Ralph had driven to within 100 yards of the overturned Piper when his cell phone rang.

"Murphy here," he answered.

"Ralph, this is Fred."

"Fred" was Fred Waltham, Chief of the Chicago-based Great Lakes Region of the National Transportation Safety Board. "Yes sir, what's up?"

"It's not "what's up," it's what went down. There was a bad one up near Milwaukee, a Cessna CJ2 with seven aboard. It was a leased jet with six bank officers and the pilot. Apparently not much left but rubble, other than the tail section."

"Must have done a header, straight down," muttered Ralph.

"We have the tape with Milwaukee Air Traffic Control, and it appears they tried to breech a storm front. She may have iced up. Anyway, we need you on this one," he commanded.

"OK, Chief."

"What's the story down there?"

"Oh, it was just a female novice's misjudgment. She's only 22, apparently pretty shook up, but she's basically fine, considering. Why not send Garrison down here? He can handle it and may even get lucky with the young lady."

"Like a Christmas present, Ralph?"

"Why not, Chief? I feel charitable. How do I get to that crash site?"

"I have a plane on the way to meet you at Lambert Field. It should be there within the hour. You can turn your car in there and I'll have Garrison fly down and pick it up. He can drive it back to Chicago tomorrow. I'll have him stay over, to comfort the young lady, so to speak."

—

Ralph Murphy lit a cigarette as soon as he departed the lounge area after deplaning in Milwaukee. He hunched his massive shoulders against a strong west wind outside the hard glass doors of the terminal. It would probably be several minutes before Curtis Jones, the local FAA official, would arrive at General Mitchell Field to drive him to the Cessna crash site. Enough time for a smoke. Ralph had worked with Curtis before, and they got along well. The light was beginning to fade; large storm clouds hung in the western sky, bringing on the already early darkness even earlier. Hadn't he read recently that this was the time of the shortest days of the year?

Not going to get much done tonight, thought Ralph.

The glow of the cigarette lit his deeply pockmarked cheeks and then faded, off and on like the beacon of a lighthouse. Ralph had heavy-lidded dark eyes and coarse eyebrows. His upper lip curled downward on the left side, the result of a mini-stroke two years earlier. His doctor had warned him about his smoking and his weight. He had given Ralph some pills for high blood pressure and elevated cholesterol, but Ralph was not a good patient and had no one at home to remind him to take his medicine. The pills languished in his medicine cabinet. At 5' 9", 240 pounds he seemed to be a heart attack waiting to happen, except that Ralph Murphy was somehow able to deflect stress. His attitude was that of a classic investigator, and when he found himself in a stressful situation, he would transfer that stress to others, to a co-worker, his boss or someone involved in an accident. He never internalized the stress. After-all, it wasn't he who caused these accidents. His job was to find out the cause, and as far as Ralph was concerned, he was the good guy and everyone else was a suspect. He had the arrogance of total innocence.

By the time the two inspectors arrived at the Israelson farm, it was pitch dark and sleeting. A spotlight truck had been driven to the scene and illuminated the once proud tail of the downed Cessna, still glistening white through the hard icy rain. The rubble was a boiling mass of charred metal strewn over a wide area of the unplanted muddy field. A caustic odor hung in the air.

Ralph approached the sheriff. "Hi, I'm Murphy of the National Transportation Safety Board and this is Curtis Jones of the Federal Aviation Agency down in Milwaukee."

"The big boys, huh?" nodded the sheriff.

"Yeah, we be the Feds," said Ralph, intentionally slurring his words.

The sheriff allowed a grudging smile that quickly faded. "I'm Sheriff James and this be Deputy Alexander," he said, white teeth gleaming to let Ralph know that he had caught his racial slur.

Ralph asked, "Find anything?"

"Naw, haven't really looked. Just trying to seal off the area and keep the ol' curious eyes away."

"OK, let's be sure someone stays with it all night and we'll start tomorrow morning at first light. That's around 8:00 this time of year. Any place to stay around here?" asked Ralph.

"There's a Motel 6 about four miles up this here road, 'bout six, eight miles out of town," the sheriff replied.

"What town would that be?" asked the inspector.

"That be Waupun." Again, the wide smile.

"OK, bro, see you in the a.m.," Ralph grinned and poked him on the shoulder.

———

For the next two days Murphy and Jones sifted through the wreckage. They determined within the first two hours that the plane had plunged straight down, nose first, as all but the rear section had been pulverized. The bulkhead at the rear of the jet and the tail section were still intact. The inspectors were able to retrieve much of the luggage from behind the bulkhead, although it was badly charred and soaked from the rain. They found Steven Schwartz's bronze Star of David welded into the steel bulkhead. The so-called black box, which was actually bright orange, was found about 200 yards from the tail section and was sent off for analysis. The icy conditions had persisted, hampering their investigation, and with the temperature in the teens, it was miserable work. Ralph had seen enough after the second day, and at 5:30 p.m., he and Curtis headed back to Milwaukee.

"Bad one, huh, Ralph?"

"Yeah, usually we find more remains, but here only the back two, the Jew and another guy. All the others completely immolated. That bird must have fallen at least 20,000 feet straight down. They had to all be unconscious, if not already dead, before she hit the ground."

"What now, Ralph?"

"Now for the paper trail; looking to see if anyone had any reason to sabotage this ship. We'll check out the pilot and the leasing company and, of course, the bankers. Divorce, domestic conflicts, money problems, insurance, you know, that sort of thing. The usual. If this was a planned accident, that's where it will show." He paused for a moment.

"The physical evidence appears to indicate that the plane iced up and the pilot couldn't maneuver her out of harm's way. He probably placed too much confidence in the bird's specs given the heavy storm they encountered. The CJ2 has a ceiling of 45,000 feet, and he likely had to use all of that capacity trying to fly over the storm. My guess is that the clouds went up to over 50,000 feet. I'm sure I'll be on the next phase well into the new year."

Curtis Jones drove up to the door marked "Northwest Airlines" and slowed to a stop. A new snow was beginning to fall. The airport windows were ablaze with brightly sparkling green and red bulbs. A Salvation Army lady rang her bell merrily. "Merry Christmas, merry Christmas," she trilled.

"Well, Curtis, have a merry. Say hello to the missus and kids. I'm off to my bachelor pad in Chi-town. Maybe I'll get lucky for the holidays. Probably have to pay big for it though, and to get a safe one is real big bucks. Oh well, I'm down to two, three times a year, so what the hell. Why not splurge? They can be real dolls. I'll send you some reports to countersign in a few days, probably after New Year's. You know, co-witness stuff?"

"Yes, Ralph, you have a merry Christmas and happy New Year. Nice workin' with you again."

"Take some time off, Curt. You deserve it. I'm goin' to put in a good word for you with the Chief. I have always enjoyed working with you. Take care, buddy. See you soon!"

"Bye-bye, Ralph."

Curtis pulled slowly away from the curb, not wanting to splash slush on Ralph. He looked over his shoulder and saw Ralph with his hand raised in good-bye, frozen up over his head until he was at least 100 yards away. Then he saw his arm drop as he turned toward the entry doors.

"What a sad life," he whispered aloud, not really believing Ralph's talk about getting a call girl. Curtis flicked on the radio. It was nearing the end of Sinatra's classic, "*Have Yourself a Merry Little Christmas, Now.*" A silent tear ran down Curtis' cheek. Ralph hadn't shed a tear for himself, or anyone else, since his Charlotte had died thirty years ago.

Chapter 11

Ralph Murphy spent the next four working days between the Christmas and New Year's holidays scouring the personnel files of the six passengers and the pilot of Cessna flight CY-394. Five of the seven were married; only Steven Schwartz and Carol Krebin were single. All seven lived in the Chicago area; the farthest out in the suburbs was Bunky Owens, the pilot. They were, however, spread out all over the suburbs, except for Elmer Galloway, who lived with his wife and teenage daughter in a fancy condo on Lakeshore Drive. None of them had any obvious marital problems. All five marriages were of at least ten years duration. The Galloways' led the way with 25 years, but Ralph knew he would need to do some more digging on that score. Sometimes marriage rifts were not easily discernable.

The bank's human resources department had released some basic information as requested, providing details on the pension, disability, medical, 401(k) and life insurance programs of each of the six bankers. Ralph sifted through this information with care, looking for anything out of the ordinary. All had elected the usual coverage. Haskell and Galloway had chosen the maximum of three times earnings for the life insurance, while the others had elected the minimum coverage of $50,000. There were no claims against their disability coverage, nor were there any major claims against any of their medical coverage, although Schwartz had medical bills of $1,800 two years earlier for an operation on his shoulder. No excess coverage, no borrowing against the 401(k) programs, nothing in their employment records to indicate financial or medical problems.

The one item that puzzled Ralph was that five of them were checked off as *"yes"* on BOLI coverage, whatever that was. He picked up his phone and dialed the number for Judy Jenkins of the First Gotham HR department. After punching his way through the usual menu of options, Ralph heard the perky voice.

"Judy Jenkins, Human Resources, can I help you?"

"This is Ralph Murphy of the National Transportation Safety Board. We're investigating the plane crash that killed several of your executives."

"Yes, Mr. Murphy. How can I help you?"

"The personnel records that you sent out have been a great help, but I do have one question."

"OK."

"On your form there is a box labeled B-O-L-I." He spelled it out. "What does that mean?"

"Oh, yes. Well, that stands for Bank Owned Life Insurance."

"What exactly is that, Miss Jenkins?" he asked.

"That means the bank has life insurance coverage on the employee. Well, we only have it on those employees who are grade 14 or higher, basically anyone who is at least a vice-president. We have lots of vice-presidents."

"How much coverage would the bank carry on these people?"

"Do you mean the six who died?" she asked.

"Well, yes. Five of them were checked off for BOLI."

"You know, Mr. Murphy, that is a good question, and I just don't know the answer. I'll have to ask my supervisor and get back to you."

"Could you find out now while I wait?"

"Let me check to see if she is in. Just a minute."

While he waited, Ralph rubbed the stubble on his neck and chin. *I should have shaved, but since there is hardly anyone in the office, what the hell*, he thought.

He loosened his tie and took a sip of cold coffee.

Judy came back on the line. "My supervisor told me that we don't have that information here at the bank. That program is administered by an outside agency called Smith, Hay & Ward. I have their number. Ready?"

"Yeah, go ahead," said Ralph as he turned the page on his note pad.

"It's 312-261-9384. They are located on Michigan Avenue in Chicago."

"I'm calling you from Chicago. Where are you, by the way?"

"Oh, HR is here in New York City."

"How's the weather there?"

"It's cold and windy, but clear."

"Same here, also cold and windy; typical Chicago weather for this time of year."

"Is there anything else I can do for you?"

"No thanks, you've been a great help. Have a Happy New Year!"

"Thanks, same to you."

Ralph pressed the bar in the cradle of his phone and immediately dialed the number that Miss Jenkins had given him.

"Smith, Hay & Ward, how may I help you?" came the honeyed voice.

"I want to speak to someone about the B-O-L-I program you administer for the First Gotham Bank."

"That would be Mr. Harry Harkness."

"Hardness?" he asked.

"No, H-A-R-K-ness," she spelled.

Ralph pressed the phone to his ear. *Got to see someone about my hearing*, he thought.

"Hello, this is Shelly Martin, may I help you?"

"May I speak to Mr. Harkness?"

"I'm sorry. Mr. Harkness is on vacation until next Monday."

"Oh yeah, the week between Christmas and New Year's is like that."

"Who's calling, please?"

"This is Ralph Murphy of the NTSB. Oh sorry, that's the National Transportation Safety Board. We are conducting an investigation of the Cessna crash near Racine, Wisconsin that killed seven people last week."

"Yes, Mr. Murphy, I heard about it. How can we help you?"

"Well, Miss--uh...."

"Martin."

"Thank you. Well, we had received information from First Gotham Bank's HR department on the victims and noticed that they were all covered under a so-called B-O-L-I program."

"Yes...." Shelly said, hesitantly.

"Is there someone I can speak with about this?"

The person in charge of the First Gotham Bank BOLI program is Chris Masters. Let me get him for you. Can you hold for a moment?"

Shelly put down the phone and ran down the hall to Chris's office.

"Chris, there is a guy on the phone from the NTSB--National Transportation Board, or something, asking about the First Gotham BOLI program."

"OK, Shel, I'll take it."

"Hello, this is Chris Masters, may I help you?"

"Yes, this is Ralph Murphy of the National Transportation Safety Board. I understand that you are the administrator of the B-O-L-I program for First Gotham Bank."

"That's correct, Mr. Murphy."

"Well, we have information that five of the seven victims of the Cessna crash up in Wisconsin were covered under the program."

"Uh--I...."

"Oh, I got the information from the Human Resources department of First Gotham."

"Yes, Mr. Murphy."

"Anyway, is it possible that you could tell me how much coverage the bank carried on the victims?"

"Well, Mr. Murphy, I am fairly new on the job, and I will have to check with my superior to see if we can release that information. Usually it is totally confidential, you understand."

"Yes, of course. Listen, my office is also here in Chicago. Could you check and call me back?"

"Of course, Mr. Murphy. I should be able to get back to you in short order." Chris hung up and ran back to his desk. The home phone number for Mr. Harkness was in his rolodex. He dialed the number with shaking fingers.

"Harkness here," replied the deep voice.

"Mr. Harkness, this is Chris Masters."

"Yes, Chris. Is everything OK?"

"Well yes, but we just got a call from an investigator from the National Transportation Safety Board asking about the First Gotham BOLI program. He wanted to know how much coverage was on the victims of the crash last week."

"What did you tell him?" Harkness asked cautiously.

"I told him it was confidential and that I would have to check with my superior."

"Good lad, very good. I need to check this out with our legal department and get back to you. I'll call right away."

Chris suspended all other activity until the return call, which came about twenty minutes later.

"OK, Chris. We need to be sure of this man's identity, but if he is, in fact, with the NTSB investigation division, we should cooperate fully."

"Mr. Harkness, I forgot to tell you that his office is here in Chicago."

"OK. Call him back and make an appointment for him to come into the office around 9:00 tomorrow, if possible, and ask him to bring photo identification. Oh, and Chris, I am going to join you for this meeting."

"Are you sure, sir?"

"Yes, we need to be careful. We're dealing with a federal investigator."

"I see what you mean, Mr. Harkness. I'm glad you'll be here."

"It wouldn't be fair of me to ask you to handle this all by yourself, Chris."

"Mr. Harkness, could you come in early, before the meeting, so that we can talk about it? There are some things that I have uncovered regarding the First Gotham Bank account that I would like to go over with you ahead of time."

"Fine, Chris, I'll see you at 8. Is that OK?"

"Perfect, sir, thank you."

Chris called Murphy and repeated the Harkness instructions, including the fact that Harry would be attending their meeting.

"That's fine, Mr. Masters. No problem. 9 a. m. works fine for me."

"Great, do you know where we are?"

"Oh yes, just up on Michigan Avenue. I'll see you then."

Murphy hung up the phone and went back to his paperwork, but his mind kept coming back to the BOLI program. *How much coverage?* He thought.

—

That evening Sarah had wanted to do some bargain shopping and literally dragged Chris along to carry the presents they were going to exchange. He had seemed unusually distracted, which she interpreted as boredom. She knew that Chris was not very interested in material possessions, and would rather spend his time with his head buried in a book. However, when he failed to answer her repeated question about which sweater to buy, she put her hands on her hips and shouted, "Christopher Masters, hello!"

Chris looked around the crowded store thinking that everyone would be staring at them. The general hubbub of murmuring shoppers had muffled Sarah's voice, and none seemed to be paying any attention to them.

"I'm sorry, Sarah. It's just that something happened at work today that has me bothered."

"What's that, Chris?"

"Well, we got a call from a Mr. Murphy of the National Transportation Safety Board, a government agency. He is investigating the airplane crash up in Wisconsin that killed those First Gotham executives who were covered under their BOLI program. Anyway, he is coming in tomorrow at 9 o'clock."

"Have you said anything to Mr. Harkness?" she asked anxiously.

"Yes, I called him, and he is going to join me for the meeting with this Mr. Murphy, but that's not what is worrying me."

"What is it, honey?" she asked gently.

"I'm concerned about whether or not to tell this guy about my suspicions about First Gotham Bank, you know, the high death rate even before the crash."

"Uh-huh."

"I feel like this Mr. Murphy should know, and maybe he will be able to do something about it."

"I don't know, Chris. You should be real careful. He is a government agent, for God's sake, and your suspicions are just that, no more than an educated guess."

"Sarah, the history going back several years makes it more than just a guess. Although I'll admit it is strictly circumstantial evidence."

"Did you mention your theory to Harry?"

"No, but I did ask him to come in early so that I could go over it with him."

"I certainly wouldn't say anything to this inspector guy unless Mr. Harkness gives you the go-ahead," she cautioned.

"Don't worry, I'm not that stupid," he said angrily.

"I didn't say you were stupid, but sometimes you get so caught up in the mathematics of a situation that you just blurt it out without considering the consequences."

"OK, Sarah, I'll be careful. I'm sure Harry will know how to handle this situation."

—

At 8:03 the next morning Harry Harkness came to see Chris Masters at his cubicle.

"Could you come down to my office, Chris?"

Chris followed him down the hall, and they settled into the armchairs in front of his desk. Harry had carefully closed the door to his office after he had ushered Chris in before him.

"OK, Chris, what is it that you wanted to tell me about the First Gotham Bank?" he queried.

"As you know, we have been gathering actuarial data on the five banks that you assigned to me, including First Gotham."

"Yes, go on."

"Well, I have noticed that First Gotham seemed to have an unusually large number of claims, even before the airplane crash. Two of them were double-dippers, which are more noticeable than other claims. Anyway, I checked the death claim history and found that they had claims greater than the actuarial expectations in three different years--1993, 1998 and this year."

"Chris, that is probably an actuarial anomaly," observed Harkness.

"Possibly sir, but the only other bank to have higher than expected claims in any one year was Central States in 1998, and that included the largest double-dipper claim I have seen since joining Smith, Hay & Ward."

"I suppose you are going to tell me the double dip was with First Gotham?" asked his boss.

"Yes, sir," he confirmed.

"Is there anything else, Chris?"

"Yes, I'm afraid so. I also ran total return numbers and here again noticed that unlike the other banks, First Gotham had always made the optimum return, even in the years when interest rates on treasuries were below par."

"And those years were?"

"1993, 1998 and this year!" His voice throbbed with the adrenaline that surged through his body.

"Well, well." Harkness stroked his pointed chin. "You know, Chris, sometimes we let our imagination run with an apparent bit of malfeasance, and all it does is lead to trouble. In this case for both First Gotham Bank and Smith, Hay & Ward. I think you should just forget about all of this. It sounds like a tempest in a teapot to me."

"A tempest in a teapot, sir?"

"Oh, I'm dating myself. It's an old expression meaning much ado about nothing--oops, there's another one, but you get the idea."

"Then what should we tell Mr. Murphy?" asked Chris.

"Let's first get him to understand how the program works in general. Then he will want to know about the accident victims, and we can certainly give him that information, and...." Harkness paused, "and let's just leave it at that."

Chris nodded in agreement. Sarah had warned him not to push his theory with the Federal investigator, and now his boss was saying the same thing. Still, he felt like it was a cover-up to protect First Gotham Bank and Richard Trace. Why had Harkness hesitated? Was it because he really believed Chris, but was protecting his precious BOLI program? Chris recalled how Harry had dismissed his reaction about the ghoulishness of the program when he had first joined Smith, Hay & Ward last summer.

As he left the office, Harkness touched his arm. Chris could not bring himself to acknowledge this attempt at solidarity, turning away so as not to make eye contact.

"Let me know when this Mr. Murphy arrives," said the older man.

"Yes, sir," replied Chris softly.

Chapter 12

The morning of Ralph's meeting with Chris Masters and Harry Harkness was a Thursday, the day before New Year's Eve. The historic millennium celebrations had come and gone and this was just another ho-hum change of years. For Ralph the day promised to be more exciting than any holiday. It was, in effect, the real beginning of his investigation into what might become a really fascinating case.

By 8:45 a.m. he was outside 500 Michigan Avenue. His appointment was 28 stories up in this building. Ralph huddled against the marble facade and cupped his hands over his Bic lighter, his ol' reliable Bic, and lit his third cigarette of the morning. The fingers of his right hand were stained a dirty orange from his habit. He inhaled deeply and blew the filtered smoke slowly out of his mouth. It was so cold that it was impossible to tell a normal breath from a smoke-enhanced one. He paced a few feet and took another drag, filling his lungs with the sweet-sour intoxicant that gave him a buzz his morning cup of coffee could not touch. Ralph had made a conscious decision that he would live with the consequences of his less than environmentally and medically correct lifestyle. In spite of what he had said to Curtis, sex had long since ceased to be a reality for him and these little pleasures would have to suffice.

He wanted to be on full alert for this morning's interview, and hoped this last Marlboro would do the trick. At 8:55 he stubbed out the cigarette in the container that, by now, already held several butts, some still simmering in the cold morning air. Ralph had looked around the entry and found it easy to identify his fellow smokers. There were four others having their last smokes until the mid-morning break, when they would all gather again in a designated smoking area. He knew that if he worked in this building they would become his closest acquaintances outside his immediate coworkers. Smokers shared the disapproval of the rest of society and bonded together in a very strong community. One could always, always get a light, and usually bum a smoke if you ran short. He had lit many a cigarette for a stranger who eventually became a known confrère.

At 9 o'clock sharp Ralph Murphy reported to Miss Honey-voice.

She was almost what he had expected, plus at least 40 pounds. *Takes good care of herself, otherwise*, thought Ralph. Blond--honey-blond—hair was in place; makeup--just so--perfect.

"May I help you?" Sally asked. The honey in her voice had gone away.

Could it be me? he asked himself.

Ralph struggled with his overcoat, and said, "I'm here to see Chris Masters and Mr. Harkness. Ralph Murphy of the National Transportation Safety Board."

"Yes, Mr. Murphy, they are expecting you." Her voice perked up noticeably.

He shook the left arm of the coat loose and asked, "Where can I put this?" gesturing toward the heavy overcoat now draped over his left arm.

Sally rose and offered, "Here, let me take it for you," holding out her arms as if to receive a sack of garbage. Her disdain was obvious. Ralph handed her the heavy garment, relieved to be rid of it for a while. He brushed down his sports-coat, spending the most effort on the left lapel which had accumulated a fair amount of white ash. He had to resort to licking his fingers to wet it down and lose the powdery look. His black trousers were noticeably rumpled, and the wide soles of his wingtip shoes apparently hadn't had any polish applied for some time. And then there was his tie, which in color and design did not match anything else in his "ensemble." Sally looked him over, and as she escorted his coat down the hall to the closet, she shook her head in disgust. Ralph was too busy with his brush-up to notice.

"Mr. Murphy, I'm Chris Masters. It's nice to meet you." Chris held out his hand and Ralph grabbed it and shook hands with gusto.

"I'm pleased to meet you, too. It's sure good to get out of the cold for awhile."

"Yes, when I came in at 7:45, you could see every breath, even inside the train."

"It's still that way."

"Please come back to our conference room," said Chris, who then turned to the receptionist.

"Sally, we will be at least an hour."

"OK, Chris, I'll hold your calls." The honey was back in her voice.

Well, of course! This kid is six feet, 180-190 and looks like a movie star, he thought.

When they got to the conference room, Harry Harkness was waiting. "Mr. Murphy, this is Harry Harkness, head of our division," gestured Chris.

"My pleasure, Mr. Harkness."

Chris said carefully, "Mr. Murphy, I don't want to offend you, but we will need to see some identification before we begin. The confidentiality issue, you know?"

"No offense taken. I'm impressed that you respect the confidentiality of your clients. Too often companies just open up their files to us without question."

Ralph Murphy produced his government ID card which Chris examined with curiosity, then handed it to Harkness. Everything seemed to be in order.

"Do you mind if we make a photocopy?" asked Harkness.

"No, no, help yourself."

Chris pressed the intercom button on the large round conference phone in the middle of the oblong table. Shelly appeared and quickly accomplished the copying and returned the documents.

"Now, Mr. Murphy, how can we help you?" asked Harkness.

"Well, you know that I am investigating the recent crash of that Cessna jet that killed those six bank executives from First Gotham Bank, plus the pilot. He was an independent hired for the day. I found out from the HR department of the bank that five of the six victims were covered under this B-O-L-I program--Bank Owned Life Insurance? When I asked for the amount of coverage, they told me that the program was administered by you folks and gave me your number. Then, when I called, I was told that you were on vacation and that led to Mr. Masters.

"By the way, do you mind if I call you Chris?" he asked, turning to the younger man.

"Oh, no, no, no! I prefer Chris. I don't feel old enough to be called Mr. Masters, especially by an older...." Chris stopped in mid-sentence and reddened noticeably.

"It's OK. Chris, I am an old fogey. No problem. Could you fellas tell me how this program works, how the bank benefits from these policies?"

Chris looked at his boss, who nodded assent. He cleared his throat and looked across at Ralph.

He took on an almost professorial air. "The banks, and for that matter, many large companies, can and do insure their key employees for fairly large amounts of life insurance under the rationale that they need to have an asset to offset the emerging liability caused by post-retirement programs such as health insurance and retirement benefits. OK, so far?"

"Yeah, I think so, but don't they have to die for the bank to collect?"

"Yes. And the bank is then reimbursed for the cost of putting up these benefits during the retirement years. We also know, statistically, that the most expensive benefit year is the last year of life, primarily because of terminal illness."

"OK, let me make sure I understand. The banks can insure employees. Let's say key employees."

"Yes, they usually limit the BOLI programs to vice-presidents or higher."

"They can insure them even after they retire?"

"As a matter of fact, they are insured for the rest of their lives, whether they retire, quit or are fired, even if they go to another bank."

"But you said the purpose was to cover future health and retirement benefits. What is there to insure if they don't retire from the bank?"

"Well, Mr. Murphy, if they work at a bank long enough, usually five years, they become vested in their retirement benefits and can collect after age 65. However, the real reason has to do with what is called actuarial science."

"What's that, Chris?"

"That is the study of probability when large numbers or events are concerned. So, even though many of the insureds never complete their careers with First Gotham, for example, the bank is able to continue their coverage because they need to keep all the policies in force, whether or not the insureds remain as employees, in order for the actuarial predictions to be accomplished."

"I see. In other words, they need the death claims of the entire group to cover their costs."

"That's true, in theory anyway, but that's not the real reason for these programs."

"Oh no?"

"No, the real reason is that they build their asset base with a tax sheltered investment. The money invested in these BOLI programs grows tax free, well, technically tax-deferred, while inside the insurance "wrapper," and the death benefit pay-outs are also tax-free."

"Chris, you're losing me."

"Mr. Murphy…"

"Call me Ralph."

"OK, Ralph, by "wrapper" I mean that investments, any investments, that comprise insurance cash value are free from tax, as long as they stay within the insurance contract."

"Why is that?"

"That's the law of the land, and it's upheld by the politicians who are beholden to the insurance lobby."

"I always thought that the insurance companies paid lousy interest."

"Ralph, if an insurance contract can earn 6 percent, for example, and do it without tax, it is the equivalent of almost 10 percent with tax."

"Here, let me show you." Chris got up and wrote on the board to illustrate his words.

"If $100 is reduced by a tax of 40 percent, rounded off, the net is $60. The $100 could represent a 10 percent investment gain, and the $60 a 6 percent gain. In my example, 10 percent taxable is equal to 6 percent net, that is, non-taxable. So, if an insurance contract earns 6 percent on what would otherwise be a taxable investment, but the wrapper shelters it from tax, it becomes the equivalent of a 10 percent investment. Not too shabby."

"What if they earned 10 percent with no tax?" asked Ralph.

"That would be the equivalent of over 16 percent, but the insurance companies, at least in the BOLI programs, invest very conservatively, mostly in government treasury notes that pay anywhere from a low of about 5 percent up to perhaps 8 or 9 percent annually. This is how the banks make out on these programs, and the real reason they put so much money into them. It's called arbitrage."

"Arbitrage?"

"A fancy word for reinvestment of assets," interjected Harkness.

"So where does the insurance come in, the death benefit, that is?"

"Ralph, it is like a bonus on the investment. The BOLI program has actuarial assumptions about the death rate and claims. We can pretty much mathematically predict the number of deaths in any group of insured lives if we know their ages and gender and have a large enough group. For insurance companies with millions of insured lives, we can be accurate down to a tenth of 1 percent each year. That kind of accuracy is not possible annually with a group of say, 5,000 lives, but it is possible to be accurate within 1 percent over a five year period, and except in a very unusual case, we can expect accuracy within 5 percent in any given year."

"An unusual case like our accident here?" asked Ralph.

"Yes, certainly that will skew the numbers."

"Chris, something is still bothering me. How is it that these banks are allowed to continue coverage on employees who leave?"

"You remember that I mentioned earlier that the banks need to have the coverage from the entire group payoff in order to cover the emerging post-retirement liability of the retired group? That can be demonstrated by cost studies. So the courts have upheld challenges to this concept. Have you ever heard of 'insurable interest'?"

"Well, I've heard the term."

"What it means is that it is against public policy for a person, or some company, to have life insurance on someone where it can be shown that they would not suffer a loss in the event of his or her death. So we traditionally have coverage that protects families if the father dies, or businesses which have coverage if the key person dies. The law requires that insurable interest need only exist at the time coverage is taken out. So, you can have situations where a wife could have insurance on an ex-husband, for example, or a business could keep it on an ex-president. Since those are examples of bad public policy, the courts support the discontinuance of those policies. However, there are many cases to support the continuance of employer owned life insurance for the purpose of covering the emerging liability situation."

"This is amazing to me. OK, gentlemen, let's get down to brass tacks. How much are we talking about in this accident?"

"The total coverage on the five who were insured is slightly over $2.8 million," stated Harkness.

"Wow! That is some number," breathed Ralph.

"Yes, well, when I first joined Smith, Hay & Ward, the numbers also seemed staggering to me. Even though it is a lot of money, it is really a very small part of the annual return for a bank the size of First Gotham. In their program we would expect 10 to 12 death claims annually for around 5 to 6 million dollars," said Chris.

"So this accident would represent about half the expected claims for the year?"

"That's right, but we would discount an accident like this as a non-recurring event, at least from an actuarial standpoint," replied Chris.

"How many death claims has First Gotham had this year?" asked the inspector.

Chris shifted his weight and looked at his hawk-like manager. The older executive put his index finger to his lips, as if to signal *No!*

"I would have to look that up to be sure," replied Chris evasively.

Harkness' smile was almost imperceptible. Ralph sensed the tension between the two actuaries. That slight smile had been a red alert to the investigator's trained eye. He leaned forward on the table. His eyes had narrowed to slits. Ralph Murphy spoke with deliberate force. "Chris, why don't you look that up? It seems to me as if you gentlemen need to compare notes. I can just go downstairs, have a smoke, and return in 15 minutes if you prefer," Ralph suggested, continuing to stare at both of them.

Chris looked at Harkness like a naughty child who had been caught by a parent. An uneasy silence fell over the room. Ralph knew that silence was the most powerful force he possessed in a situation like this. He continued to stare at them. The seconds ticked away, sweat began to form on the executive's brow. Chris coughed and cleared his throat. Ralph continued to stare through his hooded eyes. The pressure mounted. Finally, after more than a full minute, Harkness broke the silence.

"That won't be necessary, Mr. Murphy. We have given you the information you need to complete your investigation. The actuarial results are confidential and have no bearing on this matter. Also, these claims won't be processed until next year in any event, so it could well be that our total claims for next year have already been realized even though the deaths occurred in this year. Do you see my point?"

"OK, gentleman, let's move on to other matters." Ralph had decided on an alternate strategy during the silence.

"Who do you deal with at First Gotham?" the investigator asked.

"We report the program results to a man named Richard Trace. He is the president of the First Gotham Insurance Agency," answered Harkness.

"Then you have met him?"

"Oh yes, on several occasions. He is a very competent executive, very experienced."

"Well, I'll need to contact Mr. Trace. I'll need his phone number. In New York City, right?"

"Yes, it's 212-683-9301." Chris answered automatically.

"You have it memorized?" Ralph was incredulous.

"I have a way with numbers," Chris replied, smiling.

"Oh yeah, math major. Gentlemen, you have been a great help. I'm sure we will be in touch again before this is all over. Thanks for your time and information."

"See you soon then, Mr. Murphy."

"Make it Ralph."

"OK, later Ralph!" smiled Chris.

"Goodbye, Mr. Murphy." Harry Harkness nodded gravely.

"Yes, nice to meet you, Mr. Harkness," said Ralph formally.

Chapter 13

Two hours later Chris Masters emerged from the far elevator. He was alone, and turned toward the Michigan Avenue entry where Ralph had waited patiently, going through half a pack of Marlboro cigarettes.

"Hey Chris, got a minute?" called Ralph.

"Mr. Murphy, aren't you cold?"

"Naw, I went inside several times during the last two hours. I need to talk to you about this First Gotham situation."

"I don't know, Ralph. Mr. Harkness was pretty clear about the position of the firm with regard to that matter. I don't know that there is anything more to say."

"Listen, kid, I have been in this business longer than you have been alive, and I know, **I know** that there is more to this than the deaths caused by the airplane crash." His eyes burned into Chris's. "Can we go somewhere and have a sandwich so you can tell me about it?"

Chris shrugged weakly and followed Ralph down the sidewalk. His mind was churning with conflicting emotions: Sarah's warning to leave it up to Harkness; Harry's insistence that they not get into his actuarial theory; and the danger of losing his job over this whole thing. All these thoughts were churning in his head, but so was the veracity of his mathematical evidence.

When they had settled in the cozy deli, Ralph leaned forward across the shiny white table and whispered conspiratorially, "I think you have something to tell me, and if you hold it in, it will eat at you for the rest of your life. You should know, up front, that if you don't tell me voluntarily, I can get a federal subpoena and force your company to give us the information, which would be a hassle for all of you, and the final result will be the same. If you tell me what's up I can just take it from there and no one will be the wiser, except you and me. In any event, I think there is more to the death claims at First Gotham Bank than you and Mr. Harkness let on in our meeting."

Chris listened with incredulity at what was being laid out to him. How could he be involved in this kind of deal after only six months on the job? Should he go against the advice of both his fiancée and his boss and explain his findings to this virtual stranger across the table? He was certain that what he knew about First Gotham was accurate and true. It was not just an actuarial anomaly as Harkness had said. Math did not lie.

Ralph seemed to sense that Chris was wrestling with the decision to talk or remain silent. Again he relied on the power of silence and slowly chewed his hoagie sandwich as he stared directly at the young man. Finally, the silence was broken.

"Ralph, you have asked how many death claims First Gotham has had this year. Including the five in the accident, there have been more than twenty, for nearly 11 million dollars."

"Are you telling me that the actual death rate was about double the expected rate?"

"Yes, and if you were to take out the five in the accident, the death rate would have been nearly fifty percent higher than expected."

"What does that say, Chris?"

"That says that, at least from an actuarial standpoint, the odds of this many excess death claims is highly improbable."

"How improbable?"

"Almost impossible, Ralph. Even if we tossed out the accident from our findings."

"What are you saying, kid?"

"Ralph, let me level with you. My background is mathematics. I have a master's in advanced mathematics. Smith, Hay & Ward hired me to analyze their BOLI program in the banks. We started with five banks, including First Gotham, but our plan is that in time we will use this program for about fifty bank clients. We are talking about hundreds of thousands of insured lives, and many billions of coverage. Some individual banks have over five billion of total coverage on their employees. Then there is COLI, Corporate Owned Life Insurance, for billions more coverage. This is a big, big program in American business, and Smith, Hay & Ward are at the forefront of this market. For the people in our company, like Harry Harkness, it is there whole business life."

"Whew!" whistled Ralph.

"Anyway, before the accident, I was feeling uneasy about the results showing up in our numbers for First Gotham Bank. It seemed ghoulish. At first it was just a gut feeling because they seemed to have more claims than the other banks, but then I noticed they also had more double-dippers."

"Double-dippers?"

"Oh, sorry, insureds covered by more than one bank."

"How could that be?"

"People leave one bank job and join another bank as an executive, and are signed up on the BOLI plan at their new bank."

"Double-dip. Two banks are making a claim on the same person, right?"

"That's right, and it's possible that we could have triple-dippers at some time in the future, although I haven't seen one yet. I have seen several double-dippers, and First Gotham somehow seems to get a good portion of the action. Our program tracks many aspects of these plans, including the investment performance. We noticed that in years when treasuries dropped below a 6 percent return, most bank BOLI programs were less profitable than desired. They all want an IRR, that is, an Internal Rate of Return, of at least 6.5 percent. Usually, the treasury return alone gives them that amount or more, and the actuarially expected death claims make up any shortfall. However, when treasuries drop down to 5 or 5.5 percent, the death claims have to makeup a larger deficit. Follow?"

"I'm tracking, kid. Believe me, I'm tracking."

"Prior to this year, the only two times the treasury rates dropped below 6 percent was in 1993 and 1998, that is, the only two times since the BOLI programs started in 1987. We noticed, well actually it stuck out like a sore thumb, that First Gotham happened to have higher than expected death rates in each of those years, and only those years, until this year, when it happened again. Treasuries went below 6 percent and their death rates were higher than actuarially expected even before the accident. Only one other bank has ever had a higher than expected death rate in any year, and that was Central

States in 1998, and, get this, two of the largest claims that year were double-dippers."

"Let me guess, with First Gotham, right?" queried Ralph.

Chris nodded.

"Mr. Murphy, I am trained to believe in the elegance of mathematics, and this means that something, or somebody, is maneuvering the randomness of returns at First Gotham Bank."

"Son, you are making a very convincing case, very convincing! The Cessna crash may have been a planned accident, or it could have been an unforeseen accident pointing out a whole lot of other planned accidents. In any event, in my 26 years in this business I have come to realize that these things don't just happen by themselves. Someone is behind all of this," Ralph paused, then asked, "Have you met this Richard Trace?"

"I met him briefly at their offices in New York City."

"What was your impression of him?"

"He seemed very arrogant to me. Also, when we brought up the subject of the actuarial projections, he was quick to change the subject."

"That's no surprise given our discussions. Ok, Chris, leave Mr. Trace to me. I am sure we will need to have further dealings, but I don't want to get you in trouble with Mr. Harkness. Is there some way we can stay in touch?"

"How about calling me on my pager and I will get back to you from a private place as soon as I can get free," replied Chris.

"That's perfect, Chris. Good thinking." Ralph smiled and took the last bite of his sandwich.

—

As Ralph Murphy trudged through the sidewalk slush, he contemplated how he would approach Richard Trace. He wanted to be sure to get an appointment as soon as possible without giving Trace a clue that he was a suspect. He would make it seem like a routine investigation. The more he thought about it, the more complicated it seemed to get. There were the other federal agencies to consider. At this point he was the main man on the investigation, with Jones of the FAA as his backup. For most accidents of this size, that was about as far as it ever went. They would issue a preliminary statement within a week covering the basic facts, and then the rest of the details would be gathered over an extended period of time and a final report issued at the end of several months. Ralph wanted to remain in charge of the investigation. He knew that if he revealed his suspicions about the bank, the FBI would have to take over the case and he would become a bit player. After 26 years as a federal employee he knew the drill, but that did not mean he had to like it. The trick would be to keep control by pretending to investigate the victims, rather than the perpetrator, for the longest time possible.

Ralph thought about his first manager, Jim Kennedy, and the words of advice he had given him his first month on the job. *Don't be too anxious, Ralph!* At the time, Jim's admonition had not made much sense, but with experience he had come to know, full well, the wisdom contained in those words. There was no need to hurry the investigation. The required public disclosure, the routine facts, could be finished by the next week. His investigation of Richard Trace could then begin at a comfortable pace. If this guy Trace was involved in the deaths, he would have to have professional accomplices. No one could have committed so many murders in so many different locations without some outside organization helping him. If young Masters was right in his calculations, it was possible that there had been dozens of death claims over the years. What did he say? 1993, 1998, and again this year. Ralph ducked into the entry of a building and lit another cigarette. He leaned against the wall and took a deep drag, letting the smoke out slowly. The noonday horde of office workers was emerging from the nearby buildings and was scurrying off toward luncheon appointments. His office was still seven blocks further south across the river. It was cold and wet. Ralph took another drag, pursed his lips and blew a misshapen smoke ring.

Shit, haven't got that right since my stroke, he thought.

He hunched his overcoat up on his neck and stepped back onto the crowded sidewalk. With each heavy step he became more resolved to slow the investigation. He would do his background work very carefully. He would use the power of government intimidation to gain access to all the information possible before involving the FBI and certainly before confronting Richard Trace. And, he would start with Chris Masters. The kid was smart as a whip and could supply enough circumstantial evidence to convince the Chief to give him the green light. Once he had figured out the likely scenario, he could give Trace the "Columbo treatment" to flush him out. The veteran investigator smiled at the thought.

Ralph crossed the Chicago River and continued on through the Loop to his office building. The only other employees on his floor were the receptionist and a file clerk. They were absorbed in a conversation about the latest horror flick, *Scream 5*, and just barely noticed his return. He walked down the aisle separating the drab cubicles in the large open room. His space was the next to last on the left, just two openings from Chief Waltham's glassed-in, end office. Next Monday this room would be all abuzz with activity, but today it was like a cemetery. The fluorescent light above his desk flickered and hummed softly. He had often noticed the flicker, but the humming was only audible because of the quietness on this last workday afternoon of the year.

Ralph shrugged off his coat and flung it over the back of his chair. He fell into his seat with a groan, stamping his feet to shake off the ice. Warmth began to return to his body, from his torso out to his hands and feet. He heard Tracy and Vicki laughing conspiratorially at the far end of the central hallway.

The tired man picked up the phone and dialed the pager number that Chris had given him.

"Please leave a numeric message after the beep," instructed the message.

Ralph punched in his number. In a few minutes his phone rang.

"Chris Masters here. Ralph?"

"Yes, Chris. On the way back to my office I was thinking that there is much more that I need to know before I call Mr. Trace. I was hoping you could help me with additional information."

"Sure, Ralph. What do you have in mind?"

"I'd like to have the details on all the First Gotham death claims in those special years."

"1993 and 1998?"

"Yeah, and, of course, this year."

"OK, things are quiet here so I can copy that info without being noticed."

"Then a year-by-year summary to show how the pattern differs in those years, and an explanation of how the claims seem to increase in down-investment years."

"Sure."

"And, also, Chris, show the double-dipper situation, especially the pattern in up-claim years."

"Ralph, I was kind of hoping to get home early tonight, you know, to…."

"Hey, kid, no problem. Save it for next week. Any chance we can get together next Tuesday morning around 11 o'clock at the same place?"

"We have a staff meeting that morning. Could we make it at 12:15?"

"That's fine, Chris. I appreciate your help on this. You and the missus have a happy."

"Thanks, Ralph. See you Tuesday."

Ralph replaced the phone. He took out his notepad and wrote.

1) Cessna CY 294 crash: Waupun, Wisconsin, December 20th, possible planned accident.
2) Motivation: $2.8 million insurance payoff to First Gotham Bank.
3) Who benefits? The bank and possibly Richard Trace, personally.
4) How? Don't know. Need to get personnel records without arousing suspicion.

5) Check with Fred on Monday. How were the deaths (murders?) accomplished?

   a) If a one man show: His proximity to the death scenes. Need travel pattern.

   b) Deaths occurred all over the country. Will need to have the exact dates and locations. Need access to credit cards and telephone records. Expense reimbursement records. Must be a HR function.

   c) Hired help? Phone and travel records. Credit bureau to see if we can trace the money. Yes, follow the money to the hired help. He would need to make a payoff. OK, debts, marital status, all of that stuff.

6) Get circumstantial evidence from Masters.

7) Chief Waltham: How much to tell him so that I can keep control of the case?

8) Will work with the FBI, IRS, etc only when necessary.

Ralph put down his pen. He looked at the clock over the Chief's door. It read 2:45. The chatter at the other end of the room had ceased. He stared at the words on his pad.

"My God!" he whispered aloud. "Chris was right; this is ghoulish."

Ralph stood and went to his window. He pulled down the slats in the blinds. The heavy gray sky was already darkening. If he left now he could beat the traffic on the Eisenhower Freeway and get to his apartment in Des Plaines by 3:30. He could take a nap, get up around 7:00, and fix himself a Marie Callender pot pie in the microwave. Then he could watch the big ball come down in Times Square on TV at 11 o'clock, and be fast asleep when the new year officially came to Chicago. What the hell, it was already January 1st in Asia, for sure, and probably even in Eastern Europe, if he had his time zones right.

"What's the big deal anyway?" he muttered.

On the way out he wished Tracy a happy New Year. Her friend Vicki was nowhere to be seen.

Chapter 14

The week between Christmas and New Year's Day was beautiful in New York City. The economy was in a bit of a funk, but you couldn't tell by the millions of bright, sparkling, holiday lights. It seemed as if everyone in the city was out on the streets with shopping bags full of goodies. The after-Christmas sales were in full swing, and the merchants were using the economic slump as a reason to buy. On sale! On sale! Many items were half-price, even popular items were slashed at least 25 percent.

Richard Trace had no such luck. He had been contacted by Mr. Manfredi, who happened to call asking after his mother, Viola Manson Trace. He had been informed that the full $625,000 was due on Thursday. It was not as if Trace was unprepared for the call. He had been adjusting his accounts to be sure to be fully prepared for it. Johnny Pestrano was not someone to disappoint, particularly when it came to financial matters. When they had their first dealings in 1993, Trace had to ask Johnny how to make a transfer that couldn't be traced. The answer was that he should visit the Cayman Islands in the Caribbean and open a numbered account using a fictitious corporation.

Earlier that first year Trace had opened a home equity line of credit at First Gotham, secured by a lien against his home in Alpine. At the time he had a $375,000 mortgage against an appraised value of $650,000. The bank allowed up to 80 percent loan-to-value, so the line had been set-up at $145,000. He had needed to draw down $125,000 that December, but he was able to replenish the line in February 1994 after receiving his bonus. As his house increased in value, the line of credit kept pace. His latest appraisal had come in at $2.3 million, and his first mortgage was down to $280,000. His current line was at $1.5 million, and he had a balance due of $200,000. When the call came, Trace mailed a check to the account of his dummy corporation, WAT, Inc. (Without a Trace, Inc.), for $650,000, and requested that his Cayman Bank wire $625,000 to the neighbor bank that held an account for one of Johnny Pestrano's six Cayman corporations. Within an hour of receiving the funds, that bank disbursed them to the five other banks, 20 percent each. Trace knew the routine and had confidence in the Cayman banker. Nevertheless, he was greatly relieved when Manfredi called to tell him that Viola had reached her destination safely and that all was well.

Trace leaned back in his soft leather chair and clasped his hands behind his head. He closed his eyes and pressed his thumbs into the nape of his neck. The tension released, and he let out a deep sigh. Another successful year, but why in the hell couldn't that crash have come earlier in the year? The economy was still in the dumpster. There was no telling where treasuries would go next year. Johnny's fee had gone through the roof. More frightening though, was Trace's impression that their days of doing business together were over. Johnny had been damn unfriendly, even threatening. The tired man was hurt that the thirty-year relationship apparently meant nothing to Pestrano. Hadn't he been a loyal customer and a pretty good one at that? Johnny had collected nearly $1 million in fees from him, for Christ's sakes! Trace was angry, hurt and confused.

He opened his eyes and swung the chair around toward the window. The building up the street had a green "Happy New Year" sign, which blinked off and on every few seconds. A light snow was falling. Trace smiled. In three days he and Diana would be on the beach at the Landlubber's Club in St. Maarten. They preferred the Dutch eastern side of that tiny island where they had spent the first two weeks of January for the last several years. Maybe in another year they could buy that condo outright, especially now that the bank would be getting over $2.8 million in claims from this crash in Wisconsin.. That should assure a good claim return next year in any event. For now they would have to be content with renting.

He decided to go home early; there was nothing more to be done this year. Diana had lined up a charity benefit for New Year's Eve, and it would be a late night. He was relieved that it was in Fort Lee, so they wouldn't have to come back into the city. If he left now he could be home in Alpine in about an hour. That would give him time for a nap before getting into his tuxedo for the party. His shoulders sagged with the thought of it. *I'm down to taking naps to be able to make it through the night*, he thought sadly.

—

Johnny's Ristorante hummed with activity. This was one of its big nights of the year. It was family night. Every year Johnny Pestrano would close his place to outside customers and open his kitchen and dining room to the family. This year 43 of the 49 descendants of Harry Pestrano, now 92 years old, had made it into New York to celebrate. Katie Rizzo had even brought the latest edition: four-month-old Elly, Harry's 12th great-grandchild. While Harry was the patriarch, the leader of the family was Johnny Pestrano, as he had been since age 33. That year, 1981, he had become Don. Even Harry kissed his ring. The respect and love for Johnny bordered on worship. Whenever anyone in the family had trouble or needed help, it was Johnny who got the call.

Earlier in the day he had gotten the word that his fee from Richard Trace had been received and disbursed. After paying off his operatives and expenses, that assignment had netted the family slightly over $300,000. It was a good payday, but Trace was becoming erratic, possibly even expendable. He would have to monitor that situation closely.

Johnny hugged Katie and chucked the infant under her chin.

"She's a real cute Pestrano, uh Rizzo." He smiled at his nephew Alfredo, his sister Sophia's son, "Mr. Manfredi".

He and Anna had two daughters, now both in college. Angela was at the University of Redlands in California, well into her junior year abroad in Siena, and had stayed in Italy over the holidays with her cousins in Milano. It was the first holiday she had not been with them and they missed her smiling face. At the same time they were envious, as Milano was their favorite city in the mother-land. Mia was a freshman at Yale studying dance and drama, and had just announced that she had a leading role in the *Swan Lake* production that would be presented in early January.

Everyone was excited for her, and she was dancing around the room, full of this good news. Johnny and Anna basked in the glow of their extended family. They were proud of their girls, and knew that they would escape the family business, which gave them a sense of relief. Johnny had decided that someday Alfredo would be the Don. He had the right leadership qualities.

Yes, someday I'll be ready to turn over the ring, he thought.

Alfredo had handled the Trace contracts with comfortable ease and without a hitch. He had gotten the usual good assistance from Duk Lon Ki in San Francisco, but working with their network was a significant part of the job. Johnny would be ready to step aside and enjoy his immediate family and spend more time traveling within a few short years.

His nephew needed some more grooming, but Katie had brought stability into his life, and now, with this cute little Elly, he was a family man. To Johnny, it was important to be a family man.

"Hey, Dad, you old paisano!" Johnny opened his arms to his father. They embraced warmly.

"Another year, Johnny; another good one. I just keep hanging in there."

"Harry, you'll live forever. It's in your genes."

"Then it's in all of our genes. Look at this crowd," he marveled, "Your mother would have been proud of this gathering, God Bless her! How's business son?"

"Got things on cruise control, no sweat."

"That's good to hear. Some party, Johnny. You are good to do this for the family."

"It is my pleasure. It is a joy to see all of our family together," exclaimed the Don.

"I miss Angela, but I'll bet she is having the time of her life with Salvatore and Maria. They just bought a new Alfa Romeo sedan, and with her charm I can just bet she got to drive it on the way to Lake Como." he laughed.

Harry nodded his head, "Yeah, I used to love to drive fast cars. Now the kids drive me around, and I just sit in the back like a big-shot. It's not as much fun, but OK I guess."

"Dad, you are a piece of work," said Johnny, giving him another hug. "You're my idol."

From across the room Sal Graffini raised his hand to get Johnny's attention.

"Dad, Sal's signaling me, I'll see you in a few minutes."

"Sorry to interrupt you Mr. Pestrano, but it's your daughter on the phone. She's calling from Italy."

Since it was 8 p.m. in New York, Johnny quickly calculated that it would be 1 a.m. in Italy and already into the new year.

"Happy New Year, Honey. How was it?"

"Oh, Daddy, we are at the Villa d'Este and the fireworks on Lago de Como were spectacular," she gushed.

Johnny smiled as he remembered the beautiful lakeside resort where he and Anna had stayed many times.

"Please say hello to Mr. Mancini when you see him."

"OK. How is your party going?" she asked.

"Well, it is just getting started, but nearly everyone is here. We do miss you though. Let me get Mama and Mia so you can talk to them."

Anna and Mia were summoned by Sal and were soon chatting excitedly with Angela. Johnny stepped back into the hallway and pushed out a breath.

Yes, I want to step down and just enjoy my family. Maybe in another year or two Fredo will be ready. He'll soon be just about the same age I was when Dad gave me the ring. The thought brought a wide smile to his face.

Sophia looked at him and said," Well, you look like the cat that ate the canary, brother."

"Oh, I was just talking to Angela from Italy," he said to deflect any suspicion.

Sophia raised an eyebrow skeptically, "I know you too well to fall for that line Johnny, but I also know that whatever it is will have to wait until you are good and ready."

"You've got that right, Sister. Let's enjoy the night. Have a happy New Year. I love you!" he said, hugging her.

Johnny knew that she had guessed the reason for his enigmatic smile, and was bursting at the hope that her son would ascend to the position of Don.

Not quite yet, Sophia, maybe in another year, he thought to himself.

Chapter 15

On the first Monday of January, the NTSB offices were only slightly busier than during the previous week. Ralph was working on his second cup of coffee when Fred Waltham leaned into his cubicle.

"Got a minute, Ralph?"

"Sure, Chief."

"How's the Cessna investigation going?"

"Well, Chief, it's got a strange twist to it."

"How so?"

"Could we go in your office to talk about it?"

"Sure, Ralph, come on."

Ralph got up, leaving the coffee behind, and followed Chief Waltham into his enclosed, glass-paneled office. They sat side by side in the badly worn green naugahyde metal framed chairs in front of his desk.

"Chief, I got the personnel records of the bank employees who were in that jet, and it turns out that five of the six were insured by the bank, for a total of $2.8 million."

"Ralph, that's not unusual. Key man insurance, I think they call it."

"No, Fred, that's not it at all. This is called B-O-L-I, Bank Owned Life Insurance."

"It's probably just another name for it."

"Chief, I visited the company that administers the program for First Gotham. They are right here in Chicago up on Michigan Avenue. A firm called Smith, Hay & Ward. There's a kid, Chris Masters; he's the one who handles the program for them. Smart as hell."

"Ralph, where is this going?"

"Give me a minute. These banks, see, they have thousands of employees insured for billions, with a big "B", of coverage, and they are insured for life, even if they leave the bank."

"I thought that key man coverage was only good if you stayed."

"That's what I thought, but this is not key man insurance--it's BOLI. They cover these people against the cost of future benefits. Chris called it "emerging" something or other. Anyway, here's the rub: First Gotham of New York has had much higher death claims than predicted.

This Chris Masters is a mathematician, and he tells me they can predict the number of death claims within 5 percent in a group of this size, and this First Gotham Bank has had claims 50 percent higher in certain years."

"Well, couldn't that just be a sort of averaging out?"

"It might be, Chief, but it seems to fall only in years where the earnings are down. It's almost as if they make up lower earnings with higher death claims."

"Sounds like something out of Hollywood. You sure this kid, Chris, is not just imagining things?"

"I don't think so, Fred. He is convinced that these numbers are so out of whack that I can't be natural randomness, as he puts it. Something or somebody is helping nature along."

"Holy Smokes, Murphy! You mean to tell me the bank, or someone in the bank, had these people killed up in Wisconsin?"

"It could be, Chief, and what's more, there could be many other planned deaths over the last several years."

"Is there any evidence of sabotage of that Cessna?"

"Not that Curtis and I could determine. By the way, I want to tell you that Curtis Jones is a great guy to work with, not like some of those other FAA stiffs. He's a real pro."

"Thanks for the heads-up, Ralph. I'll let Kathy Thompson over at FAA regional know how you feel. So, what do you guys make of the accident?"

"It appears that the pilot had too much confidence in that bird, got in over his head in that front, iced up, and lost control. On the audio tape he said he cut himself during the turbulence. Then she plunged straight down from well over 20,000 feet."

"That doesn't sound like a murder plot to me."

"I agree, Fred, but this insurance situation at the bank needs to be followed up."

"Oh, I don't know, Ralph, it seems pretty far-fetched to me."

"I have an appointment tomorrow afternoon with young Masters to get details on the unusual death claim patterns that he has observed at First Gotham. If they are as damning as I think they will be, I will want to get your help in how we should proceed to get confidential personal information about a certain bank official who seems to be in charge. We may have to involve the FBI if this goes the way I think it might."

"OK, Ralph, we can talk about it tomorrow afternoon when you get back from your appointment." Waltham patted Murphy on his shoulder as he left the office. He returned to his paperwork and didn't give it another thought. Fred had seen Ralph go down this path of dreams of glory before. He would just ride it out, and squash it at the appropriate time.

—

The next afternoon Ralph Murphy met Chris at the Yorktown Deli as planned.

Chris greeted him warmly. "Hi, Ralph. Great to see you! How was your New Year's?"

"Pretty quiet, I'm afraid. I'm a bachelor, kind of a stay-at-home bachelor. My work is my life, as they say."

"Did you watch the bowl games? The Michigan-Washington game was fantastic!"

"I'm not much for sports anymore, Chris. Must be old age. How did you do with those figures?"

"Here's what I've done, Ralph. First, you have a history of the plan's death claims since inception in 1987, showing the actuarially expected results in column one and the actual results in column two. You can see that First Gotham was at or below expected results in all years except 1993, 1998 and last year. In 1993 they were 44.4 percent higher than expected, and in 1998 fifty percent higher. Then, of course, last year they were 76.9 percent higher. Since I have four other banks in our data, I have included them as columns three through six, labeled B, C, D and E. You will see that only in 1998 did bank B exceed actuarial expectations, and that was primarily due to the double-dips. If you remember there were two of them, both with First Gotham." He paused to be sure Ralph was keeping up with him.

"Next, I did the same comparison based on amounts of total claims with similar results. Then, I decided to calculate the average claim amounts to see if there was any difference. You will see that in each year of excess claims, the average amount of the claims is also higher, and most significantly, higher in 1998 for both banks involved in the double dips. These populations are small enough to be affected by one or two large claims."

"Populations?"

"Oh, yes, the number of people in each bank who are covered under each program we call a population."

"I see," nodded Ralph.

"These charts show pretty clearly that from an actuarial standpoint these claims are more than would be expected by natural randomness."

"I remembered 'randomness,' but forgot 'actuarial,'" said Ralph, half to himself.

"What's that, Ralph?"

"I was just recalling my talk with Chief Waltham yesterday at the office. I couldn't remember the word actuarial."

Chris grinned. "No problem, Ralph. Now, I have pulled the profile on all death claims in 1993, 1998 and last year. You will see that there are quite a few. If they have a green check mark in the upper right hand corner, they are double-dippers with another bank, but not necessarily with one of the other banks in our select group. Remember, we cover over fifty banks which have BOLI programs. In 1993 there were 13 death claims when we expected 9; in 1998 there were 18 when we expected 12; and last year there were 23 when we expected 13. In 1993 we had one double-dipper; in 1998 there were two and last year there were also two."

"Were any of the crash victims double-dippers?"

"No, Ralph. All were fairly long term First Gotham employees."

"Chris, last week you mentioned that you had already had more than expected death claims for last year before the accident. So, if we subtract 5 from 23, then they would have had 18 when 13 were expected, right?"

"Precisely, Ralph, and that's why I was already suspicious before the crash and before you came to our office. In fact, I had been talking to Sarah, my fiancée, about what to do."

"Did you find any claims that seemed suspicious?" asked Ralph.

"The only possibilities seemed to be the violent acts, the shooting of a branch manager in Detroit and a car accident in Florida, both in 1998. Oh, and Ralph, here is a graph that shows the distribution, by month of death, in all years since plan inception. You will see that in the years in question, the preponderance of claims occurred in the last third of the year, after September 1," said Chris.

"Preponderance?"

"Sorry, the 'majority' occurred later in the year, as if someone had realized that the investment results would not be sufficient and set up a procedure to increase the number of claims."

"What is your suspicion, Chris?"

"I think that when it became clear that the numbers would not work out from natural causes, then hits, I think they call it, were ordered."

"In the hit years, are the claims arranged by date of death?" asked Ralph.

"Yes, upper left-hand corner shows the dates." He pointed to the top pages of more than 50 claim sheets in the pile, "just for those three years."

"How many of the, what is it, 54 claims, occurred after September 1?"

"I think it is 31, if I remember, certainly over 50 percent in the last third of the year. Once again, it's not a statistically random occurrence rate."

"Chris, could you give me like a cover sheet so that I can have my boss understand all these numbers. I have a hard time organizing it in my head."

"Sure, Ralph, I have already done a summary which I think will be just what you need."

Chris excused himself and went to the counter to order a sandwich and some pasta salad as Ralph had arrived earlier and was already halfway through his old standby, the hoagie.

Ralph began to leaf through the pile of papers and was drawn to the green check marks, the double-dippers. In 1993, there was Conrad Jenkins, $750,000 with First Gotham, and $600,000 with Irving Bank and Trust in California. An insulin reaction led to cardiac arrest on November 9, 1993. In 1998, there was a Lily Yang-Peterson, $825,000 at First Gotham and $700,000 at Central States. She died November 4, 1998 of an unknown disease, and Sandra Turland, $800,000 at First Gotham and $750,000 with Third Southern of Memphis. Date of death October 28, 1998, suicide. Last year there was John S. Barton, $595,000 for First Gotham, $280,000 for Midwest Freedom, died November 11 of a heart attack in Palm Springs and Marilyn Madison, $800,000 at First Gotham and $850,000 at Plymouth National, date of death November 18. She had a heart attack in Nashua, New Hampshire.

Ralph noted that four of the five double-dippers had died in the fall, and that three of the five were women. Only one, Sandra Turland, had not been disease-related in some way. Chris had said, he remembered, that claims on women were higher since the same amount of premium bought more coverage because they were a better risk. He shuddered at the thought of his own risk profile.

Don't think they'd take me, he chuckled. *I wonder if we will find Trace went to California on November 11 and to New Hampshire on November 18 of last year? I doubt it. This smells like murder for hire to me. We are going to have to find the money trail first, see who his contacts are, then flush him out.* His mouth went dry in anticipation of that last part of the hunt.

There was no doubt about it. The hunt was on in earnest and Chris Masters was the lead dog.

—

When Chris returned with a basket full of bread and pasta, Ralph asked, "Do I remember your saying that women had bigger claims than men?"

"Yes, that's generally true."

"I noticed that three of the five double-dippers were women, and that all of those claims were late in the year."

"Yes, I noticed that also," replied Chris.

"They were also all over the country, and mostly of different disease-related causes."

"Ralph, I don't want this question to sound weird, but can't diseases be induced, heart attacks for example, by chemicals?"

"I seem to recall stories of injection of poisons and that sort of thing to create the impression of a heart attack or an insulin attack....Wait a minute, that guy in

San Francisco, his death was due to an insulin reaction leading to cardiac arrest, it says right here. Look, Chris, you leave this to me. We have our sources, and if that sort of thing has been going on, we will have experts working on it."

"Ralph, I have every confidence in you and your people."

"Thanks, Chris, I'll let you know if we need additional info. I think I should go now. We probably shouldn't be seen together."

Ralph deposited the papers in his briefcase and buckled it closed for the first time in months. He held it tightly under his left arm as he left the crowded restaurant. He turned and waved to Chris, who waved back, his mouth too full of food to smile. Ralph did notice, though, that his eyes were smiling.

Chapter 16

On this first Tuesday afternoon of the new year a few more of Murphy's coworkers made an appearance at the office. Some were pretty bleary-eyed after a long weekend of TV football games and beer. Fred Waltham had been through the employee reentry syndrome many times and was quite forgiving of their indolent proclivities, although he tried not to show his liberal tendencies.

At 3:30 Ralph Murphy knocked sharply on the glass panel inside the frame of his door, and swung it open about a foot.

"Have a minute, Chief?"

Waltham closed the maroon cover on a report he was reading. "Sure, Murph. Do you have that information we talked about?"

"Here it is, Chief." Ralph held up the two inch thick ream of papers.

"Come on in," Waltham said as he rose from his chair. "Let's have a look."

"Chris Masters made up a cover letter for you. It'll help explain the graphs and the claim sheets. There are a lot of statistics and things I didn't want to get confused about when trying to explain them to you. Why don't you just read this first?"

Ralph dropped into the tired old chair in front of the superintendent's desk. He mused on the fact that he'd spent many hours in this very chair over the years. They had grown old together on this job. He wasn't sure which was holding up best, although the ugly ten inch crack in the naugahyde, which had been mended by some green duct tape, probably rivaled his stroke as its most prominent blemish. He patted the metal arm of the chair, trying to be quiet so that Waltham could concentrate on Chris's cover letter.

Ralph had learned not to interrupt the chief at times like this. Some years ago he had been on the receiving end of a lecture about the virtue of silence in certain situations. Fred Waltham had a way of getting his point across without raising his voice or even mentioning the subject at hand. He kind of chewed around the edges of your rear end so that at the end of the session you would get up to leave and your ass would fall off.

Waltham studied the papers before him; finally he looked up. "He certainly is convinced!"

"What's that, Chief?"

"Ralph, are you with me?"

"Uh, yes sir. I kind of drifted off there."

"This matter may or may not need to go to the Bureau, but for now there is no evidence that the crash was crime-related, and that is our main charge, to investigate the crash. So, I want you to concentrate on the evidence at the crash scene and forget this murder theory for now. As soon as you have credible evidence that a crime has been committed, or if you simply can't get needed information, then come and see me. I'll try to keep your load of other cases as light as possible. Murph, I know that you like to operate as a lone wolf, but this is way too far out for us to get involved. Just do your job and keep me up-to-date." Ralph looked at the back of his hands, examined his fingernails, and finally looked up at Fred Waltham.

"OK, Chief, but I really thought that this could be significant evidence, even though it is circumstantial."

"Murphy, you should know by now that we deal only in hard evidence at NTSB."

Ralph returned to his cubicle. The usual hum of activity around the office had returned. Phones rang, drawers slammed, machinery spit out paper--then printed, collated or shredded it. Muffled voices from other spaces portrayed anger, amusement, frustration and mystery. The fluorescent light flickered above, but he couldn't hear the hum anymore.

Well, it was clear that he couldn't count on the support of the Chief on this matter, but Ralph was committed to getting to the bottom of this First Gotham situation, no matter what it took. He reviewed the notes on his memo pad and checked off item number 5. He would need some basic info on Mr. Richard Trace. The HR department at First Gotham would probably not cooperate unless forced to, and it was too early for confrontation.

Ralph picked up his phone and dialed Chris's pager.

After an hour his phone rang.

"Chris here."

"Chris? Ralph. I need more background on this Mr. Trace."

"Ralph, I only met him once, and that was only for a few minutes. I really don't know him."

"Didn't Mr. Harkness say he knew him fairly well?"

"Yes, but he doesn't want to talk about it any more. He has made it clear to me to butt-out as far as the First Gotham situation is concerned."

"OK. Is there any way you can get me Trace's address or social security number? That way I can pull a credit report and it may reveal financial transactions that would be helpful."

"Well, yes, just a minute. Let me see if he is enrolled in the BOLI program at First Gotham, as it has all that information. Oh my God! Ralph, Trace refused to be covered under his own program. What a snake!"

"Is there any other way we can get that information?"

"Ralph, I have to go. I'll let you know if I think of anything."

Ralph stared at the silent instrument. Had they reached a dead end?

—

Chris pondered Ralph's request as he sat in his cubicle. He knew that Shelly had files on each of the bank executives, and she would be going home soon. Harkness had already left. He was still on reduced hours after returning from vacation. Could he trust Shelly with the fact that he was investigating one of their best clients against the explicit orders of their boss? The question answered itself in his head. There was no way he would involve her in this dangerous activity.

"Goodnight, Chris! See you in the morning," Shelly sang out as she walked past his cubicle.

"Oh, goodnight, Shel. Have a good one."

Chris sat for several minutes in the quiet office. There was no sound anywhere near their end of the hall. He decided to walk to the front of the office, past the reception area, to the men's room to observe any activity. Everyone had gone; he was alone in the office. He hurried back to his cubicle, stopping briefly for a notepad, and proceeded to Shelly's cubicle. She kept the files on the bank personnel in a locked four-drawer file next to her desk. Where would she keep the key? Logic told him to try the right front drawer of her desk as she was a very methodical and organized secretary, and that would be the easiest place to retrieve it when needed. Chris slid open the drawer silently and saw that while the drawer had many supplies, there were no keys. He looked over her desktop where everything was neatly arranged and in order, but no keys. He noticed that there was a shallow tray in the middle of the chair well, which he carefully slid open--nothing but paperclips, pens and sticky-pads. The seconds he had been in her cubicle already seemed an eternity. Where could the key be? Would she take it home?

He noticed a row of files in some holders attached to the back wall behind her desk which were color coded according to a scheme that had been worked out by Harkness prior to his being hired. He was very familiar with the color codes, especially for the five banks under his charge. One of the folders was the familiar blue and brown of First Gotham Bank. With a pounding heart he removed the inch thick file from its holder. Yes, it was a First Gotham Bank file, with tabs for various sub-sections. He thumbed through the sections and there it was: Richard N. Trace, President. He opened the file on top of Shelly's desk. To his amazement it had his social security number 019-38-6905, his home address--624 Birch Road, Alpine, New Jersey, and even a copy of a personal check that he had made to the Boy Scouts last year, apparently at the request of Mr. Harkness. Chris quickly copied the information and returned the file to its place. He looked around to be sure that everything was in its original condition and slowly backed out of the office.

"Yo, sir!" came a voice from the entry end of the hall.

Chris literally jumped in the air at the unexpected voice. His mouth was parched, his heart pounding as he turned to see that it was the custodian, going about his normal business.

"I'm sorry, uh, you startled me," he stammered.

"Yeah, heh-heh, that happens sometimes. Sorry to scare you." His face was lit up in a grin of pure pleasure. The scare had made his day, maybe even his week.

Chris hurried past him, said his goodnight, and was off to the elevators.

I've got to reach Ralph before he leaves his office, he thought.

Once outside the building Chris used his cell phone to dial the now familiar number.

"Ralph Murphy."

"Ralph, it's Chris. I have the info you need. Ready! Social 019-38-6905, address--624 Birch Road, Alpine, New Jersey. Checking account with First Gotham-- 013330066789. Do you need anything else?"

"No, kid. How did you get the information?"

"It was an adventure. The next time we get together I'll tell you about it. Right now I just want to catch my boat to the train station and get home to Sarah," he spit it out.

Ralph could tell that he was highly stressed and probably had indeed had quite an adventure getting this information.

"Great job, Chris. Get home to the missus."

Ralph utilized the NTSB's account to access the credit bureau information. He entered the Full name, address and social security number of Richard N. Trace into the computer once the authorization code had cleared, and within minutes he heard the clicking hum of the office fax machine receiving the data.

Trace had a mortgage of $280,000 against his multi-million dollar home, and a home equity line of credit of $1.5 million with First Gotham Bank. The balance owing was $200,000—no *wait*, it had just been increased by $650,000 last week, and now stood at $850,000.

"Wow, that sure was some withdrawal!" Ralph whispered to his otherwise empty cubicle.

He scrolled down the list of credit cards. Most of the balances were small, except for the American Express card, at $15,000 plus, and two store cards in the name of Diana W. Trace which showed signs of an expensive Christmas season. Still, they were not out of line for a wealthy corporate executive. Trace undoubtedly had a corporate credit card which would not be on the report. Ralph returned to the $650,000 withdrawal from the line of credit. *Find where that went and we probably have our killer*, he thought. *I wonder what the going price of a murder for hire is these days? Probably up near one-hundred grand, so probably five or six additional death claims*, he calculated. *Just about what Chris had said the excess claims were for the year before the crash of the Cessna.*

Ralph realized he was at a crossroads in the investigation. Either bring in the FBI now and turn the investigation over to them, or confront Richard Trace and try to draw him out. Ralph chose the course of action that he knew would be hard to justify, but he figured after these many years he deserved his shot at the brass ring.

Chapter 17

The next morning Ralph was up before dawn. He stumbled into his small kitchen and hit the "on" switch of his "Joe DiMaggio" coffee maker. The orange glow cast a dim light over the cramped space, much like a photographer's dark room. Ralph opened his refrigerator, and the bright white light made him blink several times. He pulled the semi-frozen raisin bread from its place on the second shelf, broke off two joined slices, and shoved the rest of the loaf back and closed the door. The soothing orange glow was easier to take at this hour. He broke the precut slices apart and dropped them in his toaster.

While breakfast was heating up he walked slowly down the hallway to the front door and retrieved the Tribune from its accustomed place outside his door. He had followed this routine for many years. When he returned to the kitchen, a dull gray light from outside was beginning to mix with the orange glow. He switched on the overhead light which was encased in a opaque white globe--at least it was white when he bought it.

Ralph sat heavily on the corner bench he had made for himself in younger and more ambitious days. He leaned his elbows on the round wooden table. *What should I do?* The question had bothered him ever since his decision to go it alone. He realized that he had awakened several times during the night, always with the same question.

He took out his notes and found the number: (212) 683-9301. It would be just after 9 a.m. in New York City. His stocky fingers shook as he punched in the number.

"First Gotham Insurance." The accent was heavily nasal.

"I'm calling for Mr. Richard Trace," said Ralph cautiously.

"He's on vacation until the 18th."

Ralph thanked the lady from Brooklyn and replaced the phone. There were at least ten days before he would be able to have a face-to-face interview. The words of his first boss echoed in his head: *Don't be too anxious, Ralph.*

—

By the time Ralph got to his office, his brain was fully engaged. Even after a fitful night's sleep, he was fully alert. He considered his options and concluded that he had taken this investigation as far as he could without help. In order to develop incriminating evidence, the power of the FBI, especially to subpoena information, would be vital. He approached Waltham's office and knocked on the window pane in the usual way.

"Come in, Ralph," called the chief.

"Morning, Chief. Do ya have a minute?"

"Sure, come on in. Have a seat."

"Chief, you know I have strong suspicions about this guy at the bank. Yesterday I called his office and found out that he will be on vacation until the 18th. That's nine days. I realized there wasn't much more we could do but to try to flush him out when he gets back."

"You mean go to New York and confront him?"

"Yes, not very smart, I guess. Anyway, the Bureau could gather a lot of information in the next week and a half by using their subpoena power to force First

Gotham to release his personnel files, his travel vouchers, credit card charges, that sort of thing."

"Hold on Ralph. I thought I told you to confine your investigation to the facts of the crash."

"Chief, part of my investigation has to be if there was any reason to suspect foul play, for financial gain or revenge, you know, all those things. Well, it certainly looks like this bank, and especially the president of the insurance subsidiary had substantial financial motivation.

"We know that in the three years when the investment performance did not hold up, the death claims went way up, and that's not even including the airplane crash. We know that the majority of the claims came late in the year and that they were among the largest claims that have been processed."

"Ralph, how did you get this information?"

"The young fellow at the actuarial firm has lots of data on this bank."

"Anything else?"

"Yes. His credit report showed a withdrawal from his home equity line of credit of $650,000 just last week at the end of the year. I hope that the FBI can get his personnel records to see if his income is tied to the death claims, and he must have a corporate credit card which will show travel expenses. It's possible that he acted alone, but not very likely."

"Well, Ralph, the $650,000 withdrawal could be payoff money, but it still seems far-fetched.

"The FBI can also get access to his personal checking account and credit card records. Well, you know, I just ran out of options trying to do it all myself."

"Ralph, we don't want to get egg on our faces, and if this proves to be just the imagination of a young kid we will be the laughing stock of the entire federal bureaucracy.

"Yes, Fred, but if it's true, we can't just let a killer go free. He may even keep killing."

"I'll take it under advisement. Don't do anything until you hear from me. I mean it; keep this under your hat." Ralph had been warned.

—

Ralph had previously worked with an agent from the FBI. She was Barbara Knudsen, a specialist in white-collar crime. On that previous occasion, Murphy had been instructed to meet her in the Bureau offices in Elmhurst, out near O'Hare Airport. The FBI offices were on the 11th floor of a pristine building in that leafy suburb of Chicago.

Kind of like Des Plaines with tall buildings, Ralph remembered.

Ralph recalled that he had met with Barbara and her boss, Thomas Garcia, in the leather and glass conference room. He had explained the case to them and he and Barbara had follow-up meetings, two of them, and the case was referred to the West Coast office. She had been easy to work with and seemed to have an independent nature. He especially remembered her crossing her legs under that glass table. She had great legs, and very dark hair for someone with a Scandinavian name. He decided to take a chance and call her to discuss the case, which was becoming an obsession.

Ralph dialed her personal line and was relieved that she answered on the second ring. He had dreaded having to go through an operator.

"Barbara Knudsen, FBI," she answered crisply.

"Miss Knudsen, this is Ralph Murphy of the NTSB. Do you have a minute?"

"Sure Ralph, I remember you. The Quick Air case out in Denver, right?"

"That's the one," he said with relief. "Listen, I have a rather unusual situation that I need your advice about and was hoping we could meet out there in Elmhurst after work this afternoon."

"Let me check. Yes, that would be fine. How about the Windsock, it's out by the airport on Mannheim Road."

"That's perfect. I'll see you at 5:30 if that works for you."

"5:30 it is, see you then."

Barbara hung up her phone and held her head to one side. *I wonder what this will be all about. He was a nice old guy, so what's the harm?*

—

"It looks as if you have built quite a file on this case already," she said.

"It's not as much as it looks like. That's why we called for your help."

"Can you give me your take on this, Mr. Murphy?" she asked.

My "take," he thought. *Was that Generation X talking, or the tail end of the Baby Boomers? In any event, she is no more than in her late 30's. Nice sturdy figure, probably a black belt in judo or karate, maybe both, and I'd bet she could throw me on my butt in 3 seconds flat.* "You must have heard about the crash of a Cessna Citation up near Milwaukee just before Christmas, huh?"

"Oh sure, that was a big news item," said Barbara.

"Anyway, Chief Waltham had me investigate the accident with an FAA guy up there. We determined that it was a weather related accident due primarily to pilot error. Well, actually pilot overconfidence. We see that all the time. He thought that airplane was indestructible. Sometimes mother-nature is more powerful than even a veteran pilot expects, and this guy had over 12,000 hours of flying experience. When we have an accident like that, part of our routine is to check the victims to see if any of them had a reason to sabotage the flight. All of the passengers worked for the same bank. Oh, by the way, the jet was leased so the pilot did not actually work for the bank, except for this job. The bank was First Gotham Bank of New York."

Barbara interrupted, "Do you mind if I take notes?"

"No, no, I understand. Please go ahead."

"Anyway, we discovered that the bank had a program they call BOLI, which stands for Bank Owned Life Insurance. The program covered five of the six executives on that flight."

"Mr. Murphy, I'm familiar with Corporate Owned Life Insurance. Can I assume this is just the version owned by the banks?" asked Barbara.

"Yes, that's my understanding." Ralph was glad that Chris had given him the background on this point. "When I talked to the HR people at First Gotham, they referred me to a company here in Chicago that administers this program for them."

"Smith, Hay & Ward?" asked Barbara knowingly.

"Yes, how did you know that, Barbara? I hope you don't mind if I call you Barbara?"

"No, no, Ralph, I prefer it, and besides, I feel we know each other from before. My dad is in the insurance business, and I've heard from him that they are among the leading specialists in that field. It is quite a specialized market."

"Barbara, you probably understand this stuff much better than I do, but there is this young man at Smith, Hay & Ward who had already been suspicious of the death claim rate at First Gotham even before the Cessna crash. His summary is the first three pages in the file there, and the rest of the papers are the individual death claim sheets, 54 of them during the three years when we suspect foul play."

Barbara opened the file. "Is it all right if I read the summary?"

"Yes, I was kind of hoping you would read it first, then I can try to answer any questions you may have."

As she read the report, Ralph looked around the crowded restaurant. He noticed that there were smokers in the bar area, and even though he was dying for a smoke, he dared not leave the table and take the risk of losing her interest. He quietly sipped his beer and waited for her to finish the report. He rested his left arm on his scuffed brown leather briefcase. Like Ralph, it had seen better days. Ms. Barbara Knudsen's youthful vitality was intimidating.

Barbara looked up from the summary pages. "Ralph, this is pretty strong actuarial evidence, and First Gotham has certainly benefited out of all proportion to expectations. How do we connect this Richard Trace to the deaths?"

"He is the president of the insurance subsidiary, and we believe that his income is somehow tied to the overall investment return on the BOLI program, which includes the death claims. So in the down years, we believe he had to arrange for extra death claims in order to make his bonus, or something like that."

"What led you to that conclusion?" asked Barbara.

"There was a withdrawal from his line of credit of $650,000 just last week." Ralph noticed that Agent Knudsen raised her eyebrows slightly at this revelation.

"Oh, we got his social security number and address so we pulled a credit report. It's at the back of the file." The Bureau agent nodded with understanding as this was standard operating procedure for Federal Agencies.

"It seemed to me that there was enough to bring the Bureau into the investigation, but my boss didn't agree. That's why I have come to you. I have been ordered not to approach the FBI in any official capacity."

"From what you have shown me there is certainly enough evidence, even though it is mostly circumstantial. I can tell you that I have always felt somewhat uncomfortable with the BOLI concept ever since my dad explained it to me. It just is a crime waiting to happen, and all that is needed is opportunity and reward, which we certainly have in this case. Understand that I will be doing this on my own, outside of bureau authority. I'm more than willing to do it because I have watched my dad strive to conduct his business honorably for over thirty years, and it is a constant battle against schemes like this that make it such a difficult, misunderstood business. I can see from your evidence that this can be a real opportunity to clean up part of the problem."

"So, we have enough to go on?"

"Yes, Ralph, there's more than enough, that's for sure. What else can you tell me?" she asked.

"I called First Gotham and they told me that Mr. Trace is on vacation until the 18th, so we can't see him for nine days. It seemed to me that you could get quite a bit done in that time. To be perfectly frank with you, this case is intriguing to me. I really wanted to investigate it on my own and catch this guy. You know, Columbo style."

Barbara laughed and took a sip of her wine.

Ralph shrugged his shoulders. "But investigating airplane crashes is a lot different than this stuff. We don't have access to company records like you do. I want to pursue this to a final conclusion and was hoping that you would help me, even join up with me."

"Ralph, let me do some deep background checking which will fill in some of the blanks. I have a friend who used to work in our New York office who can contact First Gotham for the needed information. When we approach Trace, you should make the contact under the guise of investigating the airplane crash. That way we can get in front of him without arousing suspicion. A guy like this is a definite flight potential. We want him right there in New York City where we can keep an eye on him."

"I'll call my friend in New York tomorrow morning and get him on it right away," said Barbara. "Can you arrange your schedule to come with me to New York to meet with this Mr. Trace?" she asked, her tulip shaped lips turning upward in a slight smile.

Ralph nodded with vigor. He moistened his own lips. He would get his shot at Richard Trace after all. They clicked glasses to acknowledge their new partnership.

Chapter 18

The next morning Barbara called her friend in New York, Bernie Gerson, owner of the Cool Detective Agency, Inc. Bernie had thought up the name and had been told many times that it had attracted clients to his services. He had been a special agent with the FBI for 14 years prior to becoming an entrepreneur in 1998. Barbara had sent him three insurance fraud cases which had helped him launch his private career after he had left the Bureau.

"Hi, Bernie, this is Barbara Knudsen in Chicago. How are you?"

"Great, Barb, how's my favorite FBI agent?"

Barbara knew that Bernie had a soft spot for her.

"Bernie, I know this is a lot to ask but I would like to send you a file for investigation. This is not a Bureau case. It was brought to me by a NTSB investigator who can't get cooperation from his agency. I don't see any way we could pay you...."

"Barb, after the leads you have given me over the last few years, I owe you."

"Well, we need to get deep background on a Mr. Richard N. Trace, president of the First Gotham Bank Insurance Agency, Inc. Social is 019-38-6905. Personal address: 624 Birch Road, Alpine, New Jersey. We need his complete personnel file at the bank. We have confirmed that he has accounts there as well, and a line of credit. Part of the package will be a photocopy of personal check he wrote to a charity for a business acquaintance out here. He is a possible suspect in a multiple murder plot over a number of years starting in 1993."

"Another insurance deal, huh, Barbara? But this one sounds much more sinister than the usual fraud deals we have worked on together in the past."

"Bernie, this could be the grandfather of all insurance crime cases if it turns out the way we expect. I will send a cover sheet along with the rest of the written material. It is over sixty pages. This is an outside deal; the bureau isn't in on it. I'm sure you understand."

"Will you be coming to New York?" he asked hopefully, with a smile in his voice.

"It sure looks that way. This guy Trace is on vacation until the 18th, and shortly after that we will want to call on him at his office. I got called into this case by this NTSB investigator, a Mr. Ralph Murphy, kind of a frumpy old guy. You know the type. He knows his stuff though. He did a good job of background given the lack of help from his agency. We thought we would have Murphy approach Trace about the airplane crash, which we hope will seem perfectly normal to him, sort of non-threatening."

"So this Murphy will be in on the sting?" asked Gerson.

"It is really his deal and besides, I thought it would be a good cover."

"I agree, but do you think there is any danger to him?"

"There is probably plenty of danger to all of us, but not on the first appointment. The evidence so far seems to indicate a murder-for-hire scheme. We think Trace is a greedy corporate type who has somehow made contact with some professionals who do the actual jobs for a fee. When and if we get to that stage, you and I can keep Murphy out of the heavy action."

"Good, just checking. Wouldn't want to lose a potential source of business," he chuckled.

"You always have been a wise-ass," she retorted, knowing that his chutzpah would be an invaluable asset in the coming days.

—

Bernard Gerson assembled what appeared to be the official authorizations and papers. He arranged an appointment with the supervisor of the Human Relations department of First Gotham Bank, Gladys Mason, who responded nervously to what appeared to be an inquiry from the Federal Bureau of Investigation. She had never before dealt with government officials.

"We will discuss the details of this inquiry when we get together. I strongly suggest that you do not discuss this with anyone in the meantime," Mr. Gerson ordered in a deep baritone voice, knowing that it would intimidate a law-abiding corporate officer.

Gladys replied. "Yes sir!" Her hand trembled when she put down the phone.

—

The following morning, a Friday, Bernie Gerson settled into the easy chair in front of Mrs. Mason's desk. He produced a subpoena on official court stationery. He also produced his identification badge and photograph, which he kept encased in a leather folder in his inside coat pocket. Gladys inspected them, her curiosity showing. It was the first time she had ever seen a official FBI badge and she was both terrified and impressed.

"How may I help you, Mr. Gerson?" Her voice trembled. She grasped her hands together in an attempt to control the outward manifestations of her inward fear.

"Ms. Mason, I know you must be nervous about this. We often see that reaction. Let me assure you that this inquiry has nothing to do with you personally. We are conducting a routine investigation about the airplane crash in Wisconsin that killed six of your employees just before Christmas."

He could see that this statement had a calming effect on her. She unclasped her hands and patted her professionally coiffed hair.

"Thank you, Mr. Gerson. I'll admit your call did have me unnerved."

"Ms. Mason, we need the personnel records of a rather high ranking official of the bank, a Mr. Richard N. Trace, the president of...."

"Ah yes, our Mr. Trace, of the insurance subsidiary," she said knowingly.

Bernie sat up. He could not help noticing her obvious animosity toward Trace.

"I take it that you know him, then?" he quizzed.

"Oh yes. He is always so demanding, a pushy sales type, you know? He must call me five times before each bonus payment."

"OK, Ms. Mason. We will need a copy of his employment contract with the bank and any pre-appointment papers, which we realize go back several years. We need those to check out his previous employment. Then we will need his credit card records. I assume he has a business credit card?"

"Yes, all of our executives do."

"And I'll need his expense reimbursement records, especially his air reservations. You know, the works...."

"What is he suspected of?" she asked, arching her carefully drawn eyebrows.

"I'm afraid I can't reveal that, Ms. Mason. In any event, you are not to reveal the contents of this conversation to anyone. We do not want Mr. Trace to know he is being investigated."

"Well, he is on vacation anyway. He goes to the Caribbean every January for two weeks. St. Maarten, I believe." She dragged out the double a's for effect. "I think they have a condo on the beach. He's often called me from there about his precious bonus."

"Yes, well it's just as well he is away so we can get this part of our investigation done in his absence. Now, Ms. Mason, we understand he has accounts and loans, lines of credit, that sort of thing here at First Gotham. We are going to want to see those records as well, without anyone knowing that we are looking into his financial matters."

"Mr. Gerson, I can have Dave Traynor over in operations get that information and bring it to my office. We can trust him to keep his mouth shut," she said conspiratorially.

Bernard Gerson smiled broadly. *Just what we need: a cooperative witness, actually, more than cooperative. This lady is full of enthusiasm. Doesn't seem to cotton to ol' Trace,* he thought to himself.

"Why don't you do what you need to do, and I'll disappear now and be back at, say, around 3:30, okay?"

"Could you make it 4:30? The staff will be mostly gone by then, and we can have more privacy. I can stay as late as I need to tonight. My husband is away on business, so I'm alone," she blushed as she realized that this sounded almost like a come-on to Gerson.

"Okay, Mrs. Mason, I'll be back at 4:30."

—

When Bernie returned, Gladys Mason greeted him and promptly dismissed Angel, the receptionist.

"Thanks for staying on and keeping me company, Angel. I'll be fine with Mr. Gerson. See you tomorrow."

Gladys walked ahead of Bernie Gerson down the carpeted hallway to her office. She was a large woman, nearly six feet tall and wide bodied. Bernie, by contrast, was just under six feet tall and very slim. Women like Gladys made him think of his mother when he was ten years old: bigger and stronger, yet somehow comforting. He felt comfortable with her, especially after she had indicated her enthusiasm for the assignment.

"Mr. Gerson, there is a lot of information which I have organized to give you a chronological picture of our history with Mr. Trace since his hire date of February 1, 1988. You will see that he has been quite successful with the bank. I hadn't realized how successful! Sometimes the executives on incentive compensation can make more than higher ranking officers on straight salary."

"Yes, I understand Ms. Mason, they have sort of a different mind-set than those of us who make a fixed amount," he smiled knowingly.

Gladys smiled back. "Exactly, Mr. Gerson." Their conspiracy was sealed.

Bernie began to leaf through the files, which were nearly three inches thick. "Can you give me a summary, kind of hit the high points?" he asked.

"To me, the high points are that he has always made his incentive bonus, and it has gotten larger each year. It's now more than triple his salary. It is based on the Bank Owned Life Insurance program meeting its earnings goals. That's in his employment contract. The other highlight is that he has methodically increased his line of credit, but he has only used it three or four times, always paying it back when he gets his bonus. The most recent withdrawal was just last week for $650,000."

"Wow! How much will his bonus be this year?"

"This year, based on last year's results, just under $1 million, and he has over $850,000 out on the line of credit-including the $650,000 drawn down last week. So, he will be able to pay it off again."

"When was the previous withdrawal?" asked Bernie.

"He drew down $200,000 last spring."

"How about before that?"

"Let's look at the records. Here it is--December 1998 for $350,000, paid back in February 1999."

"Can we see the records of his checking account for the same dates?"

"Yes, that would be further back in the file, near the end. Let's see, the last entry, just last week, deposit of $650,000, then a check to WAT, Inc. for the full amount."

"How about last spring?"

Here's the deposit of $200,000, then a series of checks to what appear to be contractors. They probably did some home improvement."

"And 1998?"

Gladys flipped back two pages. "Here it is. The $350,000 deposit, then the next entry, a check to WAT, Inc. for the same amount."

"Does the bank have the account for WAT, Inc?"

"I don't know, Mr. Gerson, but I could have Mr. Traynor check that out."

"Do you have copies of the returned checks?" he asked.

"Well, we have the microfiche, but I didn't ask Traynor for that information."

"Mrs. Mason, I think we are going to want to know about this WAT, Inc."

"Yes, Mr. Gerson, I understand! I will have Mr. Traynor retrieve that information Monday morning first thing. I should have it by 9:00 at the latest."

"Just the WAT, Inc. checks. The back side should tell us where this corporation's bank account is located. By the way, are there any other checks to them?"

Gladys leafed slowly through the register, working backward by date. "Here's one for $175,000 in December 1993." As she continued, the entries lessened decreased and finally she said. "There are no other checks to WAT, Inc. Just those three."

"Mrs. Mason, I...."

"Please call me Gladys."

"Gladys," he smiled. "My aunt was also a Gladys, kind of the Auntie Mame of our family. I will call you Monday morning. I'm afraid we have, that is, this Mr. Richard Trace, has a problem. You have been a tremendous help. I thank you and the Bureau thanks you for your help and for your confidentiality. It probably goes without saying, but I am required to remind you to say nothing about this to any of your staff or superiors," he said authoritatively.

She nodded her head as he spoke, "You have my word on that."

Bernie gave her a big grin. "It has been nice doing business with you, Gladys."

Gladys smiled. "It has been my pleasure, Mr. Gerson!"

"Call me Bernie."

"Oh, thank you, Bernie," she blushed.

Chapter 19

By 9:30 Monday morning Bernie Gerson had talked to Gladys. The line of credit withdrawals had been deposited to an account in the Cayman Islands. They had the number, but it would be very difficult to get any information on the account. Nevertheless, it was clear that Trace was up to no good. Bernie suspected that he was buying the services of a professional killer. There was no evidence of personal involvement. Trace's travel records and expenses were actually quite minimal for a major executive. He had not been to California in years, and had not been to any of the other murder sites at the time of the occurrences.

It appeared that his primary vacation destination was the Caribbean: Jamaica in 1990 and 1991, the Cayman Islands in 1993, and St. Maarten every year since 1995, and always during the first two weeks of January. Otherwise, he was pretty much commuting from Alpine to Manhattan fifty weeks a year. Any other vacation must have been taken as long weekends. There was no evidence of other travel, at least none revealed by his check register and business credit card at the bank.

In the meantime, Barbara Knudsen had received his credit card and cell phone records from the credit bureau. The credit cards had been used sparingly and were of little help. An analysis of his telephone calling card was tedious work, but had revealed at least one gem. There was a foreign call to a number in the Cayman Islands that turned out to be the Caribe International Bank and Trust. There had been only a few other calls to this number over the years. Five had been made in late 1993, then only one between then and late 1998, when there were three more. There was another lull until this last December when there were another four calls.

When Barbara reported these calls to Bernie, he told her about the Cayman Islands account that had been set up in the name of WAT, Inc. to receive these deposits. While they both knew that it would be nearly impossible to get any cooperation from that bank, especially in the short time-frame they were dealing with, the mere existence of the account spoke volumes.

—

The personnel and bank records of Richard N. Trace were compiled by Bernie Gerson and his staff and sent, along with a cover letter, to Barbara Knudsen in Chicago. By Tuesday morning she had a rather complete handle on the personal and professional life of Richard Trace. His resume had revealed that before he took his present position with First Gotham, he had been in sales and sales management with East Coast Life in Northern New Jersey. Barbara would have Bernie check out that history to see if there was any link to his presumed current activity. On Tuesday, Bernie's assistant, Sue Henderson, had come across a Manhattan phone number that Trace had called in 1993, 1996 and 1998 using his MCI/World-com calling card number. It was to a midtown restaurant, probably for reservations. She went on to other numbers, not seeing any significance in those calls.

Bernie's investigation of East Coast Life revealed a rather ordinary insurance career. True, Trace had been Assistant Manager of the Year a couple of times in the early 70's and had been a very successful field trainer for some time. His career as a district manager had been a roller-coaster ride of ups and downs. Apparently, according to an East Coast vice president who remembered him, Trace always had trouble holding on to good people. "All his good people left for other companies," had been his comment.

In the late 80's Trace had gotten wind of a new marketing scheme out of Texas for insuring employees of large firms for a new kind of Key man coverage. He had discovered that the banks could borrow the funds for premium on this product at a very favorable rate from the Federal Reserve Bank and deduct the interest cost. He had tried to get East Coast to participate in the scheme but didn't have the political horsepower to influence any of the executive team to look seriously at the idea.

It was at that time that Trace had met Harry Harkness, who was with the leading consulting firm, Smith, Hay & Ward. They were building up their carrier network, and even though Trace had been unsuccessful in convincing East Coast to participate, he had been referred by Harkness to First Gotham Bank just after they started their program. Trace had jumped at the chance to get off the treadmill of sales management at East Coast with its constant dependence on the performance of others, and he had joined First Gotham as the executive vice president of their Insurance subsidiary, charged specifically with building up their self-insured plan, which came to be known as Bank Owned Life Insurance: BOLI. During his time with the bank, it had grown into a program covering over 7,000 employees for over $3 billion of coverage. Bernie pored over the records of his achievements at East Coast Life without finding any information that he deemed to be helpful.

—

On Thursday, the 14th, Barbara Knudsen called Ralph and asked that they get together to discuss strategy. Ralph suggested that they include Chris Masters to bring him up to speed on their progress. Barbara was reluctant at first, but then decided that Chris might be useful, given his firsthand knowledge of the BOLI program, and his familiarity with Trace and First Gotham. They decided to meet on Friday evening at Barbara's apartment in Park Ridge.

Barbara had assembled a complete file, including, of course, the information that had been obtained by Bernie Gerson in his bogus, but highly effective, meetings with Gladys Mason. Ralph and Chris both marveled at the panache of Bernie and Barbara.

Barbara's apartment in Canterbury Place was the end unit on the second floor. Neither of the visitors was used to such plush surroundings. They moved carefully through the entry area into the spacious living room as if to be sure not to knock over any of her exquisite furnishings. Barbara had laid out the documents on the large rectangular marble coffee table in front of a three place divan. She had Chris and Ralph sit there. She sat on their right in her favorite easy chair, with Ralph nearer her and Chris beside him.

The entire room was done in peach and off-white. The effect was both calming and sensual in a very feminine motif. It made both of them feel uncomfortable, as if they had intruded on a solitary woman in her boudoir. If Barbara was aware of their discomfort she never let them know it. She quickly got them to focus on the business at hand.

"Chris, it is nice to finally meet you. Ralph has told me a little about you in connection with this First Gotham case, and I have studied the data you put together for him. It would appear that you have a real flair for actuarial work."

"I have always had an interest in math, and the job at Smith, Hay & Ward is ideal in that there are literally millions of bits of data that need to be assembled, analyzed and recorded. How they all fit together is what makes it interesting and fun. In this case the information did not fit the usual expected pattern, and this made it stand out like a flashing red light."

"I'm sure most of us would never have noticed the difference from normal," she replied, her lips parted slightly in a smile.

"Can you give us a summary of what you and Mr. Gerson have discovered?" asked Ralph.

"Basically, we have confirmed what you guys suspected. His bonus of nearly one million dollars is virtually totally dependent on the performance of the Gotham BOLI program, and in those years when interest of treasuries is not high enough, there have been several additional deaths so that he has always been able to receive the bonus. We know that he also has made large withdrawals in those years and put them in a numbered account in the Cayman Islands under a company called WAT, Inc. We don't know what happens to the money once it goes to the Islands, and there is little chance that we will be able to find out. Also, none of the deaths appear to be murders, although some of them could have been induced attacks: heart attacks, insulin reactions, and the like. I suspect he has a mob contact who does the actual "jobs" and who then gets paid off by Trace. It is going to be hard to prove in any event."

"What do we do next?" asked Chris.

"Our strategy now will be to flush him out and hope that he panics and runs to his source. If he does, Bernie and his team will be on his trail."

"What do you want from us?" asked Ralph.

"Bernie and I think it would be best for you to call him when he returns from vacation next Monday, and set up an appointment for Tuesday, if possible. It is likely that his calendar will be fairly free the first few days after he returns. If not Tuesday, then as early as possible next week. Then you and I will fly to New York. The idea is to let him think it is a normal follow-up to the airplane crash.

"Do I do this alone?"

"No, Ralph, I will be with you. You can introduce me as your associate. Just leave it at that."

"Then what?"

"First, we recite the basic facts of the crash investigation, then we get into the BOLI coverage. We thought we would spend some time asking him to explain it, and why, for example, Mr. Schwartz wasn't covered. We know he elected out, for whatever reason, but Trace doesn't know that we know. As you know, we believe the crash was, in fact, an accident rather than a planned event. It probably took Trace completely by surprise."

"Yes, I believe that is exactly what happened, based on Chris' evaluation, as well as our findings on site in Wisconsin," nodded Ralph.

"Next, we will tell him that the number of death claims for last year seems quite excessive, compared to the actuarial expectancy. He will likely agree and pretend as much surprise as anyone."

"Yeah, I can just see him saying what a shame it was, and how could anyone expect such a thing," Chris said with barely disguised contempt. Barbara and Ralph nodded their agreement.

"Ok, then we will drop the bombshell," said Barbara.

"What's that?" asked Ralph.

"We will tell Mr. Trace that the death claims in 1993 and in 1998 were also excessive from an actuarial standpoint, and watch him begin to squirm. Then we will tell him we need certain information about his personal finances. From my experience I would expect him to become indignant, but at the same time try to maintain his cool. This is, by the way, information which we already have. The idea is to get him to panic and run to his source," she repeated. "Hopefully, Bernie's team will be able to observe his movements."

"Whew," breathed Ralph, "this should be exciting."

—

That Friday night's news was as depressing as the weather. The particular channel that Ralph watched had started an index at the beginning of the year tracking all violent crime in the Chicago-land area for the new year. The anchorwoman announced that the total had already reached *eight in only 15 days*, saying so with seeming satisfaction, as if it were a statistic to be proud of. Ralph shook his head in disbelief. Next came some inane story about the rescue of a cat from an attic in suburban Elmhurst, which turned his thoughts to Barbara Knudsen.

Her lips reminded Murphy of Elke Sommer, but he figured that while Elke had been an icon of Germanic beauty to him, to anyone under forty she would be, at best, an obscure foreign actress. He certainly wasn't going to say anything to Barbara about it. The weather would continue to be cold and clear, with a storm front two days away. The Bulls had lost again. They never were the same after Jordan retired. Ralph aimed his remote and pressed the "off" button. He went into the bathroom and washed his hands carefully. His hands...when he had played Little League baseball his coach had taken one look at his pudgy body, and announced that Murphy would be a catcher. *Look at these meat-hooks*, he had thought. His teammates had teased him unmercifully. They had nicknamed him "mitts." Ralph had to admit, as he held them up for inspection, they were meaty.

He reached into the cabinet and removed the plastic bottle of hand lotion. Ralph squirted the pink liquid onto his hands and squeezed it between his fingers, then rubbed it into his palms. He reached behind the toilet and pulled three tissues from the Kleenex box, holding them daintily in his left hand. The bathroom was adjacent to the darkened bedroom. Walking slowly he came to the edge of his bed and lowered his shorts to just above his knees, then sat down. He pushed his shorts to the floor and swung his legs onto the narrow bed, laying the tissues next to his side. A tank-top undershirt stretched across his massive torso. Ralph reached down. The signal had been received. He began the ancient ritual. The bedsprings responded with a complementary rhythm. He pressed his left hand into his hip and arched his back. His chest and arms were soaked with sweat, his breath became labored. It was a solitary act performed with abandon. Ralph rolled to his left side and bunched the tissues to receive his discharge. He increased his stroke, his breath coming in gasps...and then he felt the release...and again, again. His fingers squeezed on the tissue; his heavy breathing subsided.

Ralph smiled, contented. What was it Barbara had said? *No Ralph, I will be with you.* He rolled onto his stomach and peacefully drifted off to sleep.

Chapter 20

On Monday morning, the 18th of January, Ralph dialed the number of the First Gotham Bank Insurance Agency, Inc.

"Good morning, First Gotham Insurance."

"May I speak with Mr. Richard Trace?"

"Who's calling, please?" asked the same voice with the Brooklyn accent.

"This is Mr. Murphy of the National Transportation Safety Board," answered Ralph.

"Just a minute, please."

"Trace here," the voice was firm and strong, "good morning."

"Mr. Trace, I'm Ralph Murphy of the National Transportation Safety Board," he repeated. "I'm calling you from Chicago."

"Yes, Mr. Murphy, how can I help you?"

"Sir, I'm sure you are aware that six executives of the bank, that is the First Gotham Bank, were killed in an airplane crash last month, on December 20^{th,} to be exact."

"Yes, of course. It was a terrible tragedy," said Richard Trace solemnly.

"Well, I am the investigator on the case. We would like to have an interview with you since the bank had some of those people insured. Just a routine follow-up, you understand?"

"Yes, of course, Mr. Murphy. What did you say your first name was?"

"Oh, it's Ralph, Ralph Murphy, the NTSB," he stammered.

"N-T-S-B," repeated Trace.

"Could we see you tomorrow morning by any chance?"

"Well, I just got back from vacation, so I've got some catching up to do, but OK. Yes, I don't have anything else on my calendar."

"How about 9 a.m.?" suggested Ralph.

"That's fine, Mr. Murphy. Do you know where our office is located?"

"Yes, no problem. There will be two of us. I'm bringing my associate, Ms. Barbara Knudsen.

"Right, Mr. Murphy. I'll see you then."

Ralph cradled the phone, and after Barbara had heard the click at her end of the line, she pressed the bar on her receiver.

"Ralph, that was perfect. We are in business. I'll arrange for a flight later today and we will hook up with Bernie Gerson and his team tonight for a briefing. You'll like Bernie, you are birds of a feather." Barbara patted his thick shoulder.

—

That Monday night there was a cold January rain in New York City. Bernie's Cool Detective Agency offices in downtown Manhattan were much more like Ralph's NTSB offices than the elegant luxury of the FBI's Elmhurst digs. Bernie had assembled his small staff of three. They had pored over the data and could virtually recite any facet of the business life of Richard Trace. They doubled as field agents, and along with Gerson they would be the surveillance team. Barbara would wear a wire, a hidden microphone that would record the conversation with Trace. Ralph would go in clean. His role would be to introduce Barbara, then initiate the conversation, starting with a review of the accident and the insurance. He would then tell Trace that the number of accidents during the last year was far in excess of actuarial expectations. After getting Trace's reaction he would defer to Barbara to fix the hook. Ralph was happy to have the help. He realized that he would never have been able to pull off this interview on his own.

What a lucky-break it had been that Trace was on vacation when he had called ten days earlier. *What had ever given him the idea that he could be a one-man show?* This was serious business for real professionals. He marveled at the cool efficiency of Barbara and Bernie's team. They rehearsed the scene several times; equipment was checked and double-checked. The building and offices were scouted and staked out. By 8:45 the next morning they were prepared. What would be just another meeting for Richard Trace, at least initially, would be far more than that for this team of three former and one present FBI agents, augmented by one NTSB investigator.

At 9 a.m., Ralph and Barbara entered the offices of the First Gotham Bank Insurance Agency, Inc. They were announced and ushered into the plush office of Richard N. Trace, President. He motioned for them to join him at the divan and easy chairs arranged in an L-shape around a mahogany and rosewood coffee table at one side of the large room.

"Would either of you care for coffee or tea?" Trace asked courteously.

"No thanks, but I would like some water," Ralph said. His mouth was parched.

"Ms. Knudsen?"

"No thanks."

When Ralph received the heavy crystal tumbler he took a generous sip, then another. He then returned the glass to the bronze and leather coaster provided by Trace's secretary.

"I believe you have some questions about the accident in Wisconsin...." Trace ventured.

"Yes, sir, we noticed that some of your employees were insured by the bank," Ralph started tentatively. "Could you tell us about that program?"

"Sure, we started that program in 1987 to cover the future liability of First Gotham for the cost of providing postretirement benefits," Trace recited.

"How does that work?" asked Ralph.

"The bank buys coverage on virtually all of our employees who are at a vice president or higher level."

"How many would that be?" Barbara interjected.

Trace smiled at her and continued. "We have 7,000 employees in the program. The bank has a lot of vice presidents," Trace laughed easily.

Murphy and Knudsen smiled and nodded.

"How is it that Mr. Schwartz was not in the program?" Ralph recited the rehearsed question.

"Oh, Schwartz elected not to be covered."

"Then the employees can choose whether or not to be covered under the program?" asked Barbara.

"Well, not exactly. We basically want to cover everyone, but if there has been a significant medical problem within six months prior to the start date, or if an employee elects not to be covered, then he or she is left off the program."

"So the employees do have a choice?" she reiterated.

"Yes, technically, they have a choice. We notify them that the bank was setting up a plan to cover them against the cost of future benefits, with no medical exam required. In fact, in our most recent offering for new hires, we actually gave the employees a $5,000 paid-up personal policy if they agreed to participate in the plan," Trace said expansively.

"How much coverage did the bank take out on each of them?" asked Ralph.

"Well, it varied, but up to $500,000 each."

"$500,000 each? Without a medical? That would cover a lot of benefits."

"Yes, Mr. Murphy, but statistically we find that the cost of providing postretirement benefits is at least that much in many cases."

"Speaking of statistics, we have been informed that the number of death claims last year was far greater than actuarially predicted," said Ralph, right on cue. Bernie and his team listened from a van parked down on the street, tensed in anticipation.

"Yes, that accident was a terrible blow to the bank, especially coming just before Christmas. Who could ever predict such an event?" Trace pursed his lips and stroked his long nose.

Barbara then said. "Where we are having a problem, Mr. Trace, is that the actuarial predictions were exceeded **even before** the accident. As it turned out, the accident simply served to point out the anomaly."

Trace tensed at this revelation. His Caribbean-tanned face turned even darker. "What do you mean?" he stammered, obviously agitated.

"We have gone over the figures with the folks at Smith, Hay & Ward and find the same pattern occurred in 1993 and 1998." She stared straight at him.

"I don't know what that means, Miss Knudsen," Trace replied, avoiding eye contact with her.

"Mr. Trace," she continued coolly, "we need to have some personal information from you. Could you provide us with your credit card and phone calling card bills for this last year?"

"I--what is this all about? Am I personally being investigated? What do you people think; that I had something to do with that crash? For God sakes! I am simply running a business for my employer. I can't control whether accidents occur. What are you saying?" Trace exclaimed. He was almost gasping for breath.

"Mr. Trace, we are simply saying that the actuarial results defy natural randomness, and we need to check out all aspects of the case." The conversation was now between Agent Knudsen and Richard Trace. He was still unable to look her in the eye. Her stare burned into him, her eyes like lasers.

"Do I need to call my attorney?" he blurted out.

"That's up to you, Mr. Trace. If you cooperate, we can do our investigation without delay and be out of your hair in a few days. If there is nothing out of the ordinary, you have nothing to be concerned about."

Ralph sat transfixed, admiring Barbara's focused intensity.

"OK. Then, when do you want my records?" He sat up and straightened his tie. His color was returning to normal, his breathing slowed. Trace had made a decision to attempt to give the appearance that he was cooperating, at least until he could talk to Johnny.

"We will call you Thursday, day after tomorrow."

Ralph picked up his water glass and drained the remaining contents. He glanced at Barbara and noticed a slight smile of satisfaction on her lips.

"Thank you for your time, Mr. Trace. We will call you in two days," she said, her voice leaving no doubt of her resolve.

Trace rose to announce that the interview was over. Ralph and Barbara shook his hand, which was wet with perspiration. The hook was set.

—

Richard Trace followed them to the foyer and said goodbye. He then returned to his office and closed the door. He crossed over to his desk and sank into his chair. He leaned forward, elbows on his desk pad, and pressed his fingers into his temples. *They want my phone records. That could lead to Johnny. What now*? He thought. *Johnny will know what to do. I've got to reach him right now.*

—

As Ralph and Barbara descended in the otherwise empty elevator, he turned toward her. She felt his stare and turned her eyes toward him; she smiled broadly.

"Ralph, how are you? It got a little tense in there," she said, touching his arm.

"Oh, I'm fine, but I'll bet Mr. Trace is pretty shook up."

"Yes, I think we made that son of a bitch sweat!" she exclaimed.

"Barbara, you were fantastic!"

"It's just part of my job, but I'll admit it is fun to put a bastard like that in the sweat tank," she said with satisfaction.

"I really admire what you folks do, and I'm grateful that you asked me to help," said Ralph.

"Ralph, I couldn't have done it without your help." She squeezed his arm. Ralph looked down to her hand and smiled.

"Thank you for saying that." The door opened. "Well, here we are," announced Ralph, "After you, Miss Knudsen."

She stepped into the marble hallway, head held high. Ralph ambled after her, admiring her strong athletic posture. *I wish I could hold my shoulders back so straight, like that,* he thought. She turned to be sure he was following her. Her eyes flashed in triumph. He shuffled forward to catch up. When they got to the entry they were met by Bernie Gerson.

"How'd it go, Barb?" asked Bernie.

"The hook is set," she replied.

"I'll say it is!" confirmed Ralph. "You should have seen him sweat. He was gasping for air."

Barbara's light laugher echoed down the corridor.

"I think Mr. Murphy had a good time in there even though it got tense for a few moments. He was perfect in setting him up."

"OK, you guys get going now. My team will take over and keep an eye on him."

—

Barbara and Ralph hailed a cab and left for Bernie's office.

"What will happen now, Barb?" he asked.

"We hope that he will panic and run to whoever his professional killer is, and then, if we can get him to confess and implicate that person, or persons, we will have more than a flimsy, purely circumstantial case. Without some sort of collaboration, it will be virtually impossible to determine which of the deaths were murders. None of them look like murders, and that's because they were probably committed by professionals who knew exactly what they were doing. This will have to be a case where the bird sings, and the bird is Richard Trace."

"Well, he seemed nervous enough to sing to me, and if he did, it would be as a soprano," Ralph observed.

"I did sort of have him by the short hairs, didn't I?" she laughed.

"You certainly did, young lady. I'd hate to have you mad at me."

"You're too lovable for that to ever happen, Ralph."

"Yeah, sure. Me, lovable, that's a joke."

"Oh, I don't agree. You have a certain teddy bear charm," she said with a serious expression. The cab became quiet as Ralph contemplated this comment.

Barbara smiled and looked out the window at the crowded afternoon sidewalks. Ralph looked straight ahead, not daring to look at her. They arrived at their destination without another word. She had silently set another hook.

Her words hung in the air, frozen in time for Ralph. Could he dare to think she had any interest in him?

It was a question he would hold to himself for a while. They were both going to be totally focused on the entrapment of Richard Trace for at least the next few days.

Chapter 21

At 9:20 Sal Graffini walked into Johnny Pestrano's office. He stood in front of the desk until Johnny motioned him to take a seat. Sal sat on the Moroccan high-backed chair, one of a pair in front of the ornate desk. Johnny was talking to his niece, Katie Rizzo. "OK, honey. Take care of little Elly, *ciao*." He put down the phone.

"What now, Sal?" he demanded.

"It's that guy Trace again, something about an investigation," replied Graffini. "He's on line two."

Johnny looked at Sal and slammed his fist down into the leather pad on the top of his desk. A dark liquid splashed out of the mug next to it. "God-dammit! I told him not to contact me here. This guy has got to go," he said with menace.

Sal blotted up the spilled coffee with his handkerchief. "Sorry, boss," he muttered, eyes downcast.

"That's OK, Sal, no problem. Let me think about what to do with him. He's holding, huh?"

"Yes, Mr. Pestrano, line 2."

"OK. We need to pick him up and take him out of circulation. *Capice*?"

"Whatever you say, boss."

Johnny squared his shoulders and pushed up the knot of his necktie. He then ran his fingers down the smooth silk lapels of his jacket, smoothing out the material after his violent action. He forced out a long, slow breath. He lifted the phone.

"Pestrano." He spoke the family name with authority, his voice a mere whisper.

"Johnny, this is Richard. I think the feds are on to us," blurted Trace.

"How so?"

"They have figured out that the death claims were more than expected. They know the years. They want my credit card and phone records. They...."

"Stop! Where are you?" Johnny commanded.

"I'm in a phone booth in my building."

"They may have a tail on you, Trace. The feds come prepared. You are going to have to lose them."

"How do I do that?"

"Does your building have surveillance cameras in the elevators?"

"No, I don't think so."

"OK. Where do you park your car?"

"It's on level C of the garage here in the building."

"They will probably have it staked out. It will be easier to lose them on foot anyway." He paused, "How do you get to the garage from where you are now?"

"It's a separate elevator, down to level F."

"And up to?" he asked.

"Up to the 3rd floor mezzanine. The shops, you know?"

"Yes. OK, go back up to your office. 34th floor, right? Tell them you have an appointment that will last the rest of the day. Got it?"

"Yes, Johnny." Richard Trace listened to Johnny like a child taking instruction from a parent.

"Then walk down the fire stairs to 31, and take the elevator to the 3rd floor."

"What then?"

"Take the garage elevator to the first level and walk out the exit ramp and grab a cab."

"Where do I go then?" asked Trace. He heard muffled voices for a few seconds.

"Have him drop you at the Regent Hotel, westside entrance. Walk through the lobby and I will have someone pick you up at the eastside entrance. He will ask after your mother; Viola. Wasn't it?"

"Yes, that's right."

"Got it, Trace?"

"Got it. Thank you, Johnny."

Trace deposited two quarters in the slot as requested by the mechanical voice. He was sweating now. *I'm being tailed*, he thought with alarm. He walked like a robot to the elevator bank and pressed floor 34. Across the way Bernie whispered into his radio, "He's on the move. It looks like he is returning to his office." Artie Jackson, at Trace's car in the garage, and Larry Tucker, in the van outside the entrance to the building, came to full alert.

Only one other passenger joined Trace, and she got off on the 20th floor. He continued alone to the 34th floor. Trace hurried to his offices and pushed open the door to the reception area with alarm. He barely looked up at the receptionist and made a beeline to his own personal office. Again he collapsed in his chair, breathing heavily. He felt such a heaviness in his chest that he feared a heart attack. His breath was coming in gasps; he was sweating profusely. He reached out for the phone and saw that the voice-mail light was lit and blinking. He instinctively reached out and punched in the code to receive his message. It was from Harry Harkness of Smith, Hay & Ward in Chicago welcoming him home from St. Maartens and asking that he call as soon as possible. *Now, what would Harkness want? Might it have something to do with the appointment he had just endured?* His attention had been diverted just long enough that he caught his breath and slowed his heart rate. It gave him time to think about what to do next.

Breathe, think, he commanded himself. *First I'll call Harkness and find out what he wants,* he thought rationally. Control was returning; panic subsided.

Trace dialed the number that Harkness had left and soon heard the familiar quiet voice.

"Harkness here," said Harry.

"Harry, this is Richard Trace returning your call."

"Ah, Richard, how was your vacation?"

"It was great, but this morning hasn't been so good. I just got a visit from some federal investigators about that crash in Wisconsin, and they were implying that we had something to do with it," he shouted.

"Yes, well, I wanted to talk to you before they got to you and warn you that they might be a little rough. I guess you have already met their Mr. Murphy, then?"

"Yeah, that fat little pig and his sexy friend from the FBI," answered the angry executive.

"I don't know about anyone from the FBI," Harkness retorted.

"Listen, Harry, shouldn't those checks for the death claims be about ready by now?" Trace queried, suddenly inspired.

"As a matter of fact, I have four of the five here on my desk, for a total of 2.2 million," he answered cooperatively.

As Harkness spoke a strategy formed in Trace's mind.

"Listen, Harry, I want to come out to Chicago this afternoon. I can meet you in your office between 2:30 and 3:30, depending on which shuttle I catch. I'll call you from O'Hare when I get in. I want you to arrange for me to talk to that new kid of yours. Masters, isn't it?" He was now in full command.

"We will look forward to your visit, Richard," replied Harkness solemnly.

That appointment secured, Trace called United Airlines and made a round trip reservation, with the return for the 5 p.m. shuttle back to LaGuardia. The information that Murphy and the FBI broad had thrown at him could only have come from young Mr. Masters. He had looked like trouble to Trace when they had met last year--a real straight arrow. He would be sure to have Harkness put him in his place. *I have two hours on the plane to figure out how to deal with him,* he thought with determination. Trace sat at his desk for another few minutes formulating a strategy. He then rose and calmly put on his coat and walked down the hall to the receptionist.

"Nancy, I have an appointment and will not be back until tomorrow," he announced, and as he left he pulled his hat down securely over his ears.

Remembering Johnny's instructions, Trace knew that he must elude the grasp of the feds. He took the stairs down to the 31st floor exit. He pushed open the door with caution. The hallway was empty. Trace pressed the down button and waited. The seconds ticked slowly. He noticed a spider hanging down from the ceiling between elevator cars, spinning out his silky web, dangling free, building a web to catch unsuspecting victims. *The difference, little friend, is that I am not unsuspecting,* he said to himself. The car that stopped had only one other passenger, a man he didn't recognize. Trace joined this stranger and punched floor 3. The other man appeared to be headed for the ground floor. When they arrived at the mezzanine floor, the tall man burst through the doors, looking first to his right, then to his left for the garage elevator. Trace had never been on this floor in all the years he had worked in the building. He didn't see any other elevators.

My God, I'm being hunted like a common criminal! Panic began to arise in his brain. *"Think! Breathe!"* Again, he gasped for breath.

Reason told him that the garage elevators should be around the corner to his right. Sure enough, just as on the main floor, there they were, as logic would dictate. He slowed his breathing as he waited for the elevator to arrive. The door opened to an empty car. At the second floor he was joined by a woman he recognized as a business development officer of the bank, apparently on her way to her car. They nodded in recognition. Trace exited alone at level A. He made the first left turn and walked past the booth attendant and up the ramp, keeping his eyes trained down at the floor all the way. The traffic was headed west on the one way street. He ran down the line of slow moving cars, found an empty cab and ordered, "LaGuardia!"

The cab crawled along in the mid morning traffic. Trace slumped down in his seat so as not to be seen from outside the cab. The cab turned right at the next street, and was off to the airport.

—

"Have you seen Trace?" Gerson whispered into the mouthpiece of his closed circuit phone.

"Nothing, Bernie," replied Jackson from his post at the car on level C.

"Well, we last saw him at 9:29 when he left the phone booth and went back up to his office. That was 20 minutes ago. I'm going to call his office and see if he's still up there." Bernie dialed the number.

"First Gotham Insurance Agency, may I help you?"

"I'm calling for Mr. Richard Trace."

"Mr. Trace is not in. May I give you his voicemail?"

"No. When is he expected?" Bernie asked.

"I don't know. He didn't say when he would return," she said evasively.

"When did he leave?" demanded Gerson.

"I **beg** your pardon, sir!" The receptionist was obviously offended.

"Sorry, miss, can you tell me when Mr. Trace left the office? You see, we had an appointment and he has not yet appeared at our office.

"Oh, yes sir, he left around 9:30, about a half hour ago. Maybe he had trouble in traffic, or something," she offered.

"OK, thank you." Bernie punched his cell phone. "Damn, lost him!" he shouted to himself.

He pushed the start button on his three-way closed circuit phone. "Come in boys, we lost him."

Since Trace had not gone to his car, Bernie believed it meant he had contacted his professional partner, and they must have conspired on a way to get together undetected. *Boy, would I like to be a fly on the wall for that meeting*, thought former agent Bernie Gerson.

Barbara and Ralph were told that Trace had somehow shaken the surveillance team, and had vanished into thin air. They all believed he had somehow hooked up with his professional contact and was on the run. They would be put back on track from an unexpected source.

—

At 10:15 a.m. Alfredo called Pestrano's office to report that Trace had not shown up. He was instructed to come back in for further instructions.

I wonder what that crazy bastard is up to, thought Johnny.

Chapter 22

While his nephew was on his errand, Johnny Pestrano contemplated what to do about Trace. Clearly he had been exposed, probably due to that airplane crash in the Midwest in December. Individual far-flung death claims didn't have the appearance of murder, but there was always that possibility with an accident: and the feds always investigated airplane crashes. The FAA, Federal Aviation Agency, wasn't that the organization? They must have found out about the insurance coverage the bank had on those executives and put two and two together. Trace would be an easy target. He was not used to this kind of pressure and would panic. Johnny Pestrano could not afford to have Richard Trace panic. He made his decision.

It was early morning in San Francisco. The fog outside Duk Lon Ki's condo pressed against the picture window facing Alcatraz. A warm fire crackled in the living room. Ruby was still in bed. Duk was just finishing a series of stretching exercises, ending by extending his right leg above shoulder height and holding that position for 30 seconds, when a phone call shattered his intense concentration.

"Duk Lon Ki," he breathed heavily into the receiver.

"Hello, Duk, it's Johnny. Did I interrupt anything?" he asked with amusement.

"No, Johnny, I was just doing my exercises. Sorry to be a bit out of breath."

"Oh, I see," said Johnny, somewhat disappointed he hadn't interrupted a sex session.

"What's up?" asked Lon Ki.

"We have another job to do. You remember the banker, Richard Trace?"

"Oh yes, the Chinese bank president assignment!" he exclaimed.

"Yes, that's the one. Well, Trace has been fingered by the feds and he has panicked. They are investigating an airplane crash that killed six of the executives in his bank and apparently they are suspicious of the number of death claims. I'm afraid he will talk if they pressure him. We are having him picked up right now. I was wondering if you could come east and help me with this one."

"What did you have in mind, Johnny?"

"Well, Duk, I have certain reasons to want him to suffer. Let's just leave it at that."

"I think I get the picture," said the worldly-wise Asian. "Johnny, I would like nothing better than to do this guy for you. It never sat well with me that he had that Chinese lady killed. Frankly, it bothers me even to this day. Hey, wait a minute. I've got an idea!"

Johnny could "hear" Duk's smile from 2,500 miles.

"You told me some time ago that you had a Filipino friend from 'Nam who works for you."

"Right. Manny Ramiscal. So?"

"The night we went out to dinner here in San Francisco you were telling us about his rat cage. I remember that Ruby thought it was gruesome, but later she was fascinated by the mechanics of it. She threatens me all the time with "rat cage, rat cage!" when she gets angry. That woman sure likes her playthings."

"Oh yes, now I remember. Manny calls it his head cage, and...." his voice trailed off.

The phone line fell silent for a few seconds as both men contemplated the scene that the two words implied.

"Duk. That is a brilliant idea, the perfect solution. Manny runs our warehouse right across the Hudson in New Jersey. Can you come east to supervise this deal?" Johnny asked hopefully.

"I wouldn't miss it for the world. I'll try to get there tonight. Do you mind if I fly first-class? It's usually easier to get a last minute reservation that way--but it is expensive," asked Duk.

"Be my guest. For this, it's worth it!" replied Pestrano.

Duk hung up the phone and slowly shook his head.

Mr. Trace, you are going to have a miserable time tonight, he thought.

Ruby Ah Chee appeared in the doorway to the bedroom rubbing her eyes.

"What's this about the rat cage?" she demanded.

"I was just talking to Johnny about turning you in for a new model and he said that you would probably have me put in one if I did," he laughed.

"That's right, mista," she narrowed her eyes, "but seriously, what's with the rat cage talk?"

"Oh, it's just some guy that Johnny wants me to take care of in New York. Don't even think about it."

To change the subject he said, "Just look at that fog."

Her mood shifted. "Nice fire, it makes your arms and shoulders glisten after working out," she purred. "How would you like to work out with madam?"

"Did you have a head cage in mind?" he asked, eyes aglow.

She clicked her teeth together. "Head cage, head cage!" she snapped and ran across the room toward Duk. She tripped on the edge of his exercise mat and fell headlong into his strong arms. He lowered her to the mat below and they began some exercises that Duk cut short after only fifteen minutes. He had a plane to catch.

—

"Sal, I want to talk to Manny Ramiscal." Johnny had met Manny in a bar at Cam Ranh Bay in 1967. Their early attraction had been a mutual fascination for card games. Johnny had found that Manny was virtually unbeatable at any card game, not because of his intellect, but rather because of his manual dexterity. He was a magician with a deck of cards. Johnny learned that his buddy Manny was a professional magician back home in Butuan, on the island of Mindanao in the Philippines. Like most Filipinos in Vietnam, his ambition was to relocate to America. After the war he spent a few years in Hawaii. With his military record, he had become a naturalized citizen of the United States. In 1974, he got a call from Johnny asking him to become a part of the Pestrano family network reporting directly to former U. S. Army Captain John V. Pestrano. His job was "special projects."

"Manny, Johnny here. How are you, brah?"

"Johnnie, whee!"

"Manny, do you still have the head cage?" asked Johnny.

"Yeah, boss, heh-heh. Still got 'um."

"I'll have a candidate for you tonight, late tonight."

"Him must be one bad buggah."

"Not so much bad, as stupid, Manny. With a capital 'S'."

"Stupid as sheee-it, huh?"

"You got that right."

"Want um beeg rat?"

"Yes, might as well get on with it. I'll have Alfredo make the delivery around midnight tonight at the warehouse. You know the drill. Have Dimitri help. He's the big one, right?"

Dimitri Yankovich was an émigré from the Ukraine. He reported to Manny. At 6'5" he towered over his boss, who was only 5'6". There was never any doubt who was in charge, though. He had seen Manny take out much larger men in seconds with his whirling hands and feet. Dimitri was in awe of his skill in the martial arts.

"Hey, Dimitri, we have beeg sport tonight. Big boss, he wan to cage some buggah. We go trap us a rat, dig?"

"Uh, no, Manny. What you say?"

"You see, beeg man, you see. Ha, ha, ha."

Manny climbed the pull-down stairs into the attic of their warehouse quarters. He handed down two rusted-out relics of his days in the Philippines. Dimitri examined them with a puzzled look. Manny grabbed the rectangular metal enclosure. It was 18 inches long, 9 inches wide and 9 inches tall, made of brownish stained iron, with wire mesh inside the iron bars. It had a trap door across one end, and a crude lever at the back of the enclosure. He explained how the trap worked to Dimitri.

"We put da meat on dis ting," he pointed to the lever. "Den de rat comes in an when he grabs da meat, da ting goes up and da door goes down. Den we have da rat, deeg?"

Dimitri nodded slowly as the mechanics of the device began to sink in.

"Dis other ting, I'll splane later, heh, heh."

Manny left the other device, which looked like a diver's helmet, on the floor of the warehouse. It appeared to be just another dirty, rusted-out relic among many others in the large open room. Manny motioned Dimitri to follow him. They got into the truck and drove the six miles to the Dockside Inn. He knew that under the pier there would be wharf rats, and his objective was to catch one in his crude trap. He and Dimitri wandered down the pier, out to where the water lapped up over the cross beams.

"Hey, Dimi, I go down there, you hand me da trap. OK?"

"Sure, Manny."

The small man lowered himself over the edge and swung under the boardwalk. He reached up and waved his hand. Dimitri stooped down and lowered the trap by its handle. Manny grabbed it and disappeared. Under the pier, it was dark and smelled of salt water and shell fish. The water here was actually brackish, as it was five miles up from the bay. There was no breeze, and in few minutes Manny was sweating in spite of the cool temperature. He crawled across the cross-beam, the water lapping up every few seconds. It was almost high tide.

At the far end, he lashed the trap to the post and again at the other end to the crossbeam. The color of the trap blended with the oily structure. He placed a half chicken breast on the lever and carefully set the trap. By nighttime, with any luck, he would have a nice fat rat. He knew that rats hung out here because of the Dockside Inn just 300 yards upriver. By early evening the noontime garbage would backwash this way, and by the time they returned, at 10:00 or so, there would be a rat, hopefully a nice fat rat, in the cage.

Manny returned by the same route and swung himself over the edge of the boardwalk. He brushed his hands together, then brushed off his dark jeans.

"No harm, just water," he chuckled.

"What now, Manny?" asked Dimitri.

"Now, we wait till nighttime, den get um beeg rat!"

At 5:30 that evening, the detritus from the Dockside Inn had worked its way back down the Passaic River with the ebb tide. Some of it had even floated past the pier where Manny had placed his trap. Mary scratched herself and stretched, pushing off against her forepaws. Her lair was high up in the pier structure, in a place where the tide never reached. She had managed to accumulate a collection of rags, paper and leaves that gave her a comfortable nest in which to raise her babies. She had lived here for over two of her three and a half years. During that time she had produced 18 litters and over 250 young. She was a Brown Norwegian rat, again heavy with her next litter, due the following week. It was that time of her cycle that getting food was both most necessary and most difficult. Her added girth slowed her down just when her appetite was at its peak. She had to compete with her younger, faster offspring, which became more difficult to do with each litter.

Mary ventured out on her evening trek. Within seconds she picked up the scent of the chicken. It was below her to the left. She scrambled down to the crossbeam; the same one that Manny had negotiated earlier that day. The faint human odor made her hesitate, but only for an instant. From her lair higher up in the pier substructure, she knew that scent and associated it with the large two-legged creatures that occasionally walked on the boardwalk above. They had never been a threat to her.

She approached the crude trap, which blended into the surroundings in the dim light. Cautiously she sniffed at the iron bars. The aroma of the chicken was overwhelming, and she was so hungry. Mary stepped into the cage and went over to the bait. She reached out with her paws and grabbed at her prize. Behind her the door clanged shut. She spun around to find that she was enclosed in a small space. She clawed desperately at the wire mesh sides of the trap. She gnawed at the trip lever to no avail. Almost as an afterthought she devoured the chicken. There was an urgent need in her belly that could not be denied, but at what price?

Chapter 23

Chris Masters was in the midst of what seemed to be an ordinary day at the office. He was acutely aware of the meeting that was taking place in the offices of First Gotham Bank that morning between his new accomplices and Richard Trace. The statistics before him were not doing much to keep his mind off that encounter in New York City.

Just before 9 o'clock he was summoned to the office of Harry Harkness.

"Chris, I just received a call from Richard Trace of First Gotham Bank and he apparently had a visit from Ralph Murphy and some woman from the FBI. He implied that they had certain information about actuarial statistics that could only have come from our office. Have you been talking to Murphy?" he glared at him with laser-like intensity.

"Well, I did see Mr. Murphy one time after our meeting here," Chris confessed.

"Young man, we may have a problem with that. In any event, Trace is on his way to Chicago and will be in our office this afternoon. He specifically asked that you be available to meet with him between 2:30 and 3:30 this afternoon, and Chris, I *specifically* expect you to be prepared to apologize to Mr. Trace. We will speak about how this will affect your future here at Smith, Hay & Ward after that meeting. I am very, very disappointed in this turn of events."

Chris had broken Harry's rule regarding obedience to one's superior.

After returning to his cubicle, Chris gathered himself and left the office, telling Sally that he would be back in a few minutes. She assumed that he was going to the men's room. Instead, Chris went up to the nearly empty lobby of the top floor restaurant where he knew he would get the best cellular phone reception and dialed Ralph's number.

"Ralph, this is Chris. I don't have much time, but you should know that Trace is on his way to Chicago, and has set up a meeting with Harkness and me for 2:30 this afternoon. He asked Harry to be sure to have me at the meeting. I don't know what to expect since he made it clear that you guys had implied that he was manipulating the death claims," his words rushed out at Ralph.

"Oh boy! Ok, Chris, Barbara's right here. I'm going to put her on."

After a minute, during which Chris heard urgent murmurings, Barbara Knudsen came on the phone. "Hi, Chris. Listen, the safest thing for you to do is to stay in that office, in sight and in contact with as many others as possible. If there is someone you trust, tell them about your situation so they know what is happening. Please, Chris, don't let Trace get you alone if you can possibly avoid it." Her warning was clear; he was definitely in danger. He had heard enough. Five minutes had passed and it was time to return to the office and try to act as if nothing was amiss, but he signaled to Sammy to meet him in the mailroom at the end of the hall.

"What's up, Chris?" said Sammy.

"Sam, I've got a meeting with this guy Richard Trace from First Gotham this afternoon, and I'm afraid that he is really pissed at me, and, unfortunately, at the company as well. Harkness is also upset because Trace was confronted by some federal agents about the death claims at his bank, and they have figured out that the information had to come from me. I can't go into detail now, but I have been in touch with those people. I'm convinced that Trace is having people killed, and God knows what he will do to me."

"Jeez, Chris. Well, he won't shoot you here in the office. I'll keep an eye out just in case he gets violent."

"Thanks, Sammy. We better get back to our cubicles before anyone gets suspicious."

—

Richard Trace had made the noon shuttle which got him in to Chicago's O'Hare at one o'clock Central time after a two hour flight. He arrived for his appointment at the downtown offices of Smith, Hay & Ward at 2:15. Harry Harkness met him in the reception area and ushered him back to the conference room. He immediately buzzed Chris on the intercom and asked him to join them. When Chris arrived Harkness asked him to shut the door behind him.

"Chris, I believe you remember Mr. Richard Trace, President of First Gotham Insurance?" Harkness started innocuously, being as deferential to his guest from New York as possible.

"Yes sir. How are you, Mr. Trace?" Chris replied.

"Not very well after a visit I had in my office this morning. Some federal investigators had some disturbing information that as far as I can tell could only have come from your office. I'm talking about highly confidential information." His face began to redden with anger.

"Chris, I believe you have something to say to Mr. Trace," Harkness commanded.

"Mr. Trace, the information that I gave to Mr. Murphy was simply actuarially accurate, and how it was interpreted was up to him. It seems to me that the timing and number of death claims make it unlikely they were mathematically random. I'm sorry if this causes you a problem," Chris said in a soft whisper.

Harry Harkness looked at them with alarm. This was not going as he had planned, not at all!

"Ahem, Richard, I am going to let Masters reconsider his thoughts while we move on to more pleasant business. There is the matter of the claim checks. After we spoke this morning the last one arrived, so we can give you the full 2.8 million to take back to your office," the senior actuary said, in an effort to take some of the tension out of the meeting.

"Well, that **is** some consolation." Trace brightened for the moment.

"The checks are just down the hall in my office. Perhaps you gentlemen can begin to settle your differences while I am gone," Harkness said, knowing that it would be a *baptism under fire* for Chris Masters. "I'll just be a minute."

After Harkness left, Trace leaned across the mahogany table and glared at Chris. "Listen, buddy-boy, you are in way over your head--you and your fat friend Murphy. I expect a written retraction on my desk tomorrow, signed by you and Harkness. Whatever your precious statistical evidence shows is pure speculation. You don't have a right to spread theories based on the confidential records of your clients in any event. I haven't ruled out suing you guys, and if we do, it will be for millions, if not billions," he snarled.

During this tirade the skin of Trace's face had been drawn back in a vicious mask, exposing his cranial bone structure. White spittle had formed at the corners of his mouth. When he heard the tumblers of the door being opened, his face morphed back to nearly normal in an instant.

Chris blanched. He had never seen anyone display such a range of emotion in such a short span of time. He was stunned at the flexibility of Trace's facial muscles, which had gone from extreme rage to calm assurance so quickly. For the first time he fully realized the enormity of his actions and the possible consequences to his firm, and to himself. *I should have listened to Sarah and kept all this to myself,* he thought, not for the first time.

Before Trace could continue, Harkness stepped back into the room with the five checks and presented them to Trace. For the first time that day, Richard Trace felt gratified. He gave Chris a dismissive glance; he then looked back at Harkness as if to say, *it is time for the big boys to talk.*

Harkness got the hint. "Chris, I think that Mr. Trace and I have matters to discuss which don't concern you. Please remain in the office as you and I will have things to discuss when we are finished."

Chris excused himself and quickly left the conference room. He walked directly out of the office without even giving Sally a nod. He needed to get some fresh air and a soda, and he needed to give Ralph a call.

—

After Chris left, Trace turned to Harkness and, placing his large hands on the table top, said, "Harry, we have worked together for several years. First Gotham has been a loyal customer of Smith, Hay & Ward all of that time. Believe me, it is in no small part because you helped me get the job at the bank, and I will always appreciate that help. I told your Mr. Masters that I expect a written retraction of his 'theory' on my desk tomorrow morning. The FBI-- you got that, Harry, the fucking FBI-- has told me that they expect certain facts by Thursday or I'm in trouble--me, personally! I expect that retraction-- that it is all a terrible mistake. Also, I want you to get rid of that little asshole immediately. I want his ass fired this afternoon. Do I make myself clear?"

Harry Harkness nodded vigorously.

Trace continued, "Either those things get done or we pull our account and find the competition, and I am so loyal that I don't even know who the competition is, but believe me I'll find out--fast. I don't have to remind you that our account is worth millions of income to you guys each year, do I?"

"No, Richard, you are not only perfectly clear, but you are totally justified. I can't apologize enough for the behavior of Masters. We had no idea that he would be a rogue employee. It is amazing to me that he could do so much damage in such a short time. Believe me, he will be gone before the day is out, and you will have your letter, signed by me as the account executive. I hope our next visit will be more pleasant," Harkness said with a sigh.

"Harry, no hard feelings as far as you are concerned. You are a prince and always have been." Trace's color had returned to normal.

—

Once again, Chris went to the top floor restaurant and phoned Ralph. He was told that Trace was booked on a flight back to New York for 5 o'clock that afternoon and that he should immediately return to his office where he would be safest. He nodded into the cell phone and went to the elevator to descend to his office.

—

Trace punched the down button at the elevator bank outside the offices of Smith, Hay & Ward, and stared at the three floor indicators above the cars. As the car on the far right was descending to the 28th floor, he moved over and stood in front of it. The doors opened and Chris Masters began to emerge from the car, holding a large cola in his right hand. Trace saw that he was alone and pushed him back, spilling the drink all over the front of Chris's white dress shirt.

Chris sputtered, "Hey! What are you doing?"

"Let me tell you something, Masters. You better drop this whole thing and forget you ever knew Richard Trace."

He grabbed Chris by his coat labels and held him up against the back of the elevator car. "I have ways of dealing with little pricks like you. Got it, buster?"

When their eyes met, Chris was a full four inches off the floor.

Chris blurted out, "OK man, let me down."

This exchange took place while the doors were closing. As it happened, Sammy had seen Trace leave the office in a high state of agitation. Since Chris had shared his concern about the pending confrontation, he was concerned that Chris was out of the office and could possibly run into the large man. He saw Trace leave and followed at a safe distance. When he heard the commotion in the elevator he ran to intercede. Sammy forced open the doors and came at Trace, arms all akimbo, slapping and kicking like a beginning Karate student. The banker released Chris and threw up his arms in defense against the seemingly crazed young black man. Sammy managed to gouge Trace in his left eye and he yelled in pain. Chris brushed past Sammy out into the safety of the hallway.

"Who the hell are you, man?" yelled Trace.

Sammy kicked him in the shin, "Take that mothafucka!"

Trace reached out and grabbed Sammy's coat, taking a wild swing and just missing the side of his face. Sammy felt the force of the near miss and backed off, hands up, palms toward Richard.

"Whoa, man. Cool your jets," he snarled, nostrils flaring.

"I don't know who you are, buck, but if you work with Masters I will have your ass, you'll see," retorted Trace.

Sammy just smiled as the elevator doors closed on his antagonist. The older man shook himself into some semblance of order and descended to the lobby of the building. His eye was beginning to ache from Sammy's attack. *Maybe I can have Johnny take care of these guys for me*, he thought, oblivious to Pestrano's enmity.

Chris had gone to the men's room to clean up the cola spill and quiet his racing pulse. *My God, that man is a maniac. Thank Goodness he didn't pull out a gun and shoot me*, he thought. Sammy followed him as soon as Trace disappeared behind the closing elevator doors.

Chris used the automatic air dryer to blow dry his shirt. It took four applications before he was satisfied with the still-damp results. He straightened his tie and put back on his coat, which had a small rip on the left lapel.

"Thanks, Sammy. I don't know what would have happened to me if you hadn't come along when you did," said Chris.

"Anything for you, pal. I'm just sorry that I didn't hurt the bastard. What's with him anyway? He **must** be pretty pissed off at you to be holding you up off your feet," Sammy said.

"Sammy, he's out of his gourd. He knows that we suspect that he is doctoring the death claims. What he doesn't know is that we have evidence that he has been paying off someone to do the murders for the last few years so he can collect a bonus on the BOLI program at First Gotham," said Chris.

"You're kidding me!" exclaimed Sammy Sorrell.

"No, Sammy, it true. We have traced him to numbered accounts in the Caribbean where he has transferred hundreds of thousands over the years. The guy is a real bad actor. Unfortunately, he is also very influential with Harry, and I'm afraid I am going to get bad news when we go back into the office. I expect to be fired."

"No way, Chris! You are too valuable to the firm. I can't believe that Mr. Harkness would take the word of that creep over someone like you."

"The problem is that Trace controls an account worth millions in revenue to Smith, Hay & Ward. He has the leverage, and my bet is that he will use it. Our only hope is that he will lead us to his contacts who do the actual killing."

"What could you do even if you found out that information?" asked Sammy.

"It's not what I could do, it's what the FBI could do," revealed Chris.

"You mean the FBI is in on this deal already?" asked Sammy.

"Sam, remember seeing the older guy, sort of heavyset with a kind of rough orange-peal complexion who came by the office between Christmas and New Year's? Well, he has a contact with the FBI and I have met with them about the excessive death claims at First Gotham. They are in New York right now. Trace came here today because he figured that the only way they could know as much as they do would be because someone here, namely me, had spilled the beans to them. He made no bones about it at our meeting. No, Sammy, it's all over for me at Smith, Hay & Ward," said Chris with resignation.

"Then I will walk, too, man. They can shove this job as far as I am concerned. I can always do street painting and make enough scratch to get by," he said with bravado.

The two friends returned to the office. Sally greeted them as they stepped into the reception area, "Chris, Mr. Harkness told me to have you go directly to his office the minute you returned. He seemed disturbed to me."

"OK, Sally, thank you," he replied.

"Here we go, Sammy. Just as I thought," he whispered.

Harry Harkness did not even ask him to be seated. He simply told him that his services were no longer needed at Smith, Hay & Ward and that he was to get his personal belongings from his desk, turn in his keys, and leave immediately. He would be sent the usual pay at the end of January. His effective termination date would be January 15th. Chris hung his head and turned away. It was clear that there was nothing he could do or say that would change Harry's mind.

This little adventure had gotten him beaten up, at least mentally, and nearly physically, and now it had cost him his job. It was still possible that Trace would sue Smith, Hay & Ward, and they would, in turn, come after him. Then, there was Sarah. She had warned him to not push this matter; how would she react? How would they survive on just her salary? But, worst of all, what if Trace were to get away with all these murders? Chris was, of course, still convinced of his guilt, more so than ever after witnessing his enormous temper first hand.

—

Richard Trace returned to O'Hare and was inside the terminal by 4:30. He was early, but was agitated with the events of the day and in a hurry to get to his gate area. The multicolored lights above the moving walkway in the underground tunnel between concourses B and C flashed on and off, giving his face an animated scowl, amplified by the fact that he was fiercely chewing gum. It was almost as if his face disappeared each split second as the bright lights flashed overhead. Trace heeded the recorded warning to *please look down* at the end of the walkway, went up to gate area C-9 and found a relatively quiet corner in the waiting area. He dialed Harry's now familiar number on his cell phone.

"Harkness, this is Trace."

"Yes, Richard."

"When I left your office I was attacked by a tall, thin black kid who apparently is a friend of Masters. Does he work for you?'

"That sounds like Sorrell. Did he have what the kids call dreadlocks?

"That's the one. Looks like an oversized tarantula," said Trace. "I want that fucker fired, too! He almost poked my eye out."

"He is only a temporary worker for us, but I will terminate his contract. I'm sorry for all of this, Richard. I will take over the management of your account personally from now on."

"That is a good idea, Harry. I appreciate your understanding. Hope to see you in New York soon," said Trace and punched out. Only then did he grab a newspaper and sit down in the waiting area.

—

Duk Lon Ki had left San Francisco on the 10:45 United flight that arrived in Chicago at 4:21. He was to continue on to LaGuardia on the 5 o'clock Shuttle leaving from gate 9, concourse C. His flight de-planed its passengers at gate C-7. He immediately went to the nearest public telephone and called Johnny Pestrano.

"Johnny, it's Duk. I'm in Chicago. I...."

Pestrano interrupted him, "You are not going to believe this, but Trace is on your same flight from O'Hare. He went there to have it out with the actuarial firm that spilled the beans to the feds. I'm going to have Fredo meet your plane at LaGuardia outside the security stations. He'll be packing iron. You can join him and take Trace directly out to New Jersey. Manny is all set. He expects "guests" around 10:00 tonight. I'll let him know you'll be along. Once you get in the car, Fredo will give him a sedative. This stuff will knock him out for a while and when he comes to he'll be a little giddy, kind of like a friendly drunk."

"How did you find out about his trip to Chicago?" asked Duk.

"Well, when Fredo reported that he did not show up as planned, we threw out our net at all the public transportation centers and he had used his own name to book the flights to and from Chicago. We then figured that he would be going to see the actuarial firm and called them to confirm his arrival, which they were happy to confirm. The rest was easy," replied Johnny.

"When you get to your gate there in Chicago you will be able to spot Trace. He's about six-four, and will be wearing a dark overcoat and a fedora. He always pulls it down to try to hide his ears. He looks like a Vulcan, you know, Mr. Spock?"

—

At 5:05 United shuttle #676 took off for LaGuardia with two passengers linked together by a series of common events. Richard Trace was oblivious to any company other than the usual passengers, all of whom were strangers as far as he could tell. The flight was totally uneventful, even if somewhat suspenseful to the passenger who was also an observer. After many years of practice in that role he knew how to become virtually invisible.

Barbara and Ralph had checked with the airlines and knew that Richard Trace was expected on United flight 676, arriving at LaGuardia at 8 that evening. They had asked Bernie to help them get back on the trail. He was waiting just outside the restricted area of the terminal, with Ralph and Barbara outside in his car.

At 8:01 the plane pulled up to the gate at LaGuardia. Trace hustled off as soon as he could. Since Duk had been in the first class section, he had to linger and let Trace pass him on the way out of the concourse area. As soon as Trace cleared the security area, he was met by two men in heavy dark winter overcoats. The larger man held him by the elbow, and when he tried to twist free, the smaller, younger man grabbed him and said something that looked to be a warning, looking down at his left front pocket. Trace seemed to freeze and stiffen. He nodded his assent and the older man began to lead him toward the terminal exit. Just then, a Chinese man with a scar over his eye joined the group and was greeted enthusiastically by the younger man.

Wow, it looks like the professionals have arrived, and Trace was not expecting them, Bernie speculated.

He immediately dialed Barbara on his cell-phone and she answered on the first ring. "Barb, the pros have met Trace and have him in their grip. They appear to be armed. I am on my way, and if we are lucky we will be able to follow them. Be alert, they should be coming out the door in a minute or less."

"I've got them, Bernie. OK, they are crossing the street, and....Oh shit, they are going the other way. Hurry up!"

Bernie came at a full sprint and burst out the door, looking frantically for their car. Ralph began to honk the horn. Bernie turned and took one step and slipped on some black ice covering the sidewalk. He went down in a heap. Barbara got out of the car and ran to his aid. He sat up holding his elbow, his breath coming in gasps.

"Barb, I, I'm afraid I may have broken it."

She helped him to his feet. Ralph had come up to them and helped Bernie to the car. Any thought of following Trace and his captors was lost in their concern for their friend. They headed for the nearest hospital in Queens. Fortunately for Bernie, he only had a bad contusion; nothing was broken. The three of them could only imagine what was happening to Richard Trace.

"I'm not sure what we would have accomplished by following them anyway," said Barbara.

"Well, they might have led us to the big boss, whoever he is. It's a sure thing that Trace is not doing all these murders by himself. The thing is, those guys didn't seem to be rescuing him tonight. My guess is that they have very sinister plans for him. Why else would they take him away against his will?" questioned Bernie.

"What he said to Chris, you know, the threat, that sounded like he was still in bed with the pros to me," offered Ralph.

"Ralph, I think he probably still believed that all was well with the pros and their little greeting party took him by surprise. I think it is time to talk to the Organized Crime Unit of the Bureau here in New York. Maybe my descriptions will ring a bell for them. If they have a sketch artist, I think I can get pretty close, especially on the Chinese guy and the younger man at the airport. Let's give them a call in the morning, Barb."

"I agree, Bernie. Besides, you have a business to run and it is time to get them in on this case. We have more than enough evidence to warrant a full-blown investigation. You have more than paid me back for the leads I gave you. We can take it from here," she said.

"Barb, I appreciate your understanding. I just hope this all works out for Chris Masters. He sounds like a nice kid. I'd hate to see him lose his job over this deal. The thing is, with his talent he could get another job in a *New York minute.*"

"That's what Ralph and I told him, but he is really down. We will have to give him a lot of moral support when we return to Chicago. I'm afraid his fiancée will be less than supportive. She told him all along not to get involved in this thing," said Barbara.

"I don't know about you guys, but I could use a drink," Bernie offered.

"We assume you are buying," grinned Barbara.

"No way, Barbara. The drinks are on me," said Ralph.

Barbara gave him a wink and nodded her agreement. It had been a long day, and the new day had already begun.

Chapter 24

At 9 p.m. Manny and Dimitri again got in the panel truck and drove through a driving rain to the pier outside the Dockside Inn in East Newark. The lights were out as the restaurant only served lunch during the winter. The kitchen staff and wait-help had prepared for the next day
and had left by 4 p.m. The last thing they did was dispose of the clean garbage, the left-over food, throwing it into the brackish waters of the Passaic.

The two dark-garbed men walked briskly to the spot on the pier where Manny had set the trap. It was at least 15 degrees colder than earlier in the day. They wore heavy midnight blue slickers with hoods and thick leather work gloves. Manny swung down over the side of the pier and found the rusty trap in the beam of his flashlight. He began the twenty foot crawl across to the far side. There was no movement in the cage, but as he approached he saw the unmistakable mass and shape of a nice fat wharf rat.

Mary lay quiet, hoping for an opportunity. As Manny reached out to untie the first binding, she lashed out at his hand.

"Mean lil' mutha--huh, heh, heh, heh.! We got a nice un, Dimi!" he yelled.

Manny made sure the gate was securely fastened, then he cut the lashing on the outside post. The twine fell away into the water some eight feet below. Somewhere a foghorn pierced the night air. He had a tight grip on the metal handle. The cage shook violently with Mary's efforts to get at his hand. Manny laughed at his good fortune.

"Da boss would love this one," he beamed.

"Dimitri, reach down with both your hands. Grab tight, he's a fighter!"

He held the trap up to his assistant and felt the large man's tight grip. He held the handle throughout, and swung himself back up on the pier. They put down the cage, and watched the rat in the bright beam of the flashlight.

"Wow, dis is a beeg one. Must be a grand-daddy," he squealed with delight.

Dimitri turned away. Rodents of all kinds made him nervous. This huge brown rat made him feel sick to his stomach. They carried the cage by its handles back to the truck and placed it with care in the space behind the bench seat in the passenger cab for the drive back to the warehouse.

—

At 10:15 Carlo and his passengers, Alfredo, Duk and Trace approached the warehouse. They drove in a thick fog, the headlights on high beam bouncing back in their faces. Trace was still groggy from the sedative that Fredo had injected into him as soon as they had gotten in the car. If it were not for the fact that he weighed over 200 pounds, Trace would have still been out cold. As it was he slept most of the trip. The drug was mixed to keep him sedated for up to four hours, not unconscious, but groggy and compliant. The fog would enable them to move up the timetable. Visibility was down to fifty feet. Alfredo quietly opened the door of the town-car, motioning Carlo to stay with Trace. He and Duk went to the warehouse and pushed open the door.

"Manny?" called Fredo.

"Yeah, Fredo, I'm here. We ready, ol' Dimi and me. We got beeg rat ready, too. He's a hungry mutha, oh yeah." He danced around in the cold room. They had a pot-bellied stove, but hadn't yet fired it up. Just then he noticed Duk.

"Is that Mr. Duk? Johnny told me you would be with Fredo. I have heard about you from the boss. Dis a real honor for me. He told me about this bad guy we are *doing* tonight."

"Hi there, Manny. Yeah, I'm looking forward to watching this bastard taste it. He made me do a bad thing to a Chinese lady several years ago, and tonight it's pay-back time."

They locked grips in a high-five. The mutual respect in that gesture was obvious.

"Hey, we got work to do. Ready?" smiled Manny.

"Let's have at it," Duk grinned back.

"Man, it's cold in here," said Alfredo.

"Hey, you get used to it," said Manny. Dimitri nodded his agreement.

"Well, we have a date for your rat," said Alfredo. "He's pretty big, but we have him doped up.

Where do you want him?"

"In the back of da truck," said the Filipino. He pointed to the delivery style van with doors that swung out in the back. Manny opened the doors to reveal shelves on either side filled with tools. In the center was a metal pole from floor to ceiling.

"We can tie him to da pole," he smiled.

Alfredo could not help smiling and shaking his head.

"My uncle told me about you. He said you saw the humor in everything."

"Yeah, got to have um good time. I remember you from li'l boy, Fredo. You were a rascal then. You should have seen him then, Duk. A real tiger."

Dimitri accompanied Alfredo outside and they got Manny's help in half-lifting Trace out of the town-car. He was a willing participant, but he was just barely able to use his legs.

"Hey guys," he giggled. "Be cool. Just call me Slam Dunk."

The narcotic was still working. They half-dragged, half-carried him to the truck, then lifted him up and placed him against the pole in the back. Manny produced a pair of handcuffs and quickly and expertly hooked Trace to the pole by his wrists. He was not aware of his situation until his nose began to itch and he was unable to scratch it.

"Hey, can someone scratch my nose?" he giggled again.

"You get plenty scratch soon, you," replied Manny.

Duk gave a grim nod of understanding. He knew full well what was in store for Richard Trace. He closed the door and twisted the handle shut, slapping Manny's hand when he had finished.

Manny lifted the heavy head cage and carried it to the side of the truck.

"Lemme show you how it works," he said to Duk and the others. "See here, dis little lock comes undone, and she gets broke into two parts." He opened the mask like a clam shell. "Da neck hole is down here." He pointed to the rubber encased ring at the bottom of the device.

"We clamp it over his head from behind, like dis." He snapped it shut.

"Then we open dis here." He showed them how he could slide up an opening into the side of the device. "Dis same size as da hole in da rat cage."

Dimitri blanched. "No, no, Manny. You're not really going to do that to him!" he cried.

"Dat's what da boss wants. Dis guy, he one bad mudda. You don't fuck wit Johnny Pestrano," he said with profane reverence.

"Fredo, you tell Mr. Pestrano, Manny, he took care of this one, ya?"

"OK, Manny, we certainly will. Carlo and I will wait here until you and Duk get back," said Alfredo Rizzo.

"Can I stay here, too, Manny?" begged Dimitri.

"Him beeg baby, don't want to see what we do to this buggah. OK, Dimi, you make a fire for these guys. Duk and I will be back in less than an hour."

"We go down to Bayonne, down Hook Road to da pier on Kill Van Kull. I'll drive," he volunteered.

Duk Lon Ki sprang eagerly to the other side of the truck. Manny jiggled the keys, grinning broadly.

"You ready, Duk?" he asked.

"Drive on, Manny," Duk smiled.

Manny drove in silence through the fog. It was slow going. At 10:30 they arrived at Hook Road.

"Just down here, we'll turn right," Manny said to Duk.

He drove the truck to the end of the dock area and turned off the headlights. The black, oily pier loomed ahead through the thick fog, disappearing into the Kill. The fog was so thick that they couldn't even see the lights of Staten Island, just 600 yards across the water from where they sat. Duk went around and opened the back of the truck, and Manny hopped up to unlatch Trace from the pole. He dragged his now limp body to the edge of the compartment and folded him down over Duk's shoulder.

"You take 'um, I'll bring da stuff."

The four living creatures proceeded out onto the pier. Only two would return. Duk had to drag Trace along as he was a much taller man. Even with his strength it was difficult. When they had gone about 100 yards Manny called for a stop. There was no sound. He went to the side. The metal ladder was where he remembered it. He descended with the cages, one at a time and placed them on the two foot wide ledge about ten feet down from the top of the pier where Duk stood with Trace leaning against his slender body.

"Bring 'um down," urged Manny.

Duk hefted the limp body over his shoulder and swung out over the edge of the pier. He laboriously made his way down the metal rungs, then swung Trace around and seated him on the ledge. Sweat was pouring off him from every pore of his body with the effort, even in the cold foggy air. You didn't tell me it would be such hard work, Manny!" he teased.

"It make it more pleasure for you, Duk," he said with a fierce grin.

Trace eyes blinked open and he asked, "Where are we going, gang?"

The narcotic was now beginning to wear off. There was no time to lose. Manny clamped the handcuffs onto his right wrist; he had Duk help him stand Trace up against the wooden post. He hooked Trace's arms around it, and clamped the cuffs over his left wrist. Next, he tied his legs securely to the bottom of the post, feeling the first splash of water against his heavily gloved hands.

"Hey Manny, the tide is rising!" yelled Duk.

"Oh yeah, that's true," said Manny. It was just as he had planned.

Trace's still groggy body hung down from his shoulders, stretching the handcuffs and tearing at his wrists. From time to time he would start to come around. The water was now covering the ledge every few seconds, then it would recede. Manny lifted the head cage and opened the clasps with a snapping noise. It opened wide on its hinges. He slipped it over Trace's head and slammed it shut, clicking the latches closed and locked in one fluid motion, the rubber ring firmly around the tall man's neck.

"What's this?" cried Trace, trying to get at it with his hands. His wrists began to bleed with the effort. The narcotic was rapidly losing its effect with his exertion. The weight of the cage forced his head and upper body down, putting even more pressure on his swollen and bloody wrists. He moaned out loud. Duk stepped back onto the ladder, and turned the flashlight on Trace's contorted face.

Manny's eyes flashed in the dim light into a look that Duk had rarely seen before. "I fix dis mutha. He fuck with my friend Johnny, I fuck with him."

"Now for you, mothafucka!" he sneered at Trace.

He held the rat trap up in his right hand by the handle, and slid the side of the mask open. Trace rotated his left eye toward him. Their eyes met. Manny could see the fear in the eyes of the larger man. Duk stared at the scene, transfixed with amazement at the tortuous frenzy of his slender Filipino companion.

"No, no, no, please!" screamed Trace. He was writhing violently in spite of the terrible pain to his arms and wrists. Manny held up the trap and locked the two metal devices together and sprang the doors open. Mary saw her opportunity and charged into the opening. Manny prodded her with a knife he had brought for cutting the binding cord. He could see that the battle had been joined. It had been more than six hours since she had last eaten. Manny slammed the sliding door shut and bolted it down. The water was rising. It was now up to his knees. He motioned Duk to ascend the ladder, then followed, carrying the rusty trap. Below they heard the muffled cries of Richard Trace.

"Bye-bye, Miss Americum pie," sang Manny Ramiscal.

The tide was rising rapidly now, as Manny knew it would. It soon rose up to Trace's chest level. Every other wave would sweep into the cage and splash on both of the inhabitants, living creatures locked in mortal combat. Mary saw an opening and forced her way inside. In a final desperate attempt to fight off his attacker, Trace bit down with his remaining strength. His powerful jaws crushed Mary's back left leg, mangled her tail, and loosened her bowels. His last sensation on earth was the stringent taste of her discharge. His jaw slackened.

She had beaten her human foe, but now Mary now had to deal with the briny water of the Kill Van Kull, which threatened to drown her. Suddenly she sensed her escape route and used her powerful forepaws to claw her way to freedom. No sound had come from beneath the pier for several minutes. Manny turned and nodded to

Duk. They walked slowly back to the truck. The heavy fog smelled of brine and tar. The only sound was the faint murmur of traffic on the bridge nearly a mile to the west.

"Les go, Duk. Its all over," he declared with satisfaction.

Duk stared straight ahead, reliving that night when he had encountered Lily at the Mark Hopkins Hotel. Life had finally come full circle. Manny drove quietly out onto Hook Road and turned north toward the warehouse. He had his own silent thoughts--they were of the jungles in Vietnam. It was necessary for each of these men to dwell on an event far in their past to replace the grim reality of the current killing. They each understood and respected the need for silence during the ride back to the warehouse. There would be enough separation by the time they got back so that nonchalant bravado could be expressed, and even welcomed.

Chapter 25

That next morning, Wednesday the 20th of January, was icy bright. Ralph and Barbara had stayed at a small hotel near Bernie's office on the lower east side. Ralph had made himself a cup of coffee in his room, using the paper packets of coffee, powdered milk and lumps of sugar. It tasted awful. He was just starting to apply shaving cream with an ancient brush that he had brought from home when the phone rang.

"Ralph? It's Barbara. How are you this morning?" she asked.

"I'd be better if I could get a good cup of coffee."

"I noticed a coffee shop off the lobby. Can you meet me there in a half-hour?"

"You've got a deal, Barbara."

They were the first customers, and the shop was still cold. Barbara was glad she was wearing her heavy sweater.

"We need to make contact with the Bureau here in New York. Then I will call Tom Garcia and let him know that this case has developed into something the FBI should be involved with. I had filled him in on some of the background last week and he gave me permission to take it at least as far as we have gone through last night. Now it may be a while before Trace surfaces again, so we may have to be in New York for the duration. What is your status at NTSB, Ralph?" she asked.

"Actually, Barbara, I called in sick Monday. I get five weeks vacation now, and I also have accumulated several weeks of sick leave, so I can stay here as long as necessary. I should call my boss and let him know that I will be out for, let's say, two weeks for starters. I'll call him later this morning."

"I hope you agree that we had to tell Bernie to get back to his own business?" she asked, then continued, "It just wouldn't be fair to ask him to continue working on this case with us when things are so indefinite. I want to get over to the Bureau this morning and bring them up to speed on what we have learned so far. With any luck, they will assign one of their Special Agents to the case to work with us. I gather that you intend to stay on and help me?" she asked.

"Barbara, this is a lot more interesting than most of my investigations, and I really want to see Trace brought to justice. That may sound corny, but its how I feel."

By 9:30 that morning Barbara had made contact with the Manhattan FBI office and they had reviewed the case with the Bureau chief. He had assigned a young agent, Lance Henry, to the case. Barbara would be the case manager. They spent the rest of the morning with the Organized Crime Unit. That afternoon, the sketch artist made a visit to the Cool Detective Agency and made drawings of the three men who had met Richard Trace at LaGuardia based on the verbal descriptions given him by Bernie Gerson. The OCU obtained a photograph of Richard Trace and made an entry in the missing persons section of the Internet and Interpol. They settled into the rather boring routine of background investigation.

Ralph called his boss, Fred Waltham, at the Chicago headquarters of the NTSB.

"So you want two weeks off? Have you found a girlfriend, Ralph?" he queried.

"Sumpin' like dat," muttered Ralph.

"Well, keep your powder dry, ol' boy. I'll see you in mid-February. Actually, you have chosen a good time to be away. Things are usually slow this time of year anyway."

"Thanks for your understanding, boss. I'll see you soon," he replied. He turned to Barbara, "OK, I'm here for the duration."

—

Mary, the Norwegian wharf rat, had survived the trap and the cage, but she had been gravely wounded. Trace's bite had broken her left leg, and four of her unborn had been crushed. She was alone on a strange pier, in unknown waters. The water here was much more briny, and somehow colder. There didn't seem to be any other rats out here, and there was no apparent food supply. Instinct told her that she needed to return to her lair on the Passaic River. Somehow, she knew that she should swim to the west. She was able to make it to the Bayonne Bridge by the next night, having feasted on a bloated hotdog along the way.

The next day she crossed the Newark Bay from Bayonne to just east of Newark Airport, keeping the sound in the sky to her left. She knew that the sound of jet engines rising into the sky meant that she was on the right track. She took two days to work her way along the western shore of the Bay, alternately swimming and crawling along through the mud flats. As she traveled northward the water became slightly warmer and less briny. There was ample flotsam both for food and for rest. The fourth night her remaining babies were stillborn near the headwaters of the Passaic. She rested there for two days in some tall reeds next to the river and recovered some of her strength.

Old Mary's back left leg was now useless. She discovered she could float upriver with the tide, then rest offshore when the tide ebbed. Using this tactic she returned to her pier by the Dockside Inn at the end of the seventh day. Mary wearily approached her lair only to find it occupied by two younger rats. When she tried to enter, they aggressively rejected her efforts. She was an old, badly injured rat without a safe haven. She didn't have the strength of body or will to try to survive in this hostile environment. Her time had come. As a quarter moon was just beginning to show itself on the horizon, she jumped into the river and floated off toward the Bay on the next body bobbed up and down in the silvery waves for a few hundred yards and then disappeared. Richard Trace had claimed his last victim.

—

On Friday, the 22nd, Barbara and Ralph discovered that the Cayman company, WAT, Inc., was an acronym for Without A Trace, Inc., a kind of clever play on words with his last name.

Barbara told Ralph, "With the existing secrecy laws down there, we have come up empty as far as finding out where the money went after it was put in his account. We do know that there is no way to access the account, so any money left there will stay there. Even his wife cannot get at it. The bank has some sort of voice recognition technology."

"How about the credit and phone cards?" asked Ralph.

"They're mostly luxury items purchased by Mrs. Trace; or presents to her from Mr. Trace. By the way, she is apparently a well-preserved lady from the photo we have obtained. Their travel is quite limited as far as we can determine. Their life is luxurious, but pretty dull."

"Like my life," joked Ralph.

"Well, this little adventure is surely pepping it up," she retorted.

The missing person notice had gotten the attention of the media, and both the newspapers and TV reporters were requesting information from the FBI. So far they had managed to keep a lid on the publicity except for some small articles about a "missing bank executive." There would likely be an explosion of publicity should Trace be found dead, which is exactly what they expected.

While the investigation took most of the early hours of each day; Ralph and Barbara found that they were spending long hours together with little to do in the afternoon and evening. The new friends discovered a mutual interest in impressionist painting. After numerous visits to the various New York art museums they both agreed that the Chicago Art Institute had a superior collection. Ralph was particularly fond of Seurat's *Sunday in the Park with George*. The two investigators were becoming not only collaborators, but were developing a strong friendship. Lance would usually join them for lunch, but would be off to Brooklyn Heights to be with his new bride by 5 o'clock most days. Ralph and Barbara had dinner together each night, and discovered that they preferred Chinese or Italian cuisine. Their conversations usually centered on the particular activities they were enjoying, but they also had time to tell each other about their personal lives. Ralph told her about his wife, and her tragic death in a car accident some 30 years earlier. It was the first time he had talked about it in all of that time, and Barbara was the first person he had ever told that Charlotte had been pregnant at the time.

"Oh, Ralph, I'm so sorry," she had said, reaching out to hold his hand.

"It was a long time ago, Barbara. It seems like a bad dream to me now," he answered.

The next week began without any hope of a breakthrough. There was no new data, and no one had responded to the missing person announcement. The media had disappeared. It had become yesterday's news. Ralph and Barbara had decided to give it one more week before returning to Chicago. Lance Henry had been assigned another case. In this city, New York City, it was swallowed up in the swill of white noise that inundated daily life. But that was about to change.

—

Chris Masters was going through a painful period in his life. He spent his mornings moping around the apartment, watching television and reading the want adds in the *Tribune*. Nothing seemed to be appropriate for his background. In the afternoon he would meet with Sammy and shoot baskets with his friends. Sammy had grown up on the South Side and had many friends on the streets. His talent as an artist was almost exceeded by his proficiency on the basketball court. His high-school friends, predictably, called him Spider. His wingspan was enormous, and it seemed that no one could throw the ball anywhere near him without it being intercepted.

Chris was able to hide his depression during these times, but on the train ride back out to Oak Park the reality of his situation would hit home again, and by the time Sarah got home he would be in a king-sized funk.

He and Sammy had explored the idea of going to the media with the Trace story. Sammy had enthusiastically encouraged him to "expose the whole nefarious scheme." As he thought about it, the flimsiness of his case filled him with doubt. *There aren't any bodies, just numbers, and the public will not understand*, he reasoned. When he proposed the idea to Sarah, she made it clear that he would be viewed as a madman-- simply bitter over being fired from his job.

"It is time for you to put on a coat and tie and go get a job. We have rent to pay in less than two weeks, Christopher!" she shouted.

The news from New York was discouraging. Trace had disappeared. It certainly seemed like he had been abducted by the mob, but again, there was no hard evidence. Ralph and Barbara were trying to be optimistic about the case, but even they were encouraging him to look for a new position.

"Even if we solve this case, there is no assurance that Smith, Hay & Ward will take you back," said Barbara. "How is Sarah taking this?" she asked.

"She is not thrilled with me at this point," he confessed.

"Chris, I am going to arrange for you to talk to my dad. He has been in the insurance business for over 35 years, and knows all the players there in Chicago. I'm sure he can get you some interviews with various companies that have actuarial work. There are several company home offices in the immediate area."

"That would be great, Barbara. I really appreciate it," said Chris, encouraged for the first time since Harkness had fired him. *Yes, that's it. I've been fired after only six months on my first real job. That's my problem.* He had finally admitted the reality of it to himself.

Barbara's offer gave Chris a slight glimmer of optimism. He could look forward to the weekend and the next week with some hope.

Barbara confided to Ralph that she was really worried about Chris, and that she had offered to have her father help out.

"Will he be able to get Chris a job, Barbara?" asked Ralph.

"If anyone knows the insurance market in Chicago it's my dad. I just hope that Harry Harkness doesn't blacklist him. We shall see what happens over the next two or three weeks. Ralph, it's Friday night, how about a movie?" she asked.

"I was thinking of Radio City. I've never seen the show there. I understand the girls have great legs." he teased.

"Mine don't do enough for you, Ralph? All those years of ballet, and I get a put-down like that?" She grinned at him.

"So that's why you have such great posture?"

"Well, it wasn't from painting, which was my other passion," she answered. "OK, Mr. Ralph Murphy, I will attend Radio City Music Hall with you this evening," she announced formally.

"The lady does me a great honor, a great honor indeed!" said Ralph.

Chapter 26

On January 25 a deckhand on the freighter *San Juan Remo* out of Port Elizabeth spotted what looked like a diver hung up on a pier on the south side of the Bayonne docks halfway through the Kill Van Kull. He signaled to his captain who confirmed the sighting and called the Coast Guard to check it out. Captain George Batterly of the Coast Guard clipper *Liberty Maiden* and his crew were sent to investigate.

"Yo, skip, looks like a diver to me," cried first-mate Carl Shivers. "Bring her closer."

As they approached the pier Carl noticed the sun gleaming on something at the back of the post.

"My God, Captain, I think he's tied to that post or something!" he exclaimed.

Captain Batterly raised his binoculars and hit the zoom button. "Oh, my! I'm afraid you're right. We had better call the Bayonne Police Department. This looks like it could be an execution-style murder."

The *Liberty Maiden* stayed put, engines on throttle, waiting for the police to arrive. They were accompanied by the fire department dive team, which turned out to be unnecessary because it was low tide. Trace's body was entirely out of the water, which, at low tide, was four feet below the ledge on which his feet rested. Sergeant Boyce Summers was the first to descend the rusty ladder to the oily support timbers of the pier.

"Holy shit, you guys are not going to believe this one," he yelled. "This guy's face is all eaten."

"No, that must be decomposition. He's probably been there for several days," replied his partner, Barry Breem.

"Barry, I'm telling you, it's not decomposition. The rest of his body is fine. It's just his face, and his neck. There's a hole in his neck," cried Boyce.

"Henry, call for an ambulance, and Boyce, we are going to drop a harness to bring him up. Barry, get down there and give Boyce a hand," Lieutenant Parsons ordered.

The men had to cut through the handcuffs with some heavy metal clippers. Trace fell forward and Bryce and Barry just managed to keep him from falling into the water. He was then tied to the harness and hauled up onto the pier. The squad leader, Lieutenant Parsons, rolled the corpse over on its back.

"Jeez, Boyce, you are right! I've never seen anything like this before."

At age 27, Parsons was the youngest of the men on the squad. All of them had grown up in the New York metropolitan area; they had a strictly East Coast orientation. When they got back to the Bayonne precinct, they told their precinct captain about their findings.

"Sounds like a Philippine rat cage to me," said Captain Loggia. "Any sign of a rat in there?"

"No, Captain, but it may have eaten its way out through the guy's neck."

"Yeah, that's the only way out. Rats have good instincts when they are desperate. Must be a mob hit. Any ID on the guy?"

"Only a ring inscribed, 'To Slam, with Love-Diana'," replied Parsons.

"OK, we'll check the computer for missing persons. In the meantime, call the coroner up in Jersey City. Tell him I want to know the cause of death, and we need him to do fingerprints and a dental. Lieutenant, what's on the missing person screen?"

"Let's take a look. It's mostly teenagers, actually, mostly female teenagers. This guy was probably at least middle age."

"What's that these days?" asked Loggia with amusement.

"Oh, around forty or more," answered Parsons.

"Jesus, I'm surrounded by a bunch of babies," retorted Captain Loggia.

"Here's a bank executive--Richard N. Trace, age 59, 6' 4 1/2", 210 pounds, dark hair. Yep, that could be him."

"Who posted the M.P.?"

"The Manhattan branch of the FBI," replied Parsons.

"Is there a number?"

"Yes sir. I'll call them right away."

"Federal Bureau of Investigation," came the crisp response.

"Yes, Miss, this is Lieutenant Parsons of the Bayonne, New Jersey, police. We have a John Doe that matches the description of your missing person, Mr. Richard N. Trace."

"Just a moment please."

"This is Special Agent Henry. You say you found someone that meets the description of Richard Trace?"

"Yes sir."

"Where is he?"

"He's on the way to the coroner's office in Jersey City."

"Dead, huh?"

"I'll say. His face had been eaten away by...." Parsons stopped in mid-sentence at the urgent "cut" signal of his boss.

"Lieutenant, did you say eaten?"

"Well, sir, we will have to wait for the coroner's report, but he is certainly deceased."

"Are you in charge there?"

"No sir. That would be Captain Loggia."

"May I speak to him, please?"

"This is Captain Loggia."

"Captain, this is Special Agent Lance Henry. We posted the missing person notice on Mr. Trace last week. His death is under investigation by the Bureau. The circumstances of his death may compromise that investigation."

"Yes sir, I understand. What do you want me to do?"

"Look, my office is in midtown Manhattan. I can be in Jersey City in less than an hour. Give me the address of the coroner's office and we can meet there, OK?"

"Sure, it's right on the main drag, Garfield Avenue, number.... Let's see, uuh.... 2201. I'll call and tell them to expect us, Agent....?"

"Henry, Lance Henry. And, Captain, I will be bringing Special Agent Barbara Knudsen and our associate, Ralph Murphy, with me."

"No problem, see you there."

—

Loggia met Lance, Barbara and Ralph in the outside lobby at the coroner's office for northern New Jersey at 4:30 p.m. At 4:45 the coroner, Dr. Stuart

Lampkin, joined them in the small conference room just down the hall from the office. They settled into their chairs around a white laminated conference table. Stuart shook his head sadly. He had thin sandy hair and a long sallow face.

"You know, folks, I've been at this for 36 years, and I've never seen anything like this before."

"What is it Dr. Lampkin?" asked Loggia.

"This guy appears to have had his face and neck eaten by a rat," exclaimed Lampkin.

"Are you sure?" asked Agent Henry.

"Well, we found rat feces in his gums, for starters. Then the claw marks and bites would indicate it was a rat. I've seen lots of rat bites, just not like this, so concentrated."

"They tell me he had a sort of mask over his head," said Loggia.

"Well, it had been removed by the time the body got here, but, yes, that's also my understanding. There was evidence of a rubber collar--you know, black particles of rubber embedded in his neck, and chaffing that would indicate a tight collar."

"What else did you find, Doctor?" asked Loggia.

"His wrists were badly swollen and lacerated. He must have struggled something fierce. The amazing thing is that the cause of death was actually drowning. The hole in his neck--oh yes, the, uh, rat, must have eaten his way out through his neck. Anyway, that must have acted like a tracheotomy and kept him breathing, at least until the water--it was real briny water--got into his lungs. There is no doubt about the cause of death, it was definitely drowning. I've seen literally hundreds of drowning deaths over the years. Did I mention that I've been at this for over 36 years?"

"Yes, Doctor," they answered in unison.

"There were some marks on his ankles, but he seemed to struggle from the waist up for the most part."

"Could you tell how long he has been dead?" asked Barbara.

"I would estimate six or seven days. That water, being so briny and cold, would kind of preserve the body against decomposition. It is impossible to determine the exact time of death, but we can be sure it was at least 72 hours and less that two weeks."

"That tracks with the date of disappearance, right, Agent Henry?" asked the Chief, turning to Lance.

"Right," Barbara answered for him, turned to the examiner and asked, "Anything else?"

"Yes, he had traces of phencyclidine in his blood. It's a narcotic that induces drowsiness and euphoria, a kind of strange combination. He would have been like a happy drunk on that drug. I hope for his sake it was still working, but the marks of struggle would certainly indicate otherwise. Heavy exertion often has the effect of speeding the wearing-off process."

"So, his death certificate will read...?"

"Cause of death, you mean?"

"Yes, Doctor."

"Drowning is the primary cause. Animal wounds, secondary. Yup, that's what I intend to say in my write-up."

"OK, thank you Dr. Lampkin," concluded Barbara.

The four investigators walked out into the fading light of the January evening.

"What do you make of it, Captain Loggia?"

"Well, Agent Henry, how old are you?" he asked.

"I'm 26, Captain."

"You're way too young to have been in Vietnam. Well, we heard about this here Philippine head cage over there. Apparently, they have this device that wraps around the head like a diver's helmet, then they somehow let a rat loose in there and it struggles to get free. Oh yeah, they do it in a place where the water is rising up so that the rat is, uh--motivated to get out of the cage."

"And you think that is what happened here?"

"It sure sounds like it. What else could it be?"

"Do you have Filipino gangs here in Jersey?" asked Ralph.

"Not that I've ever heard of. No, I don't think so. What's your take?"

"We think he was mixed up with professionals, the mob, and that they kidnapped him and had him killed," answered Barbara.

"Maybe your mob boss spent some time in 'Nam and has a contact from over there," Loggia speculated.

"Could be. It certainly could be. We may never know. Thanks for your help, Captain Loggia."

———

After Loggia left, Barbara said, "How about talking to his wife? Maybe she can shed some light on things. I would imagine that the coroner's office will have notified her by now, so she will have a lot to deal with, but it has been over a week and I'll bet she knew what was coming."

"Good idea, Barbara. I guess you should just call her for an appointment, huh?" asked Ralph.

"I'm always the one you elect for the dirty work," she laughed.

"Well, you're certainly better at it than me, and you have the authority of the FBI," he replied.

—

Barbara had given the call her undivided attention since Ralph had suggested it, and by 9 a.m. the next morning, she had composed her presentation in her mind. She had to have several alternative lines depending on Mrs. Trace's responses, and she had rehearsed them all night.

"Are you ready, Barbara?" asked Lance, assuring her that the recording equipment was all set up for the call.

"Ready as I'll ever be," she replied evenly.

She punched in the numbers and waited while the phone rang. On the second ring a tired voice answered, "Hello."

"Mrs. Trace, this is Barbara Knudsen of the FBI. I am calling about the death of your late husband, Richard. We have reason to believe that his death was a criminal act. I am aware that you must have many things to take care of, but it is important that we have a chance to talk with you as soon as possible," she paused.

There was silence for a few seconds. Barbara waited, according to her plan. Her next statement would depend on Diana's response.

"When do I need to see you?" Diana asked compliantly.

"Could we come to your house this afternoon at one o'clock this afternoon?"

Ralph clasped his fists together in front of his face. "Yes!" he mouthed silently.

"That will be fine, Miss, er, er."

"Knudsen, Barbara Knudsen, and I will be with my associate, Ralph Murphy. It will just be the two of us."

"OK, Miss Knudsen, Thank you."

"She sounded like she was in a daze," said Barbara.

"My guess is that she suspects someone, and we need to draw that out of her," said Murphy.

—

At 9:45 a.m. Bernie Gerson called for Barbara.

"Barb, have you seen the *Post* this morning?"

"No Bernie, what's up?"

"You had better have someone go get one for you. Your boy Trace has made the front page."

A few minutes later Barbara and Ralph were staring at a headline **"MOB KILLING IN JERSEY**!" with a photo of Mrs. Richard Trace in front of her house in Alpine. She had on sun glasses and a white scarf wound around her head and neck. Her hand was held up in a defensive position, as if fending off the photographer.

"Wow, the press is after her like jackals on carrion," said Lance.

"My, aren't we literate this morning," said Barbara.

"Just thought I'd throw that in to gain some respect," Lance laughed.

"What does it say?" asked Ralph.

"Mr. Richard Trace was found murdered by the Bayonne police department this morning. He had apparently been dead for several days and had been tortured. The police would not release details under orders from the FBI. It is assumed that an organized crime family is involved.

Mr. Trace, age 59, lived in Alpine, New Jersey with his wife Diana. He was the President of the First Gotham Bank Life Insurance subsidiary in downtown Manhattan. He had been with them since 1987. Further details will be forthcoming when they become available."

"I hope the Alpine police have secured the property so that she will have some privacy," said Barbara. "Let's check to be sure they do, if they haven't already."

"Yeah, we don't need a mob scene this afternoon," said Ralph.

Lance Henry called the Alpine police and was assured that the street had been sealed off and only local traffic was being allowed in to the neighborhood. He told them to expect Barbara and Ralph that afternoon, and that they would also be bringing a van for surveillance purposes.

—

At one p.m., Barbara and Ralph arrived at the home of Diana Trace. It was in an elegant neighborhood of ivy covered walls and huge old deciduous trees with branches overhanging the road. The Traces' home was a dark brick Tudor, with a semi-circular pebble driveway behind a stone wall. It was mostly hidden from the street and appeared to have a forest behind it. From what they could see, it might have been the only house for miles around. There was no noise in the neighborhood.

A tall, willowy woman in sunglasses with a scarf over her head greeted them at the door. It was Mrs. Richard Trace. Diana guided them into the living room that looked out on a backyard with a large ornate fountain, spouting water in all directions. It was viewed through a series of large leaded-glass panes, which created a bright, iridescent scene. The light filtering into the room on this overcast January day created mottled shadows on Diana and her guests, but it produced glittering shards of rainbow colors where it hit the metal and glass edges of her avant-garde furniture. Barbara would remember the experience as if they had been in an old flickering silent movie. As they settled down in their chairs, the guests noticed that Diana's glasses were losing their sun shade and were becoming clear. She was a striking, apparently younger woman, but Ralph had been sure that the profile they had on her showed that the Traces' had been married for over thirty years--so she would be at least in her mid-fifties. *She sure doesn't show her true age*, he thought.

Barbara started by saying, "We are terribly sorry for your loss, Mrs. Trace."

"Thank you for saying that. I have had a few days to prepare for the shock of hearing that he was dead, but it is still hard. The press has been unmerciful; they are like bloodhounds."

"Yes, unfortunately, there is a prurient element in our popular press that is really obnoxious. We saw the headlines in the *New York Post* this morning with your picture. I'm afraid it will only get worse for you until the next sensational case comes along," said Ralph.

"Mrs. Trace...." Barbara began.

"Please call me Diana," she said quietly, still contemplating what Ralph had just said.

"Diana, I don't know how much the coroner's office told you, but it is clear to us that your husband was the victim of a crime--what we call an execution type murder. Do you have any idea who might be responsible for such an act?" asked Barbara.

Diana stared at her for a full thirty seconds. She seemed to be torn between two answers. Finally she said, "My husband could turn people off with his brusque manner, but he was a normal business executive. He did very well in his business, but there was never any evidence that he was mixed up with mobsters or anything like that, in spite of what the newspapers imply."

Her answer seemed well rehearsed and delivered. It was as if she had wanted them to come to her lair as soon as possible to hear this statement, then be gone from her life forever.

"Well, Mrs. Trace," it was Ralph, "we have evidence that he had a secret account in the Cayman Islands through which he moved substantial funds, including over $600,000 in the last few weeks."

"Over $600,000, my God!" she screamed. "That's a fortune for us--nearly a year's income," said Diana, without realizing that to federal employees on modest salaries it would seem fortune indeed.

"Well, yes. Do you know anything about that money, or where it went?" asked Barbara.

"I should say not. Richard never said much about his work, and especially about money. He gave me an allowance and, of course, I have my own family money, so it was never an issue for us. He kept his own checkbook at his office. What are you saying? That he was paying off some gangster?" There was a subtle change in her expression that both Ralph and Barbara sensed.

"That is certainly a possibility from our data, Mrs. Trace," replied Ralph.

Barbara pressed the button of a one-way digital pager and alerted Lance Henry in the agency van parked down the block to activate the listening device. She knew instinctively that the interview with Diana Trace would come to a close very soon. Barbara was hoping Diana would make a call that would lead them to her husband's killer, and possibly to the killer of several bank executives over the last few years.

Bernie and Barbara had concluded that Trace had been killed because his professional accomplices felt he had become a loose cannon. They had seen Trace abducted at the airport, clearly against his wishes. His re-appearance as a corpse had confirmed their suspicions. They wanted to know who those men at the airport were, and who they worked for. The sketches that the FBI artist had drawn from Bernie's descriptions had not borne any fruit. If they could link Trace with a professional criminal it would give the Bureau the impetus it needed to move the case higher up on the priority list. This visit to Trace's widow was a last ditch attempt to flush out that relationship, and so far it did not seem to be working. Their frustration level was again on overload.

"Ms. Knudsen, I can't imagine how I can help you. This is a world I know nothing about. I just want to get my own life in order, and that is going to take some doing. I don't even know which bills are paid. I may even have to dip into my trust fund to take care of things." She began to tremble noticeably.

Barbara took her hand and smiled, "Oh, I'm sure everything will be OK. He was an insurance executive, wasn't he? I'm sure he had plenty of life insurance. My father is in that business, and insurance men always have lots of coverage. They need to buy it to build up their belief in the product."

"I'm not so sure. He only had the minimum group coverage at work, $50,000, and he was eligible for $1,000,000. So, I'm not sure," she repeated, staring straight ahead as if in shock.

Barbara was so surprised at her answer that she had released Diana's hand. She looked over at Ralph to pick up the conversation.

"Well, Mrs. Trace, we will be going. We'll call you in a few days to see if you have thought of anything. I'm sure you must still be in shock over this. You have our condolences."

Diana walked them to the door and weakly waved good-bye as they got in their car and drove out the driveway to the quiet street. It was just 1:15.

"That was surreal," said Barbara as soon as they turned onto the street. "That weird light made her look like a ghost."

"You should have seen how **you** looked, especially after that business about her insurance coverage," said Ralph.

"Now that I have time to think about it, I remember my dad telling me that one of the ways to tell if an insurance person is a dedicated professional is to see if they have a lot of personal coverage. It is almost like a religion that creates a missionary zeal about the need for the product. Obviously, Trace had no such feeling for the product--just the result--the bonus money he collected when others had coverage," she observed.

Barbara poked him on the arm thoughtfully, "Do you think she will lead us anywhere?"

"If she does, it will happen soon or it won't happen at all," he predicted, "let's circle around and see if Lance has picked up anything.

At that very moment agent Lance Henry was listening to Diana's phone ringing. He patched Barbara and Ralph into his line so they could listen to the conversation.

"Johnny's Ristorante, may I help you?" came the deep European voice.

"I would like to speak to Mr. Pestrano," said Diana.

"Who's calling please?"

"Diana, uh, Diana Trace," she stammered.

"Hello," it was the familiar voice, calm and even.

"Johnny, this is Diana. I'm sure you have seen on the news that Richard was found killed yesterday. Two federal agents came to my house today. They said that Rich has been killed in a gangland execution. There was something about an account in the Cayman Islands. Do you know what's going on?"

"I can't help you Diana. None of this means anything to me." His voice was flat and unemotional.

She heard the line click.

Diana dropped the phone. She had hoped that Richard's death would evoke some sympathy from her former lover. Lance could hear her sobs through the dangling instrument. Clearly, Diana Trace had some sort of relationship with this Johnny Pestrano at Johnny's Ristorante.

"Wow. That happened in a hurry. These Traces really react quickly to pressure. Maybe that's why their pros got rid of him," whistled Henry.

"Let's get back to the office and see if any of those phone numbers match up with calls that Trace made. I seem to remember calls to a restaurant in Manhattan, but we decided that they were probably for dinner reservations," suggested Barbara. "Lance, call ahead and get that phone number. We should have you stay put for a while in case she makes any other calls."

"Or gets any calls," added Ralph.

"Got it, guys. I'll stay here for two or three hours and then join you in the office," said Lance.

By the time Barbara and Ralph returned to the Bureau office, their analysts had matched up the phone number that had been called in to them by agent Henry. There it was, late 1993 (3 calls), 1995 (one call), 1998 (two calls) and again this last year (one call). These calls had come from Richard Trace, and now his wife was calling the same number when it came to crunch time, and she was definitely not calling for dinner reservations. But how could they prove it? This Johnny Pestrano had not implicated himself in any way on the phone. So, what did they have?

Richard Trace had finagled the death claims in 1993, 1998 and again last year. He had transferred money into and out of a Cayman Island bank account in the same years, ever larger amounts as the years went by. He had made phone calls late in those same years to a Manhattan restaurateur. He had been brutally murdered shortly after the last call. Mrs. Trace had called the same Mr. Pestrano immediately after their visit. They had no proof of murder except that Trace himself had been murdered. It was possible that First Gotham Bank had simply had a bad run of luck with regard to death claims in the years in question. It was extremely circumstantial evidence, at best. Pestrano could claim that the calls were for dinner reservations, and who could dispute it? Whatever the relationship between Diana Trace and Johnny Pestrano, it would be denied by Pestrano. That was a certainty. What to do?

Barbara threw down her pencil. "There is no way we are going to implicate this Pestrano guy in any of this and make it stick. The Organized Crime unit at the Bureau now has Johnny Pestrano on their radar screen for the future. Maybe with this information they will be able to identify those sketches. I'll bet they won't want to pursue Trace's murder. Their attitude will be that the bad guys have solved an internal problem and have saved them the trouble. It is almost certain that First Gotham will not have any more excess death claims now that Richard Trace is no longer in the picture. Diana will have to struggle along on her trust fund."

"Yeah, tough life," muttered an exasperated Ralph Murphy.

Barbara shifted her weight and continued, "I'm sure the guys at the OCU will keep Pestrano under surveillance, but unless they can prove that money actually passed from Trace to him, the overall evidence is extremely flimsy. Then there is the problem of proving that there were actually any murders at all, as they all were made to appear to be natural deaths, and very effectively, I might add. Now that Richard Trace has been eliminated, we have, in a sense, accomplished our mission. It's not very satisfying, but it will have to do," she concluded.

"Kind of like those forest fires out west last fall. They say it is mother-nature's way to keep balance in the environment. Sometimes nature has a better way of keeping things in balance than we do with our backfires and burn programs. This guy Pestrano has taken care of the Trace problem in the most efficient manner, much more easily than we could ever do it," mused Ralph.

"That's a really profound analogy, Ralph. You're absolutely right on!"

"Well, Barbara, I think it's time for us to return to Chicago. We need to catch up with Chris. We should figure out how to help the kid get his job back with Smith, Hay & Ward, that is, if he wants to go back to them."

"Let's see if we can get on the commuter flight this afternoon. I'll make the call right now. Frankly, I can't wait to sleep in my own bed after over a week in the hotel," she said.

"I'm with you!" replied Ralph. "Oops, that's not how it sounds," he said, embarrassed by the double entendre.

"My, aren't we risqué," she replied. Her eyes were smiling at him.

Chapter 27

On her way back to Chicago Barbara Knudsen worked on building a case for presentation to Harry Harkness. She was aware that he would have to be totally convinced that Chris was right in his suspicions and that Richard Trace was unquestionably guilty of the crimes that he had calculated must have been committed. Furthermore, she wanted to present convincing evidence that the excessive death claims that had occurred over the years would return to normal at First Gotham Bank of New York. Using the data that had been supplied by Chris and Ralph, along with information that they had gotten from the Organized Crime Unit of the FBI, she put together a succinct ten page report. She decided that the best strategy would be for her and Ralph to call on Harkness together and make the case for Chris, without involving him, in the hopes that Mr. Harkness would be convinced that Chris did not deserve to lose his job over this matter.

When they arrived at O'Hare she suggested to Ralph that they have dinner at the Windsock. An hour later they were seated at the same table they had used two weeks earlier. Ralph had smoked three cigarettes on the way to the restaurant. He hardly noticed the smoking area by the bar this evening. Barbara explained her plan.

"I don't know, Barbara. His boss, Harkness, seemed like a tough sale to me, and he will still be upset that Chris disobeyed his clear instructions. My guess is that in his heart of hearts he really believed the evidence that Chris presented. It was clear enough to me, and he knows a thousand times more than I do about these things."

"Ralph, I have given this a great deal of thought, and I think Trace probably insisted that they get rid of Chris. After all, he was a real threat to him. He could have put pressure on Harkness regarding their account. He may have threatened to sue. Who knows what he may have done?"

"Do you think we should talk to Chris first to get his input?"

"No. If we can convince Harkness, we can encourage Chris to return to Smith, Hay & Ward. If not, we should try to encourage him to find another job, maybe even with the government. I'll bet the State Insurance Department would just love to have him, and he could probably lead them to some interesting situations," answered Ms. Knudsen.

"Well, which of us is going to call Mr. Harkness?" he asked.

"I thought since you have met him, he would likely respond favorably to you. I'm sure he will be curious to find out details about Trace's demise, and you can imply that you want to fill him in on those details," Barbara smiled.

Ralph accepted the assignment with relish, knowing it meant spending even more time with Barbara.

The next afternoon Harry Harkness again greeted Ralph Murphy at the offices of Smith, Hay & Ward. He also met Barbara Knudsen for the first time.

"Ms. Knudsen, it is a pleasure to meet you. I'm sorry it is under such unpleasant circumstances."

"Yes, well, while the circumstances of Richard Trace's death were certainly very unpleasant, the result to your firm, and especially to First Gotham Bank and their employees are no doubt positive."

"I'm afraid you are going to have to explain yourself on that point," Harkness retorted, peering over his glasses.

"Mr. Harkness, I have prepared a written report which fully explains our findings on this matter. You will see that the facts that were developed by Chris Masters have been corroborated by our findings. Mr. Trace was obviously involved in a murder-for-hire scheme with professional killers. We have the Organized Crime Unit of the FBI continuing the investigation as we speak. If Chris had not pursued this matter with Mr. Murphy voluntarily, the federal government would have sent a full investigative team into your office to go through your records."

"That's right, Mr. Harkness. When I approached Chris about this I told him that he could either cooperate or we would get a subpoena. I'll admit it was a pretty strong-arm tactic, but I was convinced that he was on to something that needed to be investigated. I've been at this for over 25 years and could sense that something was amiss."

"He should have come to me about it. He was wrong to release that information without my permission," Harry stated, folding his arms across his chest.

Barbara looked down at the table, then raising her eyes to stare directly at the older man, she said, "Mr. Harkness, we are talking about a young man on his first real job coming upon a situation that most people never have to face in a lifetime. He had the idealism of youth, which can be both a blessing and a curse. He could only see the black and white. In time, and with experience, he will be able to see the gray areas. It will take a few years

before he has the maturity and experience that you do.
Try to put yourself in his shoes. What would you have
done in this case if you were his age?"

"Hmm, I see your point. I must admit that I was
quite saddened that we had to let him go, but Trace
insisted that First Gotham would pull their account if I
didn't fire him that very day. That has become a moot
point given what has happened. Masters **was** doing a
great job for us prior to this incident," he stated, almost to
himself, as if the two federal investigators were not even
present. *Still, it violates my rule against re-hiring. Once
the toothpaste is out of the tube, it is very hard to get it
back in....*" he thought to himself.

"We encourage you to contact him as soon as
possible," said Barbara, grinning broadly.

"I will do so on your recommendation, but I am
not making any promises," said Harkness.

When Ralph and Barbara got to the sidewalk in
front of 450 Michigan Avenue, a light snow was falling.
Barbara put her arm inside Ralph's and said, "Would you
mind taking a walk with me, Ralph?"

"OK, Barbara. Where are we going?"

"It doesn't matter to me. The snow falling in the
colored lights is so beautiful at this time of the year," she
said, squeezing his arm.

"You make me feel like the luckiest man in
Chicago," he whispered.

Barbara simply leaned her head against his
shoulder and smiled. They walked slowly up the Miracle
Mile together

Kenneth Knudsen greeted Chris Masters warmly,
"Barbara has good things to say about you, Chris. I have
been looking forward to meeting you."

"Thank you, Mr. Knudsen. I appreciate the chance to meet with you. I don't know if Barbara told you about what has happened to me, well, to us, over the last few weeks."

"She did give me an overview of the situation. Let me tell you that I have been suspect of the BOLI/COLI programs for years. It just seemed ripe for the kind of abuse that you seem to have uncovered. I am sure our state insurance commissioner would be more than a little interested in your findings."

"Well sir, I do have all of the evidence we developed in my briefcase if you would be interested in seeing it," said Chris.

"You bet I would. By the way, I have lined up an interview with Robert Prescott, the chief actuary at CITA downtown. I shared your situation with him, and he is very interested in talking with you. There is no love lost between his firm and Smith, Hay and Ward. If that doesn't work out for you, I am also close to Bill Sterns at Continental American Life out by O'Hare airport. He's a close golfing buddy. The insurance business has become a fraternity of old men. We are always looking for new young blood. I have a great deal of confidence in the character judgment of my daughter, and she gave you the highest recommendation."

"Wow, I'm flattered that she feels that way," he said.." You just rest easy that we will find you a good job situation. I want to work with you on how best to expose the BOLI/COLI conundrum."

Chris reached into his briefcase and handed Ken Knudsen the thick report.

"Do you mind if I take a few minutes to glance through this information before we talk?" he asked.

"No, that's fine, Mr. Knudsen. I have been hoping to find someone to share it with who would understand what to do and how to do it," he replied.

Chris sat across from Mr. Knudsen with his hand on his chin while the older man read through the lengthy report. It took him 20 minutes. Chris could tell that he was grasping it by the nods and frequent returns to previous pages for confirmation. Finally, Knudsen looked up and said, "If there was ever a more damning expose of BOLI/COLI I can't imagine what it would show. This is dynamite!"

"Yes sir. You can see that in addition to the statistical evidence, there is all of the personal information that Barbara and Ralph developed about Trace. That is actually stronger evidence, because we have no way of proving that any of the deaths were murder, except for, of course, his own. They could all have been natural as far as the death claim reports are concerned. But, actuarially and financially, you can see why I became suspicious of First Gotham."

"No doubt about it, Chris. Especially the double-death claims--almost all with First Gotham as one of the beneficiaries. That is probably the most troubling aspect of BOLI/COLI to me, the fact that the coverage continues after employment is terminated. The lawyers have convinced the courts with smoke and mirrors on that one. Insurance is such an enigmatic business. Even very intelligent people have their eyes glaze over trying to understand the details. There is no way that companies should be able to keep coverage on an employee for 'future liabilities' unless the future liabilities actually exist. Sure, it would be more work, and certainly less profitable to them if they had to track the variety in terminations, but it could be done--and it should be done."

"You know, Mr. Knudsen, something just hit me. Throughout this entire affair I have considered Richard Trace to be the problem. What you just said makes me realize that he is only a manifestation of the core problem, which is that BOLI itself is a flawed concept. Not only that, but it is a flawed concept that can actually be fixed. The trick is to get the courts to understand how it works and what potential flaws exist," said Chris.

"We can start by talking to the insurance department here in Illinois. I know the deputy insurance commissioner personally. I'm sure he will be very interested in this material. Once we get the attention of the insurance commissioners, and there are 52 of them in the United States, we will be well on our way to making this a national issue. It always seems to take some tragedy for governmental bodies and the courts to get their acts together, but so be it," said Knudsen. Then he continued, "Would you be willing to share this information with them, and also with our representatives in Congress?

"Wow, are you sure we have enough to do that?" asked Chris.

"There is no doubt in my mind."

"My problem is that I need to make money in the meantime, and don't have time to pursue this full-time." said Chris.

"I'm sure that we will be able to fix that in short order, Chris. You have good credentials, and I have friends who need someone with your abilities."

"Are you aware that Barbara has convinced my former boss, Mr. Harkness, to reconsider me at Smith, Hay & Ward?"

"No, she didn't mention that. What do you think about that now, son?"

"Before our talk tonight, I would have probably been happy to have that job back. The work was fascinating and the pay was excellent. Now I know that the real problem is the very product they produce and service. If I felt that they would agree to work on fixing the flaws in the BOLI/ COLI program that we have identified, then I could probably return to work there. But I'm sure they would resist any changes to the max. Mr. Harkness defends the program totally even though I am sure he is very aware of the flaws, especially after this situation with First Gotham. No, sir, there is no way I would go back."

"I'm glad to hear you say that, Chris. You can do better, and I will work hard to see that you get that chance. I *do* have time to devote to this project, and I can't wait for us to get at it, starting tomorrow," said Ken Knudsen.

Later, as Chris walked down the sidewalk to his car, there was a spring in his step that he hadn't felt in over two weeks. *I can't wait to tell Sarah about all this*, he thought to himself.

Out of courtesy and curiosity Chris kept his appointment at Smith, Hay & Ward. Harry Harkness greeted him at the entrance to his office.

"Chris, I don't know if you saw it on the news, but we have received word that Richard Trace was found murdered just over a week ago."

"Yes, Mr. Harkness. As you can imagine, I have followed that situation very closely."

"Last week I received a visit from your friend Murphy and a lady from the FBI, a Ms. Barbara Knudsen. I assume you have met her?"

"Yes, Ralph introduced me to her when the situation got beyond his agencies' reach."

"They presented me with rather irrefutable evidence that Trace was involved in a murder-for-hire scheme using the BOLI program. Apparently, he received millions in unwarranted bonus money over the years. That was his motivation. I have already contacted First Gotham to warn them to be sure not to continue the compensation arrangement that made it possible for Trace to profit from his despicable scheme. They were horrified that anyone would be so cold blooded. It had never occurred to them that the bonus could encourage such activity."

"Mr. Harkness, first let me apologize to you for disobeying your direct order. Nevertheless, I felt strongly that crimes were being committed, and telling Mr. Murphy made it seem possible that someone could do something about the First Gotham situation. I couldn't see how I could possibly do anything to stop Trace, and I certainly never expected things to develop as they did-- that is, with his being murdered and all. Frankly, I didn't think ahead about the implications for Smith, Hay & Ward," confessed Chris.

"I feel that I also owe you an apology and hope that you will consider returning to the firm," offered Harkness.

"Thank you for the offer, Harry," Chris said with confidence. "I know that I was doing a good job here...."

His former boss interrupted, "I expect the claims at First Gotham will return to normal, and that we will have what you call natural randomness."

"I'm sure you're right, Harry. My problem is that I have concluded that the whole idea of a bank, or any other company, owning life insurance on its employees **forever** is just plain wrong. It should be against public policy."

Harry Harkness leaned forward in his chair, elbows on his knees. He closed his eyes. *Why did I violate my rules!* he thought. "OK, Chris, if that is how you feel, I'm sure working here at Smith, Hay & Ward won't work for either of us. I wish you well in your future endeavors," he said hastily, wishing the interview to be over. He was furious at himself for even allowing it in the first place. *Never, never violate your rules again, Harkness.*

After Chris left his office, Harry turned to his window and looked out at the darkening sky. Contrary to the opinion of the young man who had just left his office, he was still convinced that the concept which had made his firm successful and profitable was inviolable. Yet, he thought, *What if there is another Richard Trace out there? After all, there **were** thousands of companies, insuring millions of employees, for billions of dollars.* It was not unlike the question of whether or not there was life elsewhere in the universe....

Appendix

Banks in the United States are heavily regulated. All large capitalization businesses in America are required to prepare their financial statements according to Generally Accepted Accounting Principals (GAAP), which have been developed by the accounting industry along with the Securities and Exchange Commission (SEC). While GAAP creates a standard for accounting by banks, there is **not** a requirement that banks disclose Bank Owned Life Insurance (BOLI).

Most banks choose to include this item under "other assets" in their financial reports. Thus, an asset that is often in the millions of dollars (billions for larger banks) often gets buried in the annual reports of many of our largest institutions. Banks do not want to highlight this coverage because of the potential adverse reaction that it might cause should their executive employees really understand the details of these plans.

Insurable Interest: In order to insure its employees, a bank or other corporation has to have an insurable interest, which is defined by the Supreme Court as "...an interest, arising from the relation of the party obtaining the insurance, either as creditor of or surety for the **assured**, or from ties of blood or marriage to him (her), as will justify a reasonable expectation of advantage or benefit from the continuance of his (her) life. It is not necessary that the expectation of an advantage or benefit should be always capable of pecuniary estimation...." Warnock v Davis, 104 U. S. 775.779 (1881).

This general definition of insurable interest has been refined by certain courts cases over the last 120 years, so that there is recognition in most jurisdictions that an employer has an insurable interest in the life of an employee when the employer is liable for future life, medical, disability or retirement benefits of the employee. Insurance is regulated by the individual states and many of them have ratified this definition by statute, the only limitation being that the potential insurance proceeds do not exceed the total benefit obligation of the company to the aggregate group of employees.

In 1991 the Office of the Comptroller of Currency (OCC) issued Banking Circular 249, which specifically addressed the issuance of Bank Owned Life Insurance (BOLI). This circular made it clear that the OCC's interpretation of federal banking statutes is that they do not permit banks to purchase life insurance as an "investment." The OCC Circular does allow banks to purchase life insurance in two situations: Key Person indemnification and the financing of employee benefits. The Circular developed two tests: Test A and Test B.

Test A is used to determine if Key Person insurance is permitted and states that a bank may purchase life insurance on the life of any officer or director whose death would have an adverse impact on the bank sufficient to create an insurable interest. Test A also states that the bank must terminate the coverage if the insured ceases to be a Key Person due to retirement, discharge or any other reason. Therefore, under Test A, the coverage is specific as to the insured and the need.

Test B is very different. This test is used to determine coverage under future employee benefits.

The banks are given considerable latitude in establishing these emerging liabilities. Insurable interest must exist at the time of purchase, but only at the time of purchase, and may be continued as long as the bank has a continuing liability. The OCC Circular 249 allows these calculations to be made on a group basis. In the interest of efficiency it is permissible, and often expedient, to over- insure some members of the group and under-insure others. This is permissible as long as the total aggregate insurance coverage is within the allowable parameters. Unlike test A, the individual insurance policies can be maintained even if the insured leaves the firm, even if they go to a rival bank. In effect, once they are insured, they are insured for life.

This is especially true since most BOLI contracts are written on a single premium basis. It is not necessary to match up an individual's coverage with that same individual's future benefit; it is done on an aggregate, group basis.

Modified Endowment Contract (MEC): In 1988 the federal government promulgated new tax rules regarding the method of premium payment on a life insurance contract. Basically, on all contracts which are paid in fewer than seven years, any withdrawals from the policy cash value would be considered first a withdrawal of earnings until all earnings have been withdrawn, then a return of principal. This is known as last in-first out (LIFO) accounting.

Throughout the history of life insurance, the method of accounting on cash withdrawals from a policy has been on the first in-first out basis (FIFO). On all non-MEC policies, that is still the method used. The new legislation was aimed at slowing the proliferation of the so-called single premium life insurance policies, which had been designed as an investment vehicle, as opposed to a protection vehicle. While BOLI certainly was a legitimate target of this legislation, the rules for insurable interest under Test B made it possible for the banks and large corporations to dodge this tax trap.